... ... a reporter and producer, including time at Radio 4's *Woman's Hour* and Radio 2's Steve Wright show.

Jo's debut novel, *The Oyster Catcher*, was a runaway bestseller and won both the RNA Joan Hessayon Award and the Festival of Romance Best EBook Award. Her recent book *Escape to the French Farmhouse* was a #1 bestselling ebook. In every one of her novels Jo loves to explore new countries and discover the food produced there, both of which she thoroughly enjoys researching. Jo lives in Pembrokeshire with her husband and three children, where cooking and gathering around the kitchen table are a hugely important and fun part of their family life.

Visit Jo's website: jothomasautl...

or follow her on:

🐦 @Jo_Thomas01

📘 /JoThomasAuthor

📷 @JoThomasAuthor

Retreat to the Spanish Sun

Jo Thomas

PENGUIN BOOKS

TRANSWORLD PUBLISHERS
Penguin Random House, One Embassy Gardens,
8 Viaduct Gardens, London SW11 7BW
www.penguin.co.uk

Transworld is part of the Penguin Random House group of companies
whose addresses can be found at global.penguinrandomhouse.com

Penguin
Random House
UK

First published in Great Britain in 2022 by Penguin Books
an imprint of Transworld Publishers

A CIP catalogue record for this book
is available from the British Library.

ISBN 9780552178662

Typeset in 11/14pt ITC Giovanni by Jouve (UK), Milton Keynes.
Printed and bound in Great Britain by Clays Ltd, Elcograf S.p.A.

The authorized representative in the EEA is Penguin Random House Ireland,
Morrison Chambers, 32 Nassau Street, Dublin D02 YH68.

Penguin Random House is committed to a sustainable
future for our business, our readers and our planet. This book
is made from Forest Stewardship Council® certified paper.

For Bil.
So proud of you. Dream big and always keep going!
xx

PROLOGUE

'Oooffff!'

The smack to my face is an almighty shock, making my heart pound like a racehorse on the gallops, and leaving me wondering what on earth has just happened. Especially as I'd been walking along a quiet beach, by the sea, breathing in the fresh air, enjoying the peace, and about to accept Gary Barlow's invitation to join him for a cocktail at the deserted bar. I was ecstatic as he pulled out a chair for me, poured me a drink and asked me all about myself. All I could think of saying was that I love cheese and onion crisps and red wine – I often have a bottle open on the side and kid myself it's for cooking. I love watching property programmes, too, and used to try to take a late lunchbreak to catch up on them, but these days I never have time to watch them.

I take a moment for my heart rate to settle and to gather my thoughts, work out where I am and what just happened. Suddenly there's a cold wet kiss on my lips. I run the back of my hand across my mouth, then over my face, still throbbing from the slap, as the reality of the situation slowly sinks in.

As my eyes adjust to the light in the room, I roll my head in the direction of the person lying next to me: fast asleep, seemingly oblivious to the smack they've just delivered. I stare at the sleeping face, as angelic as it was when she was a baby, twenty-four years ago. Nearly the same age I was when I had her. She looks so peaceful now. A far cry from the sobbing mess that turned up a few days ago with all her belongings, plus Harry and Willy, the two pug puppies. What I thought was the roar of waves on the seashore is actually Willy snoring.

I pick up the hand that is still resting on my cheek and gently push it back to the other side of the bed. Harry is looking at me from between us and is still licking his lips.

No Gary Barlow, then. No deserted beach bar in the setting sun. I turn towards the window, feeling hot despite the rain, as the light leaks through the threadbare curtains. I hate them. I put them up as a temporary measure when I first moved in and they're still there. They make my heart sink every time I look at them. They remind me of the empty nest I left behind when my youngest turned eighteen and we had to move out of their childhood home, but it was a new start for us all. The debt my ex-husband Rob had left me with was paid off. My son and youngest child, Luke, had gone to university to study law, like his dad, and my eldest, Ruby, had eventually settled on events management. She'd gone to work on chartered yachts, then met and moved in with one of the on-board chefs and now works for an entertainment agency. My middle child, Edie, went to college to study art, living in a shared house and working in a local café, making cakes for farmers' markets and festivals.

This little ground-floor flat was my new beginning, with all the kids being settled in their lives. But none of us has actually moved on. One by one the kids have come back and have filled this nest right up. Edie's rented house-share was repossessed by the bank from the landlord and now she's back, with her boyfriend, Reggie, while they look for somewhere of their own. On their budget, it's hard. Luke took a gap year to go travelling after he and his girlfriend split up. But now he's back, sooner than expected, with no real plan to return to university. And Ruby has left her long-term boyfriend.

We need somewhere bigger, somewhere we can all live comfortably. The curtains, which I found in a charity shop, barely shut out the light, or the view of next door's garden, which is more of a dumping ground.

I lie there, listening to the deep breathing of my elder daughter and her pug snoring. I take in the quiet before the whole house wakes and next door's dog starts barking, which will set off Harry and Willy.

My phone rings and I scramble for it, but before I can get to it, it dies. 'Bugger!' I jump out of bed, exciting Harry and Willy, who bark as I look for the phone charger. It isn't where I thought it was, by my bedside, so I run into the living room, where Luke is a large lump on the sofa-bed. In the pitch black, I knock over a pint glass of water as I retrieve my charger from beside him. He's never got one.

He doesn't stir as I use one of his T-shirts, left in a ball on the floor, to mop up the water with my foot while attempting to plug in my phone. I realize that the glass was on top of my books, being used as a bed-side table . . . my college books.

I rip back the curtains, to Luke's annoyance.

'What the . . .' He groans, screwing up his face and rubbing his eyes as the morning light pours in. The room stinks so I throw open the window. Turning my attention back to my books, I use the T-shirt, a sock and some brightly coloured Oddballs pants to wipe the water from them. 'What time is it? What's all the fuss? Shut the curtains!' mumbles Luke.

'Why are those dogs barking?' Edie comes out of the spare bedroom she's sharing with Reggie, who teaches guitar online, while they save for a deposit on a place of their own. Edie rubs her head and pads to the bath-room in a pair of Reggie's boxers and a T-shirt.

'My books!' I shout at Luke, but he just rolls over and harrumphs. There may have been a muttered 'Sorry,' but I can't be sure. I head to the kitchen area, which is littered with late-night baking detritus, presumably Edie's. As soon as I plug my phone in, it rings again. I pick it up.

'Hello, Price and Rutherby, how can I help you?' I say, trying to sound like the professional estate-agent's receptionist I am and not like I've just woken up, hav-ing overslept. I look around for somewhere to sit, but clothes are draped over every piece of furniture. Having cut his gap year short, Luke's supposed to be consider-ing his options – from the depths of the duvet by the look of it. I snap the phone off and glare at him.

'Maybe you should talk to your dad about going to work for him for a bit,' I hiss quickly, clutching the phone, but he doesn't respond. I need to deal with this call!

I clench my teeth as I hear the lock on the bathroom door open. Edie is heading back to the spare bedroom. I move quickly into the hall – from there, I see Harry and Willy standing on their hind legs on my dressing-table in the bedroom window, barking at next door's Alsatian. I grab my moment, with my books, phone and charger, and run to the bathroom before anyone else can. Inside, I lock the door, slot my phone into

Luke's portable charger, put down the loo lid and sit on it. I take a deep breath to settle my shredded nerves, then redial the number.

'Hello, Eliza Bytheway here. Sorry, we seem to have been cut off. Thank you for bearing with me. I'm working from home right now,' I say, remembering how different life was just a few months ago, when my two-bedroom flat was home to me with the spare room set up as a home office, and occasionally housing visiting children. Now, I'm working from home, trying to finish my college course, and the place is bursting at the seams. 'How can I help you?' I ask.

'Well, I've been ringing for a while. I'm looking for a two-bedroom bungalow or flat,' says the voice at the other end of the line.

'How about I see what we've got and if anything interests you, I could get one of the agents to give you a ring back with some more information?' I say.

'That would be lovely. The truth is, I've got far too much room in this house these days, and it's so quiet.'

'Sounds like bliss!' I say, trying to keep the hysteria from my voice.

'Oh, it's far too quiet for me. I'd like somewhere near to town, with neighbours. I'd like to see a bit of life,' says the caller.

'I'm sure we can find something suitable for you. What's your name?'

'Betty Fox.'

'Well, Mrs Fox, let us see what we can find for you.'

I look around the bathroom. Two bedrooms, one nicely fitted kitchen, opening onto a living room with a bay window. If only I could . . .

There's a knock on the door. 'You going to be long? I'm dying for the loo,' says Ruby.

If only my flat didn't come with three – make that four – grown-up children. Boomerang kids – because they keep coming back. Love them as I do, what I really need is some peace and quiet.

'May I call you back, Mrs Fox? I'll just check our records.'

'Of course, dear. I'll be here and waiting.'

I end the call, pick up my books and the charger, unlock and open the bathroom door. My daughter brushes past before I've had a chance to leave.

'Thanks, Mum,' she says, and I smell her familiar perfume. Sweet, caramel and yet spicy, still clinging to her skin from yesterday as she slides past me. Too heavy for this time of the morning, though, before I've had a cup of tea.

There is only one thing for it. I go to the front door, remove my keys from the lock and open it, walk outside to the kerb, open my car, get into the driver's seat, still in my dressing-gown and slippers, and lock all the doors. My neighbour walks past, the Alsatian trotting amicably beside him, and I give him a nod, hoping he doesn't notice my attire. Then, just when I thought things couldn't get any worse, my ex-husband pulls up in his Audi TT, jumps out and does a double-take. He's holding a birthday card for Luke, by the look of it. He frowns at me. I take a deep breath and raise a hand, as if everything about this was perfectly normal. Then I unlock my phone, staring straight ahead, glad he can't see my toes curling under the dashboard.

'Mrs Fox, where were we? It was peace and quiet you were after?'

'No, dear.' She laughs. 'I think that was you.'

I look back towards my full-to-bursting flat, as Rob, smart as ever, delivers the card to Luke – no doubt with a little wodge of notes inside. He's let them down in being there but he tries to make up for it with birthday bribery. I glance at his wife, sitting in the Audi, glaring at me. She's practically the same age as my children and has one on the way, yet she still looks like she's walked straight out of a hairdressing salon. I could barely function when I was pregnant. And after I'd given birth, the real anxiety set in. By the time our third child arrived, an unexpected surprise, I was a shadow of my former fun-loving self. The one who had met her husband in a nightclub and loved to dance like no one was watching. I was sleep-deprived and consumed by sadness, even though I had three beautiful children.

I watch Rob hugging our son, slightly awkwardly, then slapping him on the back. Neither of them knows what to do. Willy and Harry are sniffing his ankles with interest. Luke's birthday isn't for another week, but Rob's card has come in the general region of the date, so that's something. Birthday bribery done, Rob turns back to his car and I wonder how long it will be before I can get in the shower, make a cup of tea and start on my college work. I just have to choose a subject for my final essay. It's for a foundation course at the local university, the School of Sport and Health Sciences.

I went to an open day and thought it was perfect as I want practical work I can do from home and they offer all sorts of courses in health and wellbeing, complementary health care, podiatry and sports massage. But, first, I have to complete the foundation year as I lack A levels. I was having way too much fun working different jobs to worry about details like turning up for exams. Whether I was shelf-stacking in the supermarket or peeling potatoes in the chip shop, after a shift I'd go out and party.

I smile just thinking about it. Sadly, I don't have any qualifications so this is my time. I need to finish this foundation course. Then I can decide what I want to study to get qualified. When I'm equipped to set up my own business we'll be able to afford somewhere bigger for us all to live. But I have to get the foundation course done. I've already had an extension for my final essay twice, due to family circumstances, the old feelings of anxiety and a flexible, understanding tutor, who also retrained after her children left home. But this is my last chance. Everyone else's work is in. I have just over two weeks. If I don't get it in by the end of August, before the autumn term starts, there's no way I can start a new course. I can't blow this.

I open my iPad and see the familiar advert on the side panel.

Betty Fox was right. All I need is a bit of peace and quiet.

1

'It's only for a couple of weeks,' I tell them, or maybe I'm telling myself, worrying all over again that I've made a totally rash and idiotic decision. I could pull out. I could just phone and say something's come up. I could talk to my tutor and say I can't meet the deadline, but that really isn't an option. I'm in the last-chance saloon here.

As if she's reading my mind, Edie says, 'We'll be fine, Mum,' as an attempt to reassure me.

It started as a bit of a joke, a moment of madness just before the postman delivered my mail to me through the car window. Sitting in my red Fiesta, I felt like Alan Bennett's lady in the van, except I haven't got a van or a drive to park it on. I was checking on some of our clients: that Mrs Bevington is leaving the washing-machine in her Glue Pot Lane property when she moves out, and that Mr Grey is going to cut his grass before he leaves or the buyers will pull out.

That was when the advert popped up on my screen again.

'Here's the house-sitting agency details.' I hand Edie a piece of paper with the address, phone number and anything else I could think of that might keep us connected. 'I'll ring as soon as I get there.'

'Better still, let's set up a family WhatsApp group,' says Ruby, her thumbs working frenziedly on her phone keypad.

'Brilliant!' I say, anxiety rising, the old familiar feeling. 'What's that?' I remember to ask, trying to focus.

'What's what?' asks Ruby, still typing.

'WhatsApp,' I say.

The word is bouncing around inside my head as I look at her, but I know I won't take in the answer right now because I still have so much to tell them before I leave.

'Now, Tuesday is bin day. There are plenty of frozen pizzas in the freezer. And pasta. You can always make a meal if you have bacon and eggs, omelettes, carbonara, quiche—'

'Yes, Mum, we'll be fine. Now don't miss your flight,' says Luke, who is upright now and standing in the hall in a crumpled T-shirt and boxer shorts.

'Now remember,' I try to stay parent-like, 'no parties.

I know it's your birthday next week, Luke, but no parties. And remember to shower and use deodorant. If the toilet doesn't flush properly, a double flush should do it. There's some hummus in the fridge that needs eating – it's only just past its sell-by date. It'll be fine . . . And remember to let the dogs out and don't let them sleep on the bed. Oh, and the doorbell can be dodgy. If you order things online, make sure you're awake for the delivery. And, Edie, clear up after you've been baking.'

They're ushering me towards the door, a gentle nudge, like a mare nosing her foal to its legs. So gentle that I barely notice it's happening, the three of them guiding me out. Then, when I'm on the doorstep, as I feel the drizzle hit my skin, I hug them all again and try not to cry, rubbing at my itchy nose and laughing as my chaotic family stand smiling back at me. Suddenly I'm gripped with panic and really do want to rush back inside, go back to where we were, all packed in together, safe.

'Go!' They laugh.

I take a huge breath and walk towards the waiting taxi. As the car drives off, I wave and wind down the window to shout, 'Remember, no parties. And no dogs on the bed!' When I can't see them any more, I fall back into my seat and look out of the front windscreen. I push down my anxiety. I'm actually doing this. I take more big breaths, unable to decide if I'm excited or terrified. A bit of both, maybe. But I have two weeks' holiday from work to spend in Spain, caring for a beautiful house with two dogs. It's a chance to finish my coursework in peace and quiet. This is my time. A chance at last to change our lives for good.

2

'So, remember, no parties and definitely don't allow the dogs on the bed. There are instructions for the refuse here . . '. Josep Santiago, the home-owner, hands me a piece of paper.

'Of course,' I reply, feeling as if I'm in a parallel universe.

I replay my departure from home early that morning and can't believe I'm in Andalucía! And it's hot in the mid-August sun, even on the shady terrace I'm standing on, at the end of the long dusty drive, looking out over the trees to the mountains beyond. Despite the breeze, I use the paper he's handed me to fan my face as we walk into the *cortijo*, or farmhouse.

After the advert for house-sitters had appeared on my computer screen when I was in the car in my dressing-gown, I sat there fantasizing about it for a bit.

Then I showed Ruby, more as a bit of fun than a serious suggestion. Deep down, though, I was considering the possibility but maybe I needed a gentle push in the right direction from my children. They all thought it was a brilliant idea and suggested I phone the agency and sign up.

Suddenly I found a whole load of excuses as to why I shouldn't. After a long discussion with Ruby, Luke and Edie, in which they all agreed to the house rules – no parties and no arguing – I agreed to explore the idea.

Now, here I am, standing in the cool of a *cortijo* in south-west Spain, a stranger's home, about to make it my own for the next two weeks. The house has an unusual, but not unpleasant scent, of wood and beeswax, of sun on the hard earth, jasmine, garlic and olive oil lingering from the kitchen. And there's something I don't recognize. That's when I catch sight of a leg of ham on the kitchen counter and wonder if that could be responsible for the salty, nutty smell. The outside is a glossy dark golden-brown, and where the meat has been carved, it's delicately marbled.

I look at Josep. He has curly dark hair, pushed back from his face with sunglasses, thick eyebrows over deep brown eyes, and is clean-shaven. He's wearing a well-pressed shirt and jeans and I can see a pink tongue touching his white teeth when he speaks.

He raises a hand and gestures towards two large

white, well-trained dogs. 'You do have experience of dogs, don't you? The company said you did.'

I think of Harry and Willy. 'Oh, yes . . .' I nod, gazing at his big white well-behaved dogs.

'These are Maremmas. A breed of sheepdog.'

'What are their names?' I ask.

His tight-set face softens with a smile.

'This is Mateo and Diego,' he says, as if he's introducing them formally.

I smile at them. This place is perfect – plenty of peace and quiet. I might be doing my college work from home, but nobody said it had to be *my* home. There is nothing here to stop me getting it done. In fact, I can't wait to start writing the essay.

'The dogs and I will be fine. You have nothing to worry about.'

Hesitation is written all over his face: he's wondering whether to leave or not. I know that feeling.

'I promise I'll take care of your home. And your dogs.'

They look up at him.

Behind him, on a dark-wood sideboard, I can see a picture of him laughing with a woman, who I presume is his partner. 'Is your wife joining you on this trip?' I ask.

He swallows hard. I know that feeling too. Swallowing emotions that you keep for when you're alone, not for public viewing. 'She's not. I'm not . . . It's just me.'

17

I don't ask any more questions. Instead I kick myself for being insensitive.

'And the farm?' I say, changing the subject, nodding in the direction of the track and the stone barns beyond the *cortijo*.

'You don't need to worry about that. Pedro looks after the animals. He works for me.'

'Are there many?' I say, hoping I've moved things on far enough.

'*Pata negra*,' he says, and I'm none the wiser. 'Black hoof. Black Iberian pigs. The finest pigs, producing the *bellota* ham. The very best ham. Most of the farmers around here keep pigs. But we also have chickens, sometimes cows and horses on the land. It is important to have a mix of animals to help the *dehesa*, the, er . . .' He waves a hand in a circle, searching for a translation. 'I'm not sure there is an English word, the landscape, the ecosystem. It is why we have such amazing pigs and hams, because of the terrain and the way we work with nature.'

'Ah,' I say. I know nothing about pigs and have run out of questions.

'Pedro will do everything that is needed,' he says, as if sensing I'm out of my depth. 'He's my pig man.' We stand in silence, him needing the push to leave, like I did.

I try to reassure him again that the dogs and I will be fine, and finally I gently nudge Josep Santiago out of the house, with his holdall and briefcase, much as my family had done to me that morning.

'Okay. You have all my contact details,' he says. 'Perhaps we should set up a WhatsApp conversation so we can stay in contact.'

'Just your number is fine,' I reply, still fanning my face with the paper that contains his contact details. 'I have it here.'

He puts on a light jacket and pulls out his phone, with some papers, from an inside pocket.

'Whoops!' I catch a few pages, glancing at them briefly as I hand them back. They look like hotel reservations and some addresses.

He hasn't told me where he's going or what he's doing, and why should he? I'm a stranger whose job is to mind the dogs and the house. He's told me the important things: not to throw any parties, not to allow the dogs to sleep on the bed, not to leave the house unlocked if I go out, and to call if I'm concerned about anything. I smile to myself, thinking of the instructions I left at home. I know how to run a house. It's what I've done for the past twenty-five years. With children in it.

He puts his phone away, having double-checked I've got his number. Then he wavers, as if he's about to change his mind, just as I did. But I hesitated to leave my children and hugged them hard instead. I'm not about to hug him, good-looking though he is.

'It'll be okay, I'll look after your home,' I repeat, trying to sound professional, as if I've done this lots of times. As I'm gazing into his dark brown eyes, I need him to know that I mean it. Whatever other worries he has, this needn't be one of them.

He holds my gaze, and I really do want to give him a reassuring hug.

'*Gracias*,' he says, and nods. 'The agency said you come with very good references.'

Of the two I gave, one was from my best friend, Alice, whom I met at antenatal classes when I was pregnant with Ruby – we've stayed close ever since. She now runs her own business as a recipe developer for pre-packed high-end supermarket ready meals: a friend who appeared regularly at the door with new dishes for us to eat while I was bringing up three kids on my own was a lifesaver. Alice always said she liked to get my opinion, but she was just being kind, giving me a night off from cooking for three fussy eaters.

The other reference came from Jez, a fellow student on my college course, who is retraining after life in the City and major burnout. Like me, he thinks working from home, in something like sports massage, could bring in the income he needs and a better work–life balance. Also, we're the same age in a class full of young students and seem to have bonded over an appreciation of Freddie Mercury and Spangles sweets from our childhood. He's nice. Nothing else. I don't think I see men like *that* any more, and I'm sure he doesn't see me as anything other than a mum of three adults who can remember when there were only three television channels. And the Christmas *Radio Times*. But it's nice not to be the only oldie in the class.

The references are glowing and I blush when I think of them. I feel guilty that I couldn't provide professional ones, but I could hardly ask my boss for a reference to take another job during my annual leave from the estate agency. The company has been good to me, letting me work part time while the kids were at school and around my coursework now.

I take calls from people window-shopping, dreaming of a new life in a new home, send out details or direct them to the website, organize viewings, get feedback on them and keep on top of sales progression, like whether or not the curtains are being left, or the cesspit will be emptied before the buyers move in. Sometimes people just need reassurance. It's a big upheaval leaving your home, especially if you were happy there. Right now, Josep needed to remind himself about my references and I can tell he believes I'll take good care of his home and his dogs because he seems less anxious now. I don't blame him for hesitating: he's leaving his home, his farm, his dogs in a stranger's hands.

'I promise,' I reiterate. 'Everything will be fine.'

With that, a faint smile tugs at the corners of his mouth and likewise at mine. We're going to be fine.

'I'm, er, just visiting a few clients. People I supply, with *jamón ibérico de bellota*, Ibérico ham,' he tells me. 'Just to check how things are.' That makes perfect sense to me. 'Just one thing . . .'

'Yes?' I say.

He looks straight at me, with his dark eyes. 'If anyone asks why you're here . . .'

'Yes?'

'I'd rather they didn't know where I was. Maybe you could just make something up.' He seems uncomfortable.

'Of course. Don't worry. I have plenty to keep myself occupied. I don't plan on meeting anyone.'

I look around at the tree-studded slopes engulfed in hazy sunshine and smell the warm air as it tickles the hairs in my nose and experience a wonderful sense of solitude.

Josep nods, then gives me a grateful smile, which is really very attractive and makes my stomach fizz with excitement. But I know that's down to anticipation. Like I say, I really don't look at men in that way any more, and I became invisible to the opposite sex a long time ago. Probably around the time I had my first child, followed quickly by the second, a big dollop of baby blues, then an unexpected child and the guilt that came with getting pregnant again. We'd agreed to stop at two. But I remember needing to be held, reassured, close to my husband when I was feeling lost with two small children, and took my eye off the ball. Breathing in deeply, I tell myself that's in the past. Two weeks here, on my own, is my chance to focus on the future. Looking out at the sparkling swimming-pool, the tree-covered mountains and down the valley to the small whitewashed village glistening in the sun-light, I know this is where I can finally get my work done, plan for my future, with a degree under my belt, and finally feel like somebody, instead of Mum.

Josep Santiago walks with determination to his car. He glances back briefly, gives me a nod, gets into the car, starts the engine and drives off. I stand on the ter-race watching him go, raising a hand as if I'm waving off a visitor, even though I'm the guest. Josep drives into the heat haze, a cloud of brown dust flying up from the wheels of the car as he disappears down the drive, expertly avoiding the potholes. I wonder if he's looking behind him and calling, 'Remember, no par-ties,' out of the window.

Then, I turn back and look at the terracotta-tiled terrace, the tree-studded fields all around, the orange-tinged earth, and listen. Apart from the loud birdsong and cicadas humming in the hot afternoon sun, there is silence.

3

As the sun lowers in the sky and a smile grows on my face I feel a sense of peace. Finally, silence . . . if you don't count the cockerel, the squabbling blackbirds in the hedgerow and the occasional grunt from the pigs in the surrounding countryside and woods – the *dehesa*, as Josep called it. I can live with pigs I'll have nothing to do with. I smile wider.

I feel like a kid let loose in a sweet shop. All of this and just me, for two whole weeks.

I take a photograph and send it to the family Whats-App group. At least, I think that's what I've done. *Here, safe and sound! It's beautiful! And so peaceful!* I add a smiley face and receive a flurry of immediate responses which makes me proud: I've managed to navigate the WhatsApp thingy.

Well jealous! says Luke.

Enjoy! Relax! says Edie.

Get your work finished! instructs Ruby.

I will. Thank you for making me do this! I reply, with another smiley face and lots of kisses. I get kisses and crazy faces back. I hold the phone to my lips for just a moment, missing them, but knowing that having this time apart will benefit us all. I just wish I could stop worrying about them: Ruby and her relationship breaking up, Edie job-hunting, and Luke clearly still heartbroken after his split from his girlfriend. I wish they were all here with me.

The two large white soft-haired dogs are strolling towards me, then lie down on the terracotta tiles. I bend to stroke them. They lie at my feet, pink tongues lolling as they pant. They gaze up at me, as if to say 'So now what? You're in charge, right?'

'We'll be fine,' I tell them, and they wag their feathered tails, as if they agree with me. I see a water bowl and take it to the kitchen to refill it. I plan to start work as soon as I can but, first, there's something I can't wait to do, something I've dreamed of for years: a solo swim. A whole pool to myself without worrying that someone is staring at my out-of-shape body. Not that it ever was in shape. I've always dreamed of being able to float in a pool, just me on my own. And I can't believe I've got the chance, right now.

I head inside to find my swimsuit. It's a bit faded. Once red, it's now kind of pink, and I'm not even sure it'll fit, but there's no one around to see. I pull it out of my case in my bedroom. It's actually Ruby's case, bright against the white walls of the plain, simple bedroom at the end of a long corridor off the living room. There is a mahogany wardrobe, bed and bedside table, a simple tiled shelf for my belongings, more terracotta tiles on the floor, white curtains over a large dark-wood-framed window that opens inwards. It looks out on the woodland and mountains surrounding the farmhouse. The view is breathtaking, and now I understand why people say that. I take a moment to let the sun massage my face and breathe in lungfuls of the warm woodland air. I hear birds singing, a dog barking in the distance, a donkey braying, and I smell wild thyme. I look out at the blue of the pool, sparkling in the sunshine, the orange trees in stone-walled beds. Real oranges, like little balls of sunshine.

I feel strange, as if I've been cut from my moorings. Here, I'm not just 'Mum', I'm Eliza, just me, and it's very odd – trepidation and excitement at the same time. No one here knows who I am, what my background is. I could be anyone. It's a strange, yet thrilling sensation, which fills me as I undress and struggle to pull on my tight swimsuit, wriggling and jumping from foot to foot. It's been years since I wore one: far too self-conscious. It hasn't seen the light of day since I used to take the kids to the public pool. I hated it and stopped going in with them once they could all swim.

It wasn't the swimming I disliked. I liked the weight-lessness once the water covered my body, but I hated my naked face, my body, baring it in front of strangers. I hated the showers and the changing rooms and the walk between the two. I spent the entire time wishing my thighs didn't wobble and holding an arm over my large breasts. But here there's no one. No one to see the extra pounds I carry, thanks to cheese and the children's leftovers, or the stretch marks left behind on my breasts and belly from when I carried them. I hold my breath and pull up my swimsuit with a quick final yank, so I don't have to see them either. I would never go swimming at home nowadays. But, oh, to feel the cool water on my skin, with no one watching, is a luxury and I'm *not* going to pass it up.

I wrap a large towel around me that I found in an airing cupboard in the corridor, with a pile of sheets. It was next to another door I opened that disappears down into a dark cellar and smells of salt, reminding me of the one holiday Rob and I had in Spain before we had the children and a wonderful delicatessen we discovered there – we went in daily to buy bread, ham and olives. A breeze rose from the cellar, despite the heat outside, making me shiver, and I shut the door, then found the airing cupboard.

Now I walk barefoot down the corridor to the ter-race, loving the feeling of the cool tiles under my feet and feeling daring, still in awe that I'm actually here.

Only this morning I left home in the drizzle, and didn't even bring my slippers, which have been my constant companions since I started working from home and studying. Here my feet and I feel free. I walk out into the warm sunshine, slip off my towel, feeling the mountain breeze on my bare skin, and then, without needing any encouragement, step into the refreshing water. I hesitate just for a moment, feeling strange again in my new surroundings without the kids. Then I remembered their encouragement to make the most of my time here, and although they meant work, I know they would approve of this. It's exercise! I walk down the steps into the water to my waist, where I stand on tiptoe, my arms raised. For the first time in years, I enjoy feeling the water on my skin, and then I dive in. Loosening up with each stroke, with just the dogs watching me, as I swim up and down, then lie on my back with my face to the sun, enjoying the freedom of having the pool to myself.

It's heaven! Just what I needed. So peaceful. No interruptions, no work phone pinging to remind me that every day is a work day even though I'm at home or sitting in the car.

Eventually I climb out, feeling the warm air on my skin and the water trickling over my body, enjoying the isolation and privacy of this place.

I reach the top step, and turn to look out on the dusty land, the mountains, watching the shifting patterns of the shadows cast by clouds. And nearly throw myself back into the water as a young man in work clothes strolls past, in the field on the other side of the pool, driving a small herd of excitable pigs back towards the farm buildings.

I grab the towel and hold it to myself. He must be Pedro the pig man. He's young, with olive skin, wearing a sleeveless shirt and headphones.

'Hello! *Buenos días – buenas noches*, I mean,' I stutter, and hold up a hand in a wave, the other clutching the towel tightly to my chest.

He nods, not raising a smile but looking at me with interest, clearly wondering who I am and where I've come from.

'I'm Eliza Bytheway,' I add, wishing I could say it in Spanish. I inch my hand up a little further, by way of a universal greeting.

He stares at me, and I have no idea whether to keep my hand in the air, feeling slightly uncomfortable that he hasn't returned my greeting. 'Um . . .' I wonder what to say next and if I've made a faux-pas. If so, what could it have been?

'Pedro,' he says. 'I take care of the pigs.'

I smile with relief that he's responded, but it's not the friendliest welcome I've ever had. I wonder what Josep has told him about me being here. 'I'm staying at the house,' I say, feeling a bit pathetic.

He nods.

'If you need anything, just let me know,' I say, hoping he'll say the same to me. He doesn't.

'You are staying here?' he asks, his eyes narrowing with suspicion.

'Yes, just for a while.' I don't need to offer too much information: something tells me Pedro and I aren't going to be sharing coffee breaks while I'm here. He'll be doing his bit on the farm and I'll stick to the house. But that's fine by me. The fewer distractions the better.

'Well,' I say awkwardly, attempting a smile, 'I'm sure you have things to do. Don't let me hold you up.' I raise a hand again, then quickly lower it. 'The pigs to look after.'

'The baby ones – they lost their mother,' he says, surprising me with a full sentence. Then he starts walking, still looking back at me and the farmhouse. I don't move, for fear of making my state of undress more obvious.

Behind him, on the other side of the hedge, I see the bobbing backs of black piglets following him, like a group of nursery children heading home from a day's outing, ready for a snack before bedtime. I watch Pedro pass and the pigs behind him, wondering if he's always like this or if it's just me he's taken a dislike to. As the piglets run and tumble past, I don't know whether to go inside or stand still. I haven't been this close to a herd of pigs before and I don't want to startle them. I have no idea if they're friendly or not. I stand still, watching them pass. Pedro throws a glance at me. The pigs are following him as though he's the Pied Piper. Interestingly, I notice there's little smell. I have quite a sensitive nose – I can smell an old apple core at a distance, and too much aftershave on young men can have me throwing open the windows and gasping for air.

As they pass, the piglets' ears flap over their eyes, bottoms bobbing, and they make the occasional excited squeal. When they're safely beyond me, and Pedro has turned the corner into the farmyard out of sight, I run inside to my room, the dogs following me. I shut the white nets on my window then take a shower, while the dogs wait for me patiently outside: they clearly want to be fed, and have worked out that I'm the only one here to do it.

Back on the terrace, showered, dogs fed, with a glass of wine from the open bottle on the kitchen counter, I settle on the sofa there, with the dogs at my feet and a plate of cheese, ham and olives from the kitchen: I was following instructions to help myself to whatever I could find. I hold my face up to the warm, slowly setting sun. It's perfect. I pick up a piece of thin sliced ham I carved from the leg in the kitchen and pop it into my mouth. It's like nothing I've ever tasted before. I pick up another piece, this time breathing in the briny scent, and slowly put it into my mouth. It's delicious:

nutty, cured, melt-in-the-mouth ham – I try not to think about the pigs that have just followed Pedro happily from the woods.

What more could I want? I've got peace, quiet, sun, a pool and gorgeous food. If I can't finish my work, I never will.

4

The next morning, I wake to a lick. My eyes ping open. One of the dogs is stretched out next to me, his accomplice sitting by the bed, not as brave as his friend. I take a moment to work out where I am and remember I'm in Spain. No phone pinging into life, just peace – and two soft-as-butter dogs. I see that the bedroom door is ajar – I must have forgotten to shut it properly last night.

'Off, off!' I laugh. 'You'll get me into terrible trouble with your boss!' And the dogs wag their tails.

I pad down the cool, tiled hallway in my pyjamas, far too hot for this weather, and feed the dogs, then make coffee. I decide to take it outside and go up the steps to the roof terrace. Pedro is passing again. Once again, I try to brave it out and call good morning. He looks at me, pushing his wheelbarrow, and nods.

Maybe I should have offered him coffee. But he's gone.

Two hours later, back under the shade of the terrace overlooking the sparkling pool, I've swapped WhatsApp messages with the family, scrolled through Facebook and Twitter and tried to google a few ideas, but I'm still no further ahead with my final essay for my coursework. I tap my pen on my notepad.

'Come on, what to write?' I rack my brains. 'Think!' I tell myself crossly.

I had finally decided I wanted to go to university to do the bits in life I'd skipped when I was younger. I'd left school as soon as I could and begun a series of part-time jobs. I worked to make my own money, but also to get out of the house. I wanted to move out of my parents' home, but had no idea of what I wanted to do, whether or not I should go to college. I knew I wanted a home and a family, and eventually I met Rob at a nightclub on one of my nights off. We had fun, lots of fun. I was still working out what to do with my life but he wanted to be a lawyer. So, I kept the money coming in while he studied. The years ticked by. Soon Rob was starting work and we were setting up home, getting pregnant and married in that order. My time for college seemed to have been and gone. But never say never. Now is my time. I'm doing a foundation year to make up for my lack of A levels. I'm on my way to becoming a professional. It's like, now, with the family grown-up, I've realized I don't know who I am. Who is Eliza Bytheway if she isn't a mum, juggling a family and a part-time job? What am I?

When I got pregnant, I thought I had everything. At first Rob was delighted – so much so that we even planned a second child soon after Ruby was born. It was after the third, Luke, a sickly baby, that things started to unravel. After a stressful Christmas dinner that saw me in the kitchen, tears streaming down my face, gravy burnt, Rob decided it wasn't working for him and left. With the help of my friend, Alice, I got through it. Then each of the children left home, and the family house had to be sold to pay off the debts Rob had racked up against it. There was just enough left, after the debts had been cleared, to buy some-where for me to live . . . I was alone, in a ground-floor flat, surrounded by boxes, wondering where my life had gone.

Now I've decided to find something I'm good at, work out what I want to study, then train. I would say retrain, but as I didn't train for anything in the first place that wouldn't make sense. I wish I had – then I wouldn't be in this position now. I'd love to be able to say 'I'm going back to . . .' whatever it was before I had my family. But I don't have a profession to pick up. Other things in my life had felt more important than going to college: a job that paid weekly, security, family. The things I didn't have growing up. But a job, a marriage and a family weren't the same as security. With some letters after my name, though, I'd feel I was more than Ruby's, Luke's and Edie's mum, and Rob's ex-wife.

It suddenly hit when Luke went to university to study law. After dropping him off, I drove home, shut the front door and stood with my back to it in the quiet empty flat. I remember thinking, He's going to be a lawyer so what are you going to be, Eliza Bytheway? I felt a huge sense of loss, not just for my youngest child leaving home but for me too. I had no idea who I was. There was a gaping hole in my life that should have been filled with the other bit of me, the bit that had a career I wanted to restart. But I was an empty shell, craving something to fill me.

I loved being a mum, but I felt lost and so lonely, with a real ache in my heart. Not that I wanted a man – I definitely don't want to go there again. That wasn't the answer. But I did feel totally alone. I realized I needed to go back to that crossroads, when I'd intended to go to college but instead got pregnant. I want to do the very best I can in this foundation course. It might be online and not in a class to meet other people, as I'd hoped, but I'm happy that I chose to do it.

I had a little bit of money when the house was finally

sold, the debts settled, my new flat paid for, and decided to invest in a new beginning for myself. If I can just get this foundation year under my belt, I'll be able to work out which courses I want to continue with that will help get me a better job.

I stand up and stretch, debating another swim in the pool, and look around for Pedro. He's bound to be nearby – I'll wait until later, I think.

I wander back into the house and admire its lovely features: the dark-wood window frame, looking out over the fields, dotted with windblown trees, the patterned tiled floor, the open hatch into the kitchen, and the sideboard. I take lots of photos and send a couple to the family WhatsApp group.

I sent them a message early this morning, but no one's replied yet. I'm guessing none of them are up. I decide to explore the house again, this time at a leisurely pace. First, though, I close the door on the master bedroom, but not before I get a waft of cologne, and feel a stirring I haven't experienced in a long time, a fluttery feeling, a sort of delightful shiver. I put it down to the sunshine and quiet . . .

I sit at the table on the shady terrace and pick up my pen, the first page of my pristine notebook staring back at me. I have to start. I just need an idea, a spark to set me off. I write a list of things that 'make me happy'. My children, most of the time. What else? Cheese. And that ham! I remember it melting on my tongue, disappearing to nothing, its taste lingering.

This is hopeless. I look back over my projects for the year and flick through my textbooks. I google 'health and happiness'. Scrolling through the pages of results, I read lots of recipes that I intend to try when I get home. I make a note of them on the page where my essay should be progressing. I put down my pen. The dogs sit panting, pink tongues lolling, as they move further into the shade. I sigh. Something will come to me. 'Health, happiness and wellbeing,' I repeat, pick up the pen and write it again. Still my mind is blank. I turn to Facebook for ideas and soon I'm lost in photographs of the children when they were younger, making me smile and my eyes fill with tears.

At lunchtime, I take another picture of the pool and send another WhatsApp message: *Thinking of having a dip!* I write, with a smiley face, and this time get a reply from all three children, including emojis, and capital letters – I have no idea what they stand for.

I look at my essay or, rather, the blank page that is now full of recipe ideas. My brain is fried. 'Health, happiness and wellbeing,' I repeat, and close my notepad.

I stand and walk back into the farmhouse, into the cool darkness, and pad across the patterned tiles to the kitchen. I need to find something for lunch. I start by slicing some ham. I find olives too. Big fat green ones in a pot with a wooden spoon and a lid. Ripe tomatoes – I hold one to my nose and breathe in its grassy scent. I slice some Manchego cheese to go with bread, which is a little stale now, so I toast it. I love the smell of toasting bread – so comforting. There was always toast for breakfast when the kids were growing up, when they got home from school, if they were ill, and when they got in from nights out with friends. It's the last of the bread and I'll need to go shopping soon.

I look outside, through the wrought-iron window bars to the sparkling pool. Too hot to go into town now, I think, as I take my food onto the terrace with a glass of water. I sit and pop another piece of the ham into my mouth, then a slice of firm tomato, drizzled in peppery olive oil from a bottle by the stove. Its flavour explodes in my mouth. Then I sample the salty, glistening olives coated with dried herbs, between bites of the toast I've rubbed with garlic and drizzled with oil. I wonder whether to have a glass of wine, but I don't. I'm here to work. But my brain seems to have shut down in the heat.

I'm used to my brain shutting down and to feeling hot. No one tells you what to expect when the menopause hits. It came as an almighty surprise to me. My brain went to mush and I'm always hot. It's one of the things that made me want to do my course: I needed to get my brain back. It was a bit like being pregnant again, and a constant reminder of how quickly life moves on. I shake my head. I sit and listen to the leaves rustling in the warm breeze, the birds chirping to each other as if they're passing on local news and gossip. I can hear the buzz of bees working hard, like little engines, visiting the plants and flowers near me, and in the distance a donkey is braying. I finish my lunch and the glass of water. It's too hot outside for me now, even in the shade, so I stand up with my plate and glass and head inside. The dogs follow and flop down in the cool.

I wash up and clean the kitchen: a distraction tactic so I don't have to look at the essay I'm writing, which now seems to be a series of simple Spanish recipes. I look around the open-plan living room and dining room, enjoying the cool as much as the dogs are. I sit on the worn leather sofa, and slowly the quiet becomes overwhelming. I'm not used to it. It's never this quiet at home. There's always something going on that stops me getting started on my work. Here, there's nothing and it's unsettling.

I spot a radio on a shelf. Getting up, I turn it on, and it bursts into life with music, making me jump. The two dogs leap up too.

'It's okay!' I laugh, trying to soothe them. 'It's fine,' I reassure them, then find myself dancing in front of the dogs. They begin to wag their tails and pant, and I grab a pair of paws and dance to the rhythm of the song. No one is watching – at least, I'm pretty sure they aren't. I haven't seen Pedro for hours.

When the song finishes, I collapse back onto the sofa, laughing, and the dogs jump onto me, licking my face. I puff and fan my cheeks.

'What to do with myself now?' I say to the dogs, as I ease them off the sofa. 'We'll go for a walk in a bit,' I tell them. 'It's too hot now.' I yawn, and feel the need for a nap. Well, why not? I can here. Then I'll walk the dogs and get some shopping. I walk across the tiled floor and along the corridor to my room. It's beautifully cool with the shutters pulled to. I lie down on the bed, hearing the pitter-patter of paws following me.

I wake from a deep sleep, much longer than I intended, my hand on a furry face next to me.

'No dogs on the bed!' I hear Josep's words, and imagine him adding, 'I know what you British are like about your pets.' I shoo them off, straighten the covers and brush away any of their hairs. I open the shutters. It's definitely a little cooler. The sun is lower in the sky, taking the intensity of heat out of the day and making it feel softer.

'Come on,' I say to the dogs. 'Let's go for a walk.' They look at me as if I'm speaking gibberish, which of course I am. I wonder if I should try to speak Spanish to them.

I look up 'walk' on my translation app. *'Pasear!'* I say, but still they don't move. I need to work on my pronunciation. Maybe I should attempt to learn some Spanish while I'm here. Perhaps learning a new language could be the answer to my project – health, happiness and wellbeing. It would certainly keep my brain more active. I tell myself I'll definitely try. After all, this is about me embracing new experiences and, so far, I'm doing pretty well.

5

I find a pair of well-worn dog leads hanging on a hook beside the large armoire, by the big front door. Picking them up seems to be the signal for a walk – the dogs dance about excitedly. I shut all the windows and internal doors in the house, double-checking to make sure I've locked them before I step outside. I lock the front door, put the dogs on their leads and look down the dusty potholed drive. Which way to go? I turn towards the farmyard, its barns and the countryside beyond. With all the fields around the house and the woods behind them, it seems a shame not to explore, especially as it'll be cool under the trees.

If I could see Pedro, I'd ask him for the best route . . .

'Pedro? Hello? *Buenos días?*' I call, stepping tentatively towards the farmyard. I've never been on a farm before so I'm not sure what to expect. It's very quiet. I look out at the fields but they're vast and empty. I sigh. I turn to the barns. Maybe he's in there. I walk towards them.

'Pedro?' I call, planning to stick my head into each of them to see if he's there. If he's anything like my kids he'll be listening to music through headphones and won't be able to hear a thing. I head towards the open door.

'Hey!'

His voice makes me jump as he appears in the doorway. I don't know why. Seems he's been here all along. Why couldn't he just answer? But something about the look on his face says I'm interrupting him.

'*Buenas días*,' I repeat politely, as he looks at me impatiently.

'Hey,' he repeats, less politely.

I have no idea what his problem with me is, but he clearly has one. I find myself attempting to look around him. It's possible he has a friend here. Something about him and his behaviour makes me feel uncomfortable, but I can't quite put my finger on what it is. Maybe he's just not keen on being friends. He looks around without making eye contact, keen to get on with whatever he's doing. I don't hear signs of him having company.

'I was wondering where I should walk with the dogs,' I say.

He stares at me and I'm not sure he's understood.

Suddenly, he throws out an arm, gesturing to the countryside. 'Walk where you want.' He gives a sharp, irritated nod, and the conversation is over. I let out a sigh as he turns back to the barn.

I guess I'll just see where my feet take me. I walk towards the gate into the field, looking to the left. There are pigs in the far-off corners. I plan to walk straight towards the woods, across the field. And now I can see a well-worn path, leading to the trees. As I walk, I see some of the trees have had their bark stripped, revealing orange wood beneath, and wonder why. I'm keeping the dogs on the lead as they pull me forward. The last thing I want is to lose one. I'm breathing in the hot herb-infused air as we follow the dry, hard path.

'Steady, steady,' I say, as the dogs tug at their leads, keen to explore, sniff and run. I'm hot, as we hurry across the uneven, rough, scorched ground. I wish I'd brought water. Finally, we reach the shade of the trees – heaven – and the dogs slow down, wanting to take in the smells, as do I. We walk on at a more relaxed pace through the oak trees.

Finally, we reach a clearing, like a little oasis, where the ground is covered with twigs and fallen leaves. I let the dogs off the leads to sniff around, keeping my eye on them. They happily snuffle about in the fallen twigs on the woodland floor and I sit down at the base of a big oak and think about my essay. My thoughts turn once again to home. I wonder how everyone is doing and, missing them, pull out my phone, check my WhatsApp and distractedly flick through photographs with one eye on the dogs all the time.

Finally, my thoughts snap back to why I'm here, and all sorts of ideas come to me about health, wellbeing and happiness. This is making me happy, taking time to stand and stare. Maybe I should write about forest bathing. I read in a magazine that it originated in Japan. Spending time among trees helped with mindfulness, brought down blood pressure and lowered stress. I feel better already, just taking in the light coming through the canopy of branches and dancing on the forest floor. I could write about spending time with trees to promote health, wellbeing and happiness! Excitement surges in me. This is good – really good! My spirits are lifting and my mind starting to whirr. I need to get back and use the Wi-Fi at the farmhouse to find out exactly what forest bathing is and how it works. I need to write down how I feel right now. I push my phone into my pocket.

I turn to put the dogs on the leads. I can hear them but can't see them. I call, and hear rustling in the undergrowth.

'Come on, let's go. Good dogs! *Bueno!*' I might be getting the hang of this.

The rustling gets louder and I call again, when suddenly I hear a grunt, a snort and a high-pitched squeal.

I swing round to see a huge beast careering out of the undergrowth and barrelling towards me. I try to scream for help, hoping Pedro is nearby, but I stumble backwards, over roots poking through the ground, catching my foot, and crashing into the oak tree I'd just been sitting under. I wave the dog leads at the vast white pig.

'Shoo! Shoo!' I'm swishing the leads about in a figure of eight action. The pig grunts again, still careering towards me.

'SHOOO!' I wave the leads in huge circles and suddenly it swerves, squeals and disappears back into the undergrowth as quickly as it appeared.

My heart is racing as I push myself away from the tree. It was huge, and angry by the look of it, one ear pointing upwards, eyes wide and glaring. It could have killed me. What if it went for the dogs? I need to find them and make sure they're safe.

I force myself to call their names, over and over. 'Mateo! Diego!' What if they don't understand me? I try again with a Spanish accent. The words barely come out of my strangled throat. What will I tell Josep? For heaven's sake, I can't even look after a house and two well-behaved dogs. I'm totally useless! Why did I think this was a good idea? I want to go home. Tears spring to my eyes and I hear more rustling in the undergrowth. I brace myself for the huge creature to reappear and wonder if I could make it up the tree.

The rustling gets louder and I jump at a low-hanging

branch, but my fingers slip, I lose my grip and land back on the ground with a thump. I wait with terror to be bowled over by the pig but I'll try to scare it off again. It's not going to attack the dogs on my watch.

I take a deep breath, ready to shout for them – and see them, sitting next to me, panting happily. I don't remember when I last felt so relieved. Maybe when I lost Edie in a shopping arcade. Panic gripped me until I saw her standing next to a security guard, holding his hand, as he reported a little girl who had lost her mum into his walkie-talkie. Now my heart calms and I hug Diego and Mateo, pressing my face into their soft white fur. Then, taking a restorative breath, I say, 'Come on, guys, let's get out of here', scramble to my feet and slip on their leads. We hurry back towards the *cortijo*, quicker than I've moved in a long time, limping and aching all the way.

Back in the cool of the house I pour myself some water with shaking hands. I'm furious: I wish I'd known not to go that way. But I'm not sure if I'm angry with the pig, myself or Pedro. He could have warned me not to walk through the woods, I think, adrenalin still pumping through my body. I'm going to find Pedro, I decide, to tell him that the dogs and I could have been killed. That animal should be in a pen. I stalk out of the house towards the farm buildings, ready to give Pedro a piece of my mind.

6

'A what?' Pedro screws up his face as I try to explain. I found him in one of the outbuildings, typing into his phone. He ushers me outside. 'Health and safety,' he says, in Spanish, but I get it. 'Problem?' he asks.

I just don't have the Spanish to tell him what has happened and resort to speaking English a bit too loudly. 'A big white pig! In the woodland! It was wild!'

'Sorry?'

A rush of nervous laughter bubbles up in me. I push it down, take a deep breath and start again. 'Sorry . . .' I slow right down. 'I'm Eliza,' I say, in case he doesn't know I'm here for a while, not just a day visitor. 'I'm staying . . .' Josep asked me not to say anything to anyone about him going away. Did that include Pedro? Surely Pedro knows he's gone away.

'I'm staying at the house. The *cortijo*.' I point.

'Ah, *sí*.' He nods. 'The *cortijo*.'

'I was walking, like you said' – I do finger-walking on the palm of one hand with the other – 'over there.' I point towards the woodland. 'With the dogs.' And, yes, I woof. He smiles as if he's entertained. I sigh. I'm not sure why I'm bothering, but, really, that pig scared the life out of me. Someone needs to do something about whatever is in there.

He stands there staring at me, his arms folded across his chest, and I wonder if he has understood anything of what I said.

'A big pig!' I put my fingers on top of my head as ears and oink. Yes, I actually oink.

He says nothing. I'm wondering whether to leave him or persist.

I oink again, feeling ridiculous, like I did when the children were little, playing with their toy farm and asking what noise a pig made.

The sun is beating down on the back of my head and I wondering if I'm going a little crazy with the heat or just from being on my own.

'A pig?' he says.

'Yes! It was huge. In the woods!' I'm excited by the breakthrough and rather pleased with myself.

'We have pigs, in woods.' He juts out his chin. 'They are . . . wild. *Pata negra* pigs.'

'This wasn't a black pig,' I say. 'It was a big white one, angry. Grrrrr!' Once again I hold up my fingers as ears.

He shakes his head and lights a cigarette. 'We only have black pigs here,' he says, and puts up his hands to hang down over his eyes. 'Very gentle. You must make a mistake.'

This time it's my turn to shake my head. 'It was very angry. Loose in the woods.'

'No, not a pig.'

'Well, whatever it was, it could have killed me or the dogs. I thought you should know. Maybe a boar?'

He shakes his head again. 'Our boar would not—'

'Really?'

'Yes, really!' He walks towards a stone shelter in the shade. He beckons me to follow. 'Our pigs roam free in the woods but are peaceful pigs. Very gentle. And our boar,' he points over the gate to what must be a sty, 'he is going nowhere. And nowhere near the lady pigs.'

He points again to the stone shelter, cool in the shade.

He opens the gate and I follow him back the way I came, across the tree-studded field. I didn't notice the stone shelter before.

Nervously I bend down and peer in.

The huge pig doesn't move. He barely lifts his head to acknowledge visitors, let alone charge out intent on mowing me down. In fact, he barely looks as if he's breathing, other than the huge sigh he lets out.

'You see, you are mistaken. Our boar is . . . How do you say? Lovesick?'

'Lovesick?'

'He grieves. His partner has died, giving birth,' he gestures to a barn next door, which I'm presuming is the nursery, 'and he does not leave this room. He doesn't eat and has no interest in the lady pigs. He is . . .' Pedro searches for the right word, '. . . heartbroken,' he finishes, then tuts. 'Our pigs live outside, not in shelters. He is not behaving like he should. He is not in the woods chasing dogs,' he says firmly. I gaze at the big boar and wonder if a pig can really be lovesick. Then I turn back to Pedro. Something isn't quite right. Is he teasing me? The British woman who doesn't speak Spanish?

'Well, something did,' I say firmly.

He shrugs, finishes his cigarette and stubs it out on the ground. 'Better to stay away from the woods,' he says gravely. 'From the pigs.' I'm being told, not advised. 'So you do not get wrong stick and tell Señor Josep things you do not understand.' He stares at me. 'Best stick to the *cortijo* and the dogs.'

I shiver.

'Yes?'

I stare at him and, feeling uncomfortable, I nod in agreement. What's he talking about, 'things you do not understand'? And what wrong stick?

'You are here, with the dogs. No Señor Josep?' he questions me.

Suddenly, feeling guarded, I swallow. 'He's . . . he'll be back very soon. Just a quick visit,' I gabble. 'But I should let him know about the problem in the woods,' I add, wondering if I really should contact him or whether Pedro is right and I should just stay out of the woods. It's not my business.

Pedro's dark eyes narrow. 'I can look after the dogs if you don't want to be alone. It's very . . . remote. It's no problem,' he says.

He can't be much older than Luke, I think, as he chews a piece of gum. His baseball cap is on back to front.

The dogs are so well behaved . . . But he's saying I could just go back to where I came from, if I wanted to.

'*Gracias*,' I say firmly. Something tells me it's not an option to go home. 'But I'm fine where I am.' Josep Santiago employed me for a reason. I'm here to stay.

I turn into the warm glow of the setting sun and consider going for a swim, but not until Pedro has left. He seems as suspicious of me as I am about him. I'm unsettled. I need to put some distance between him and me. I'll walk into town and do some shopping – buy some bread at least.

Back in the house I grab a basket. The dogs look up at me expectantly, seemingly excited about a second walk. 'Okay, okay,' I say. It's not like they're any bother and I'm enjoying their company. I collect their leads again, lock the front door carefully and head down the dusty track to the lane at the bottom. I don't bother to ask Pedro for directions. I'll just follow my nose.

As I walk away, I feel him watching me and can't help but think there's something he doesn't want me to see in that barn. I know when someone's trying to hide something from me – like Ruby, when I found condoms under her mattress and she was only sixteen, and Luke with the vaping machine he'd bought from someone in school, and the dried herbs Edie kept in a coffee jar in her bedroom for baking. Or when school reports that other parents had had went missing, letters about parents' evening and missing coursework. It's instinct: you don't want to be right, but usually are, that something's up. And why was he so dismissive about the creature in the woods? It was dangerous, and if it wasn't the boar, what was it? Why was Pedro not more concerned?

As I walk into town, I look at the wildflowers growing along the roadside, following the cream rock face into the small whitewashed town. It's nestled in the middle of a big green plain, with mountains all around it. I feel myself settling as I walk. The hot dust from the roadside tickles my nose, making me sneeze, but I like the heat. It's a long way from the wet summer back home where eating outside can be miserable without the sun on your face and the scent of flowers.

As I walk, I think about the work I have to do, letting my mind drift back to the words I need to put on the page for my final essay. I'm not sure forest bathing is as calm and restful as I thought. Maybe I should write about how life seems to have changed for everyone in the last few years. How we're appreciating things we once took for granted. Working from home has become the norm. Maybe I could write about the people who have chosen to work from home in hot, sunny places, like here, how they've changed their lives for the better and found happiness. I'd just need to find some people to talk to. So far the only person I've met is Pedro and I don't think he'll help me, given his unwelcoming lack of charm.

I feel my shoulders relaxing as I walk past the recycling bins on the outskirts of the town and turn the corner, past a car park. From a building somewhere high up, among the higgledy-piggledy whitewashed houses, I can hear someone playing the guitar and families talking loudly, arguing even, through open windows. This is more like it. The sound of people, families. It's much more what I'm used to.

But at the back of my mind is that beast in the woods . . . and Pedro. Maybe he's right. The *cortijo* is in a very secluded, rural location. I wanted peace and quiet . . . but maybe this is just too quiet. I swallow. And why would Josep need a house-sitter, with Pedro there to look after the dogs? And why did I feel the need to tell Pedro that I'm staying put? I'm not sure what's going on. Or even if I want to know. I'm here to get my essay done and then I'll be leaving. Whatever Pedro's problem is, it's none of my business. But I don't plan to go back into those woods.

7

I walk towards the town, the dogs beside me. The sun is less intense now. There is a small dark, grocery store just past the car park. I can hear men greeting each other and talking loudly, but they stop as I walk by. There's a smell I recognize but can't name. The shop seems to be built into the side of the mountain, and is almost like a cave, dark and cool, with a series of small caverns around it, sealed with wooden doors and bolts. I follow the narrow, cobbled road up the hill, where I find a larger shop, a small supermarket. I tie up the dogs next to a bowl of water, telling them to 'Stay!' and 'Be good!' Again I wish I could say it in Spanish.

Inside, the air-conditioning is chilly and I fill my basket with bread, milk and my usual staples. The young woman on the till greets me with a smile.

She's got long dark shiny hair and big gold earrings that catch the sun. I pick up a few other bits, and head for her till. She puts down her phone and starts putting through my shopping. Suddenly she stops, hurries to the door and calls loudly to another young woman walking past, speaking quickly and laughing. Her friend, with short red hair and similar gold jewellery, laughs and calls back. They wave, say goodbye and the young woman returns to my shopping.

She stops again and holds up a packet of cheese. 'This one,' she says, and taps it with a long, painted fingernail, 'is no good.' I wonder what I've done wrong. I watch her as she steps out from behind the till and goes to the refrigerated shelf. She comes back with another packet. 'This one is better,' she says. 'A local producer. And is on offer! Much better . . . flavour. My friend makes it. Not that you'd know about it, if you are not part of the Gastronómica Society, phfff.' She throws a hand into the air.

'The what?'

'The Gast— Oh.' She shakes her head. 'Nothing. But it is hard to get your produce noticed if you are a woman around here. But I'm sure you will enjoy it.'

'*Gracias.*' I smile and pull out my card to pay.

'Let me know if you like it.' She smiles back. Suddenly I'm lifted by her kindness. 'My friends and I eat this as tapas. With this.' She turns around, takes

a bottle from a shelf and shows it to me. It's sherry.
I always thought it was for old people, but I don't
say it.

'I'll take it,' I say, and add it to my shopping, excited
by the extravagant purchase.

'Beautiful dogs,' she says, of the two waiting by the
door.

I wish I could take credit for them, but I can't. 'Aren't
they?' I agree. I bid goodbye to the young woman and
promise I'll let her know how the cheese and sherry go
together.

With my shopping in my basket I step out of the
cool shop and smile at the two dogs sitting there
patiently in the shade where I've tied them.

I pick up their leads. I could go straight back to the
cortijo now I've got my shopping. But I look up the hill
and hear the guitar again. Instead I decide to continue
up, just to see what's there. I walk in the shade of the
houses on either side of the street, with blue and yellow mosaic tiling on the walls and on the sides of the
terracotta steps leading up to the front doors. The
walls are whitewashed, and red geraniums fill pots
along the edges of balconies and in wrought-iron
brackets attached to the walls. I can hear conversations
taking place, loud and passionate. I think back to my
own busy flat and wonder if that's what we sound like.
Somehow it feels so much warmer in Spanish as the
speakers talk at volume and over each other. I can

smell cooking – olive oil and garlic – and my stomach rumbles.

I walk further up the hill, a little out of puff now, past a small shop with brightly coloured scarves tied to a wooden board outside. Eventually the road opens out onto a small enclosed cobbled square. Around the outside I spot a couple of bars and restaurants with awnings, parasols and blackboards offering the daily specials. In the middle there's a water fountain in a stone basin. I step up to it, take a sip, then stand and look around. A big church with huge doors stands in front of what must be an amazing view. Narrow cobbled streets lead off the square, and another road winds up the hill with more houses. Maybe from there you get to see over the church to the views beyond. Perhaps all of the roads lead to the square. Again, I can hear the guitar playing and I wonder where the music is coming from. The open windows of an apartment above a restaurant on the corner? I can smell something delicious and my stomach rumbles again.

I notice a small bar with a bustling terrace area. A cold beer and some of that delicious-smelling food would go down a treat.

I follow the smell to the street just off the main square, under the apartment with the guitar playing. I stand outside a big wooden door and look around for a sign or a menu. Two men, with long greying moustaches, whom I recognize from the first grocery shop I passed, approach the door. 'Excuse me,' they say in Spanish, and give tight smiles.

'Oh, yes, of course.' I step back from the door.

'Can I help you?' the man with the longest moustache says, in English, clearly singling me out as a visitor.

'I was just wondering where the menu was,' I reply, looking around. His companion taps on the door twice. It opens and the delicious aroma of garlic, olive oil and herbs tumbles out and, with it, the sound of loud voices talking and laughing. It seems this is the place to eat round here.

The two men laugh as they slip through the open door. 'No menu. We eat the dish of the day,' one says.

'Well, that sounds good,' I say, and walk around him to look into the restaurant.

He holds up a hand. 'No,' he says.

I look down at the dogs. 'I didn't think.'

He tilts his head. 'It is not the dogs that are the problem, Señora. This place is not for you.'

I'm wondering if I've just heard him correctly. 'Pardon?'

'This place is not for you. Over there,' he says, pointing to the three small restaurants on the square, one with a wooden terrace and parasols providing a little shade.

I'm trying to understand what has just happened.

'Good day,' he says, then turns back into the buzzing restaurant and the door shuts. I'm too shocked to be angry.

I walk back towards the square and the bar with the parasols. I spot a small round table, my knees shaking a little. A beer is exactly what I need and I head towards the little table with my shopping and the dogs. I'm still reeling from my encounter with those men, and a sense of injustice and irritation is surfacing.

Just one beer before I go back and start work again. I'm a grown woman, for goodness' sake, and can hardly believe I've just been turned away from a restaurant.

I head towards the bar, but just as I reach the terrace, a couple arrives from another direction and takes the little table for two. I glance around the small busy terrace, fury building inside me.

'Come, come!' A middle-aged waiter appears, carrying a tray on one hand. He's wearing a small pinny.

'Oh, don't worry.' I'm going off the idea of the beer. Clearly this place doesn't want to take my money.

He places two bowls of French fries on a table and the small group gathered there fall on them. The smell is divine and I'm hungrier than I thought. He waves me inside. I walk up to the bar, the dogs following. He whizzes behind the counter, and reappears with a bowl of water, which he puts down for the dogs, patting them as they start to lap. He smiles at me. 'Beautiful dogs. Now, what can I get you?' he says, in perfect English.

'Um . . . a beer, please, a *cerveza*,' I say, trying my Spanish. '*Por favor*.'

He starts pouring the beer, silver bracelets and rings shining against his brown skin. He has dark hair, and a bandanna tied around his neck. A beautiful Spanish omelette is sitting on the counter.

'Would you like a slice?' he says, smiling. 'It's very good. Just made.' He's speaking with an Essex accent, if I'm not mistaken. So that was why the Spanish man shooed me this way. He thought I should be with the other holidaymakers.

'Thank you, I would,' I say to the barman, my mouth watering.

The beer, with a big frothy top, is in a shapely glass, cold condensation running down the side. I can't wait to taste it. The waiter cuts a slice of the omelette, puts it on a small plate with a fork and places it on a tray with the beer. Before I can say anything he heads out towards the terrace with the tray, pulling up a chair at a group there and beckons for me to sit.

'Oh, um, I . . .'

'You are here for Spanish conversation class, right?' he asks.

I look at the small group, where the French fries have just been delivered. My beer and the omelette have joined them. And I really want them. The group turn and all eyes are on me.

'Hi!' says a woman, in a brightly coloured kaftan and headscarf to match. 'Have you come to join us?'

'Oh, wonderful! A new member,' says a young woman with short hair.

'Well, er, no, but I suppose . . .' Spanish conversation would be good: it might help me communicate with the dogs. I promised myself a long time ago not to let anxiety get the better of me when I was trying new things. I think about my essay and inspiration strikes: these could be just the people I need to talk to about how they changed their lives and found happiness abroad.

'Oh, do sit down!' says the woman in the kaftan, her bangles jangling up her arms.

'That would be lovely.' I'm suddenly very pleased to see welcoming faces. Perhaps the man at the other restaurant thought I was lost and looking for the Spanish class. It makes sense now. I take the seat being offered to me at the table. I put the dogs' leads under the leg of the chair and they obediently lie down.

'How lovely to have a new member of the group!'

'Have you just moved here? I haven't seen you before.'

'What lovely dogs! How are you finding it here?'

'Would you like a chip?'

They're staring at me, like Buzz Lightyear joining

Woody and his friends in *Toy Story*. Luke loved that film. I get a twinge of homesickness and distract myself with a sip of the cold, refreshing beer.

'Actually, I'm just here for a couple of weeks,' I answer the first question.

'Oh, shame.'

'I'm visiting,' I say.

'Ooh, who?'

'Yes, what brings you here?'

I think about Josep: I mustn't say I'm a house-sitter.

'Um . . .' I look at the expectant faces. Knowing I have to offer something up, I shrug. 'I have work I need to do,' I add, not giving them the full picture.

They all seem to expect more, but I don't have anything. Suddenly panic rises at my little white lie.

'I'm staying with Josep Santiago. At Cortijo Santiago.' I hope this will put paid to the questions.

'Oh, is he joining you?'

I swallow, reminding myself to tell no one where he was going. But, in fact, I don't know where he went. All I know is that it's a business trip to meet clients and I have his phone number.

'He's dealing with business at the moment. I'm just getting to know the place.'

'So, you're not here looking for a new man, then?' asks an older woman, with a lot of hairspray and lipstick.

'Definitely not.' I laugh. 'I'm very much off the market.' Somehow, I like the liberation this gives me. I'm not interested in anyone. I'm not looking for a date. Why does everyone assume you're looking for a relationship when your kids finally leave and you're on your own? I just want to throw myself into my work, make a life for myself.

I scoop up a forkful of the Spanish omelette. Crispy at the edges, light in the middle, layered with sliced potatoes, seasoned perfectly . . . and then a strange aftertaste. I chew and swallow. 'Wow!' I say, and they're all watching me. 'That's interesting,' I say. 'Lots of flavours. Anyone else had the omelette?'

They shake their heads.

'Juan always makes us chips. A taste of home,' says the woman in the kaftan.

I frown. 'But you all live here, don't you?' I wave my fork around in the general direction of the pretty little whitewashed village.

'Oh, yes. We all live here.'

'I'm Marianne,' says the kaftan woman. 'Back home everyone called me Mary, but here I'm Marianne. A bit like Juan.' She indicates the barman in his calf-length jeans, deck shoes and silver jewellery. 'Back home he was a postman called John. That's the beauty of moving abroad. You can be who you want to be!' She looks at me. 'And who are you?'

'I'm Eliza,' I say, and nothing more.

'I'm Josie. I run a B&B here with my partner,' says the younger woman, checking the time on her phone. 'Well . . . I did. It's just me now.'

'I'm Eileen, golf widow,' says a woman sitting in the shade with a hat pushed down on her head.

'Sally,' says another. 'I'm a different sort of widow. I moved here after my husband died. Thought it was time to do something different . . .' She smiles, but there's a hint of sadness in her eyes.

'And now we have you!' says Marianne, her long sleeves lifting at the edges in a gentle breeze. 'So, why come to Spain to work?'

'Oh, you know . . .' I try to bluff my way out of it. They're all looking at me eagerly, like the dogs waiting to snatch any crumbs I drop.

I look at the chips in the bowl, the sachets of salad cream on a plate next to them, and try to change the subject. 'Have you tried the tapas here?'

They practically shudder.

'Juan's a bit too experimental for us,' says Sally, quietly.

'But he does a lovely cup of tea. And a fry-up if we ask him. It's not the same, but it's something,' says Eileen, who looks as if she wants to be anywhere but here in the heat.

'Well, this Spanish omelette may have interesting flavours, but I was ready for it.' I finish the little plate and wonder again about the aftertaste.

'You'll be getting yourself invited to the Gastro-nómica Society at this rate!' says Marianne, with a deep, throaty laugh.

'The what?' I ask, hearing the name for the second time that evening, as I put down my fork. Juan is there to clear my plate.

'It's a private members' club across the square,' says Marianne. She points to a cobbled street opposite, under the big open windows where the Spanish guitar is still playing, filling the evening air with beautiful music.

Juan tuts disapprovingly.

'Oh,' I say. The penny finally drops. 'The place I just got turned away from?' I wave across the square at the narrow street and the covered doorway.

'You have to be invited to go in,' says Josie. 'I don't know anyone who's been.'

I feel rebuffed all over again. The man with the big moustache wasn't sending me to find the Spanish classes.

'Behind the dark door,' says Eileen, with a shiver.

'They meet there to eat, drink and chat.' I'm sure Sally looks a little wistful.

'Only the finest foods. The meals go on for hours. You can hear singing sometimes,' Marianne explains.

'And it's men only!' Eileen rolls her eyes.

'Men only!' I blanch. 'That's a bit outdated, isn't it? Or is that a joke?' I pick up my beer and drain it.

'Another?' Juan is there smiling, pointing to my glass.

'Oh, I should go,' I say.

'Do stay for another. It's so nice to have company,' says Marianne. 'Not that we aren't company for each other, but it's lovely to have a new face.'

Juan grins. 'And another slice of tortilla?'

Despite the slightly unusual flavour, I'd feel rude refusing.

'And another couple of bowls of chips, please, Juan.'

'So, is that a yes?' he asks me.

'Okay, that would be lovely,' I say. The dogs seem quite content watching the world go by. 'Just one more.' I seem to have made his day. He beams as he clears away the empties and hurries back to the bar.

Suddenly, having company in the sunshine and eating tortilla, even with a slightly unusual flavour, is just what I want to do. What harm can one more beer do? I think guiltily about the work I'm supposed to be doing. The work I promised everyone I had to come out here and finish. But maybe this is work: I can ask these people about their life-changing decisions. I look at the cold beer with the frothy head and the tortilla that Juan has brought me, and it feels nice to be here just being me. Well, the Eliza I've told these people I am. The one who doesn't have family WhatsApping to ask where the cheese grater is and how the washing-machine works. I sip my beer. I'll just have to get up early and do my work.

'Just one thing,' I say. 'If this is the Spanish conversation class, how come no one is speaking Spanish?'

'Our teacher, Simone, moved back to England and we've never found anyone to take her place,' says Marianne.

'You don't speak Spanish, do you?' asks Eileen.

'Very little, I'm afraid.'

'Phew!' they all say, and laugh.

'Thought we were actually going to have to do some work then!' says Marianne.

After a couple of hours in fun company, I'm full and happy. I haven't laughed so much in a long time.

'You'll have to come back tomorrow. It's flamenco night!'

'Really?'

'Well, we're learning from the internet. There's a YouTube video we're trying to follow.'

I go to the bar and pay my bill. So reasonable.

I say goodbye and thank them all for making me so welcome, then set off back up the hill with the dogs in tow.

'See you tomorrow!' they call, as they, too, leave for home.

I wave and smile.

As I do, the door to the Gastronómica Society opens, and I see the man with the long moustache leave, pulling up his trousers over his belly. Gastronómica Society! Pah! I think about the young lady in the supermarket, the cheese and the sherry I bought from her. I'm fascinated by what goes on in the Gastronómica Society. Why is it so hard for her friend to sell her wares around here? Does that society really have so much sway that you can only sell produce if you're part of it? I wave again at the conversation group as they go off in different directions, and glance once more at the door of the Gastronómica Society that spurned me. I feel annoyed all over again, for me and the young woman in the shop. If I was here longer, I'd want to know more. But I'm not. And of course I won't go back to the Spanish conversation group tomorrow. I have work to do. I mustn't get distracted.

8

The following morning is a little fuzzier than I was hoping. I'd opened a bottle of wine and had a glass sitting out on the terrace last night, overlooking the pool, watching the bats fly to and fro, and the lizards running in and out of the rocks.

Instead of the morning light, my phone beeps into life and wakes me. I grapple for it and it hits the floor. I try to pick it up, but my legs seem pinned to the bed and won't move. I feel the familiar panic that haunts me every now and again when things seem unfamiliar. Like in the days after I'd had the babies, when anxiety overwhelmed me. I think that was what caused the breakdown of my marriage with Rob. I was scared, heart racing, crying, but instead of reassuring me he told me to 'snap out of it' and pull myself together: I had three children to look after. He always talked about the pressure he was under as the only bread-winner, but especially when he walked in from work to find the house in a mess, the washing-up from last night still in the sink and me sitting sobbing beside the baby in the Moses basket.

I loved my children but felt so incapable. It was only thanks to a fantastic health visitor, and my friend bringing ready meals for me when Rob was working away and all the kids had chickenpox, that I got through that time. But the love between Rob and me died and never came back. He wanted a wife and mother, and none of the mess that came with real life. By the time Ruby had gone to primary school, he had left to work in Holland where life was altogether brighter and cleaner.

The kids hardly saw him while they were growing up. It's only since he moved back a couple of years ago with his new wife that he's been in their lives once more, now that the messy part is over.

I try again to move my legs, and that's when I look down the bed to see the two dogs lying across them. Relief rolls in and my anxiety is washed away, as if by waves on a beach. I reach down for my phone and sit up. The dogs lift their heads and I stroke them. I'll shoo them off the bed in a bit. Right now, their company is so cheering. Just five more minutes.

I unlock my phone. It's the family WhatsApp group. As usual the battery is low so I grapple for the charger – luckily it's by the bed – and plug it in, then read the messages.

Luke: *Mum, how long for hard-boiled eggs?*

Edie: *How do you make those pasties you always made for us? The ones you told us were all different, with our favourite ingredients, but were actually all the same?*

Ruby: *Oh, I could eat a roast dinner. Mum, when are you coming home?*

They make me smile. It looks like I'm actually missed and they're starting to discover how much I do for them.

I type back: *Twelve minutes on hard-boiled eggs, Luke. Put them in cold water and bring to the boil. Remember to run them under cold water when the time is up. Stops them cooking.*

Thanks, Mum!

Edie, tuna and cheese puffs. Buy ready-made pastry. Ruby, not long now. I'll make a roast as soon as I'm back.

Mum, where were you last night? Was trying to get hold of you! We fancied pancakes! The little ones you used to give us with butter melted over the top . . . and maple syrup! What were they called?!

I'm about to apologize but think better of it. *Was out with friends!* I write, with an emoji. *And Scotch pancakes or drop scones!*

What friends? You don't know anyone!

I've made some! I wouldn't necessarily call the group of women I met last night friends, but it feels nice to say. It's been a long time since I did anything with friends.

Thought you were out there to work? says Ruby.

Suddenly I'm indignant and a little scratchy. But she's right, I am here to work. I did enjoy myself, though, I think, with a little smile.

When I finish on my phone, I decide to risk a swim, hoping Pedro won't be around.

The dogs jump down and follow me. I must make an effort not to let them get onto the bed again. I don't want their owner to come back and find I've let them develop bad habits because it was easier than disciplining them. I feed them and head to the pool. After a swim and a breakfast of some melon I bought from the supermarket yesterday, I feel revived and restored and ready to dive back into my work. I squeeze out a few paragraphs about moving abroad to find happiness, and it's lunchtime. I put some slices of cured ham and salami coated with dried herbs with the cheese I bought yesterday on a plate and eat them on the terrace. The young woman in the shop was right: the cheese is amazing. I can't wait to try it later with a glass of the sherry.

Then I smile to myself and think, Why not? I open the bottle, pour a glass of the light-golden liquid, raise it to my nose, sniff and taste. She was right: it's delicious.

*

As I wake from an afternoon nap, the dogs are looking at me intently from their positions on the bed. They blink. I blink back, and they return it. It's quiet. I get up, wander out onto the terrace and look at my work, but my brain feels like mush. Maybe a walk would help. The dogs are panting with anticipation.

'Okay, okay! I give in!' I've been persuaded to collect their leads from the big armoire. I walk back outside into the hot, dusty afternoon. I look towards the drive and the road. I listen to the sound of silence, just the birds singing, like they're putting on a show, and the buzzing of huge fat bees from wildflowers. Other than that, there's just the grunting of pigs, the distant donkey braying and a cockerel letting everyone know that siesta is over. I'm sure a walk into town, a chat with the women in the Spanish conversation group will give me a better idea of what to write about and perhaps some tapas wouldn't hurt while I'm there. Maybe not the omelette with the strange ingredient.

When I arrive, Josie is standing on one leg and clapping.

'Is everything okay?' I ask.

'Like we said, it's flamenco night! Josie's been trying to learn it so she can teach it to us,' says Marianne.

'She's got the YouTube video,' says Eileen.

'Can't get any internet in my apartment,' says Sally. 'Can't even do that Zoom thingy with the family.' She looks so sad.

'But you've got a lovely balcony,' says Eileen.

'I have. Plenty of room for the family.' She smiles.

'And do they come often?' I ask. It would be a good point to make in my essay: families become closer with a shared place they want to visit.

'No, not really.' She shakes her head.

'Oh.' I don't know what else to say. Then: 'Can I get anyone anything? More chips?' I say brightly, and head to the bar.

'You're back! We didn't scare you off, then?' says Juan. 'You couldn't resist my omelette!'

'Well, um, no,' I say, not wanting to hurt his feelings. 'Even if it has got a slightly unusual ingredient.'

'Ah, my secret!' He grins.

'Is it . . . ginger?' I ask. 'And maybe some mixed spice?'

'You're good!' He looks impressed, and pleased as Punch. 'Gives it a touch of something different. Makes it stand out from the others.' He beams. 'I'm trying to make my food unforgettable for the tapas competition.'

'Tapas competition?' I take the beer he's poured for me.

'Happens every year. The bars here and in the neighbouring town take part. People walk around them, try the tapas and give it a score.'

'And do you often win?'

'No.' He shakes his head. 'Never.'

'Who does?'

'The Gastronómica Society, of course. It's the one day in the year when they open their doors to the public so they can prove their food is the best and most authentic.'

My hackles rise, as they always do when I see an unlevel playing field.

'But this year, I have some new recipes to try out.' He beams.

'And is it just you?' I ask, looking around his small but busy bar. His enthusiasm is infectious.

His smile vanishes. 'It wasn't, when I moved here three years ago, with my partner. But he left. It's just me now. And my dishwasher, Sebastián.' He nods as a young boy comes into the front of the café, pulling on his apron. Sebastián waves and makes straight for the small kitchen. 'He thinks I'm crazy, that my tapas are too fancy!'

'They are!' Sebastián is filling the sink with soapy bubbles.

'But I'm determined to make a name for myself here. Back home I was plain old John, but I much prefer being Juan and all things Spanish.'

'Sounds like you've become a real local.' I smile.

He shrugs. 'I don't think I'll ever be that – I'll never be invited to the Gastronómica Society, but this place is home now.'

'Would you want to be invited there?'

'Well,' he rolls his head from side to side, 'it would be nice to see what goes on in there, and to feel fully accepted.'

'Well, from where I'm standing, it looks like your locals have totally accepted you.' I gesture at the Spanish conversation group, who are still watching Josie as she stamps, claps and nearly wobbles over.

'Sorry about yesterday,' he says. 'I shouldn't have assumed you were here for the group. I hear you're staying with Josep Santiago. He's one of the best-known ham producers around here. Everyone knows about his ham. It's supposed to be amazing.'

'Have you tried it?' I ask.

'Sadly no. It's not that easy to come by and sells for high prices to exclusive customers. But you'll know that. If you're here with Josep, you'll know his reputation goes before him.'

I nod, not wanting to confess that I don't really know anything about him or his business.

'Anyway, I know now that you're not here for the Spanish conversation group.' He leans in further. 'I can save you from having to go over, if you like. Say I need to pick your brains on some new recipes I've been trying out.'

I smile again. 'It's fine. I'm happy to join them. Could do with the company.'

'They'll be delighted,' Juan says, and carries my beer around the bar.

Across the square I see a group of men, including the portly chap who turned me away from the Gastronómica Society yesterday. They gather at the door and tap on it. The man turns and catches my eye. He smiles and nods.

'Like I say, it's that feeling of never being fully accepted,' Juan says, and I bristle.

'Well, I know where I'd rather be,' I say. 'They can keep their stuffy society. Tell me about your tapas ideas.'

'Really?'

'Yes, I'd love to hear,' I say, as the dogs settle beside me. They've drunk the water Juan put down for them, and eaten the little scraps he produced from the kitchen, which I think may have been leftover Spanish omelette.

He claps his hands. 'I can make some for you to try. I'm thinking of some amazing combinations. Really going wild with flavours, like the real Spain – colourful, loud, bold. Doing what no one else dares to do around here. Go big or go home!'

I look at him, wide-eyed. 'Sounds adventurous.'

'Oh, yes!' He's on a roll and it's lovely to see. I look back at the men filtering into the Gastronómica Society.

The fat man turns and walks towards us on the decking at the bar.

'He's the mayor, Señor Blanco,' says Juan, in a hushed

whisper. 'He runs this town and that society. He holds the power around here.'

He walks towards us and even the Spanish guitar playing from the apartment opposite fades away. He stops in front of the terrace.

'*Buenos días*.' He nods at the group and looks at the bowls of chips on the table with disgust.

'*Buenos días*, Señor Blanco. Can I interest you in some tortilla?' asks Juan, with a hopeful smile.

'*No, gracias*,' he says, regarding it with the same disdain he gave the chips. He turns his attention to me and my cheeks flush.

'My apologies,' he says. 'I didn't realize you were with Josep Santiago when we met yesterday.'

'Really?' I say, raising an eyebrow. I wonder who he's been talking to. I can't believe it's any of the women here. They clearly don't speak with the mayor often. 'And would that have meant I'd be allowed into your club?' I say, feeling for Juan, who is looking snubbed.

'Sadly, no.' He laughs. 'We have a strict men-only policy. It is a place for men to come and leave their worries behind.' Once again I'm rattled. 'I'd worry you might find us a little obsessive about our good food.' He glances at the chips again. 'But, as I say, I understand you're here with Josep. We haven't seen him for a while. Please give him a message.'

I nod slowly.

'Tell him we look forward to seeing him in the club.

There are many business opportunities we'd like to discuss. His grandfather was an obstinate man, and his father, no interest. I'm hoping that now his father has passed on, and Josep has a place at the club, he will make full use of it.'

The statement seems loaded with innuendo but I have no idea what he means. 'I'll tell him,' I say curtly.

'Good. Give him my best wishes and I look forward to welcoming him to the club soon.'

Juan coughs and takes a deep breath. 'Actually, Señor Blanco, I would love to visit your Gastronómica Society. I hear the food is excellent, as is the sherry – the best you can buy. I'd love to learn more about Spanish gastronomy.'

Señor Blanco looks at Juan. 'You want to see inside our club?' he scoffs.

'I'd love to. I've heard so much about it.' Juan pulls at the hem of his T-shirt, like an excited and slightly nervous adolescent.

Señor Blanco turns away, chuckling to himself. Juan flushes and looks up at the balcony across the square, above the Gastronómica Society, where the guitar player moves back into the shadows. Someone's got to do something about this, I think.

We sit in silence, apart from Juan, who is standing with a tray and a small bowl of peanuts. He flicks one towards his mouth in frustration and misses as we watch the mayor walk back to the club.

'I have to go. I have B&B guests turning up,' Josie says. The rest of us are still watching the mayor as he enters the Gastronómica Society, loud chatter spilling out onto the square before the door shuts. Then the Spanish guitar starts up again and we all breathe out as one.

'What a pig!' says Marianne.

'I came here to get away from men like him!' says Sally. The sun seems to disappear behind a cloud, giving an altogether more sombre feel to the early evening.

'I think,' I say, gazing at the doorway, 'you need to go for it and win that tapas competition, Juan.'

'If only I could.'

9

The fairy lights come on around the decking, in the late-afternoon light, a breeze whipping up.

Juan places lit tealights on the tables from a tray he's carrying.

Josie looks at her phone. 'They've been delayed,' she says, meaning her B&B guests, and lets out a long sigh. She pushes her phone back into her pocket and sits down again.

'Tell me to shut up if I'm being too nosy.' I feel as if I've forgotten how to make conversation with new friends: I'm used to chatting with my children or as part of work and college, and can't remember the last time I talked to new people, with their own stories. Why did I let myself become so lonely? 'What made you come here?' I ask. What was the happiness they were all looking for? 'Was it what you wanted? The happy-ever-after?' As Juan passes, I ask him for a glass of red wine.

'I was a hairdresser back home in England. Chris was a plumber. We had everything, nice house, cars, friends.' Josie sighs. 'But our friends were all having family, children. We weren't. In the salon all the talk was of family, babies due, grandchildren. It started to get harder and harder to listen to it. You hear everything from behind the hairdressing chair, even if you don't want to.'

Josie sips her drink and grimaces. 'Actually, I fancy a glass of wine too,' she says to Juan, putting aside her cold tea. 'The guests won't be here for a while.'

'I'll join you,' says Sally.

'Bring the bottle, Juan.' Marianne waves.

The wine is poured and Josie clutches her glass of Rioja. 'After another miscarriage,' she takes a sip, 'I was on the settee at home, watching *A Place in Sun*, and I thought, Why not? Chris was fed up with his boss and we just decided to go for it. Buy something to do up and run a B&B.'

'That's fantastic!' I say, sipping the peppery, full-bodied red wine. It's glorious.

'Well, for a while it was, when we were doing the place up. That was the exciting time. We were the envy of all our friends, doing what they wished they could do. But we really had no idea what we'd taken on. Everything was so much harder than we expected, expensive . . . and the paperwork . . .'

'Tell me about it,' says Marianne, lounging on the settee like an artist's model.

The other women agree.

'But everything's okay now?' I smile encouragingly, hoping she's going to tell me she's found happiness.

She shrugs. 'Not really, no. Once we'd finished the building and were finally getting customers through the door, life took on a pattern of changing beds, cleaning, greeting guests and seeing them off. Chris decided he didn't want to run a B&B. In fact, he hated it and wanted us to sell. I couldn't bear the thought of going back to the hairdressing salon and hearing about other people's celebrations. So . . .' She takes a deep breath and a swig of wine.

'So?' I ask, as if I'm talking to one of my children around the kitchen table after a break-up with a boyfriend or girlfriend.

'He said it wasn't working and left,' says Josie.

'He went back to the UK?' I ask tentatively.

'No.' She gives an ironic laugh. 'Moved in with a woman he met on his morning bike rides over the mountains here. They set up a bike-hire business together closer to the coast.'

I think of Rob, with his new wife and child. I wish he'd stayed to see our children grow up. 'Oh, love.' I lay my hand on hers.

She sniffs and blows her nose into a paper napkin, then lifts her head. 'I wouldn't go back. It's hard work, but I wouldn't change it. I came to this group because I thought it would help my business to learn Spanish, but actually, having a community here every day to listen to me when things have got tough has been the biggest help – having people to talk to when pipes burst or I can't understand the letter I've had from officials or I've got a booking mixed up. Thank you!' she says, with a smile. They all raise their glasses.

'To the Spanish conversation group!' says Marianne.

I smile. I can understand Josie's pain and can't help but feel I've fallen into something special here – like I've finally found my tribe, like I'm not alone. 'To the Spanish conversation group!' I lift my glass.

10

Juan puts out some bowls of crisps and nuts. The fairy lights twinkle and the tealights in their little glass holders flicker, like fireflies at dusk. I'm sitting on the decking outside the bar, and the warm breeze is lovely. The dogs are content, happy to sit and listen as long as Juan and I keep offering them titbits from the leftover tapas, which they sniff suspiciously.

I feel a warm glow and know I should be getting back, but I don't want to leave yet. It's not quite dark, and I don't want to return to the empty *cortijo*.

'I was working for the boss of a construction company before I took early retirement. I liked it there, but he was always having affairs and I had to try to keep tabs on his whereabouts and make stuff up when his wife, or mistress, would drop in looking for him.' Eileen chuckles, the wine and conversation seemingly relaxing her.

'Do you have children?' asks Josie.

'A son,' says Eileen. 'But he and his dad don't see eye to eye . . . He came out as gay when he was twenty. I'd always known, of course, but his father couldn't accept it. Life became so full of anger. My son blamed himself for that and moved out. We barely see or hear from him. I hated the emptiness once he'd gone. Derek suggested moving out here and I agreed, thinking it might bring us closer together. But it just brought him closer to his golfing buddies. I've been lonelier since we moved out here than I ever was at home. If it hadn't been for this group . . .' She sips her wine.

Eileen clearly doesn't want to say any more, and Sally joins in quickly. 'I was a supermarket delivery driver. I loved it! Most of the others hated the job – especially at Christmas time. People could get very upset if they were missing anything from their list. You'd be amazed how suddenly everyone is desperate for Brussels sprouts and red cabbage. It would ruin their Christmas if they had to have broccoli and carrots instead. And I loved driving. Plus it got me away from my husband. Miserable sod. He had so many things wrong with him in the end, but he'd never listen or take his tablets. Never missed a day or an evening in his club. He used to clear glasses in exchange for pints. He was there more than he was at home. I used to sort all his medication for him and remember his hospital appointments. And never one word of thanks.'

We're all feeling her pain.

'Then, after he died, the house became mine and I could do what I liked. Start afresh somewhere. But I got ill. A long spell of chemo, and I was put on sick leave. Once I got the all-clear, my kids thought the best thing I could do was sell up and retire out here. They came with me. We bought an apartment with a shared pool. They wanted to be nearer the sea, but my budget just couldn't stretch to that. Anyway,' she takes a deep breath, 'they left, promising they'd be back for family holidays and the like, but they're busy, I know that. And the apartments are as good as worthless since they put up newer buildings nearer to the coast. I put my place on the market three years ago. I've only had two viewings, and one was a nosy neighbour!'

'To think we've all been coming to these get-togethers, even after our Spanish teacher left, and we never knew any of this about each other,' says Marianne, looking around with a watery smile.

'What about you, Marianne? What brought you here?' asks Eileen. 'I can't imagine you being a golf widow!'

'No.' She laughs and then stops, sparkles of tears in her eyes. 'I, erm, was married. Had two children.' She shakes her head. 'All a bit boring, but I worked in the local building society. Spent my day at a computer screen. Went home to a husband who barely acknowledged I was there. Once the children left home,

I realized it was just me and him . . . well, me, really. So, I started taking art classes at the local adult education centre and I . . .' she gives a small smile, '. . . I met someone. We didn't mean for it to happen. It just did.' She looks lost in bittersweet memories. 'And when it did, we knew we couldn't waste any more time. If we were to be together, we had to go for it. I told my husband, then my children I was leaving. Tom told his. I felt such guilt, but also knew we all deserved a chance to be happy. So, we thought it was best to move somewhere where we didn't cause any further upset, neutral territory so to speak, and decided on Spain.'

'How lovely,' says Josie.

'I packed what I could. My husband wanted to make things tricky with the finances, but I told him I wasn't interested. I walked away from the marriage with what I took into it. A suitcase. I met Tom as agreed at the Premier Inn at the airport. I was so relieved he was there, I just burst into tears!' She sniffs. 'He sat me down on the bed and made me a cup of tea, then asked if I took sugar. I remember thinking, I've given up everything for a man who doesn't even know if I take sugar in my tea.'

My nose prickles and my eyes fill with tears. Beside me, Sally sniffs.

'But it was the best thing I ever did,' she says. 'We did so many things together that I'd never have done by myself. I felt thirty years younger!'

'Oh, that's so good!'

'So, it all worked out, then?' I ask, happy for her.

'Well, until we went to late-night fireworks at the beach on New Year's Eve. He went to get drinks and . . .' she takes a deep breath, '. . . that was it. He had a heart attack and died there and then.'

For a moment nobody says anything.

'That was it, over,' Marianne goes on. 'I moved out of our apartment into a cheaper one, and here I am.'

'You didn't think about going back?'

She shakes her head. 'I couldn't. I'd caused too much hurt,' she says, and glugs her red wine. 'But I didn't regret doing it,' she says, her voice cracking. 'I thought I'd spend my days painting and my nights making love. Long and short of it, it turns out I'm not that great at painting.'

She laughs, which makes her boobs wobble, and we can't help but join in.

'I'm more of a good copier than a great artist!' she says.

I feel more relaxed than I have in a very long time.

'The thing is,' she says, 'I'm not even his widow. His family were able to mourn him, but I wasn't invited to the funeral. They shut me out. I wasn't allowed to grieve.' She focuses on me. 'And what about you, Eliza, how did you end up here?'

'Oh, I was married . . .' I stop myself. How did I end up here, in life, in general? 'I'm divorced. I have three children.' I suddenly miss them dreadfully. 'And . . .' What else is there to tell? That's it. 'I've spent my life robbing Peter to pay Paul and trying to keep our heads above water, sometimes drowning, but I wouldn't have it any other way. I loved having my kids. I'm just not sure what else there is about me.'

'And you're staying with Josep Santiago?' asks Marianne, one of her pencilled eyebrows raised.

'Oh, yes, and I'm doing a foundation course at college so that I can go to university and train, but I can't quite work out which course I want to do.' I grab that thought with relief: it gives me some sense of identity, a whole new Eliza Bytheway.

Suddenly, we hear loud voices and laughing as three men leave the Gastronómica Society.

Josie's phone bleeps into life.

'Oh, the guests are nearly at the B&B. I'd better go!' she says, draining her wine. She puts some euros on the table. 'Thank you! I loved this evening, getting to know you all better.'

We all raise our glasses. 'To the shit Spanish Conversation Club!' we say and laugh.

'Goodnight, ladies. Enjoy your chips!' say the men, as they amble past, bursting our happy bubble. We watch them as they walk away laughing, feeling their disdain.

'I know where I'd rather be,' says Eileen, glaring at them.

I look around this group of brave women and my eyes narrow, my hackles rising. The men saunter away, hands in their pockets, unsteady on their feet. 'You all came here for a reason,' I say. 'You all stayed. You wanted a better life. You didn't put up with the rubbish life was throwing at you then and you shouldn't have to now.' I jut my chin towards them.

'But that society runs the town. We'll always be outsiders, the ones who came here for the sun and sangria. We'll never feel this is our home. It's like we're in a strange kind of limbo,' says Eileen.

'We need to show them we don't want to join their society,' I find myself saying.

'What do you mean?' Sally says.

'Show them that we don't want to join their society!' I repeat.

'How?' Marianne wonders.

'It starts with winning the tapas competition,' I say, fired up by the stories I've heard, the determination to adjust to new surroundings. These women should be proud of what they've done, not belittled. 'Juan?' I say, fuelled by injustice and red wine. 'Show them you're here to stay and can create dishes that are as delicious as anything they have in that club of theirs! I think we should try a couple of different tapas dishes every night and show the Gastronómica Society that they do not have the monopoly on good food and fun,' I say, enraged on behalf of the women of the town.

'I'll get planning!' he says, clapping his hands together.

'Nothing too adventurous, mind,' says Eileen.

Like the children I took to the seaside, dipping their toes into the water tentatively but soon jumping in and out of the waves, I don't think it'll be too long before Juan has a group of guinea pigs happy to try his tapas ideas.

'See you tomorrow for my new recipes,' says Juan, delighted as we all stand to leave, including the dogs. 'Thank you!' he says to me. 'Tonight, wine drinking, tomorrow, tapas. You are a very good influence!'

'Or a bad one!' I laugh. 'See you tomorrow.' Now I have to come back.

'Just one thing,' Marianne says, wrapping her shawl around her tanned shoulders as Juan takes our euros and puts them into the till. 'I don't know if you've noticed but Juan is a terrible cook.'

There could be a flaw in this plan.

Large drops of rain start to fall as I walk back down to the car park and up the hill to the *cortijo*. By the time the house is in sight, the rain is falling heavily. The dogs and I run the last few hundred metres and I shut myself in with my back against the door, laughing. Lightning flashes and there's a clap of thunder. I run to my bedroom, the dogs following, and we all dive under the covers where we fall into a heavy sleep.

11

I wake up, thinking about the women at the Spanish Conversation Club and their stories, how they've come to be here, how so many of their best-laid plans have gone awry. They've all overcome adversity but the happy-ever-after has eluded them.

I get up and the dogs follow – I really must stop them sleeping on the bed before I hand back the keys to this place in just over a week's time.

Talking of keys, I realize I forgot to lock up last night. A couple of glasses of Rioja and a thunderstorm and my brain turns to mush – it seems to go hand in hand with hot flushes and itchy skin.

I mustn't let that happen again. Who knows who or what might have got in? My mind goes into overdrive and I remember the huge creature that ran at me in the woods, wondering if it's still there. Not that I'm going back to find out.

I go down to let the dogs out, and as they trot in front of me, keen to get outside, I notice the door to the cellar is ajar. Must have blown open in the storm last night. I shut it and smell salt on the mountain air.

Despite the early-morning sunshine greeting me as I open the door onto the terrace and the pool, there are puddles, reminding me of last night's winds and rain. Something makes me shiver. I see my notebook in a puddle. I retrieve it, holding it up as the rainwater drips off it: my thoughts and ideas are running off the pages into a blue puddle. I shake it out and lay it in the sun to dry. Now what? I look around. I hold up my phone and, almost without thinking, photograph the mountains in the sunshine and send a picture with a smiley face to the family WhatsApp group. Then, after double-checking that no one's around, namely Pedro, I nip back to my room, pull on my swimsuit and slip outside for a morning swim. It's still early. I was awake, my mind racing about the big boar in the woods. The sun hasn't even had a chance to hit the pool and warm it up. Despite that, I plunge in. It's bracing but invigorating.

I come up for air at the end of a length under water, and run my hands over my face, shaking the water from my ears. I hear a strange noise. I glance around, water dripping from my nose and hair. 'Pedro?' I call, as the water drips down my face. I listen, and identify snuffling, grunting and a bit of squealing.

I head for the steps, pull myself out of the pool and grab my towel. 'Pedro?' I call again, my heart starting to race.

I hold the towel to me, slip into my flip-flops, squelch around the pool and peer around the back of the villa towards the farm track and the barns. 'Pedro?' I call again. Nothing.

Suddenly a car is bumping and weaving its way down the track. I don't recognize it. I shield my eyes with a hand and pull my towel around me as tight as it will go. Do I run away now? Or should I stand there and try to pretend I'm not a middle-aged woman in my swimsuit, with a towel that's threatening to fall off and reveal my overweight, unfit body?

It's too late. He's seen me. It's like one of those bad dreams when you're naked in front of an audience.

He stops the car and cuts the engine. The driver's door creaks and a tall man gets out. I think I may have seen him going into the Gastronómica Society, but I can't be sure: there's always a stream of men, in similar short-sleeved checked shirts, who knock on the dark-wood door.

I swallow. 'Can I help you?'

'No,' he says, and smiles. 'I don't think so.'

He walks to the pig nursery in the yard and opens it. A herd of piglets runs out noisily, jostling each other, tumbling and squealing, which must have been the noise I heard. They're running about, over and under each other, as if they haven't a clue which way to go. I find myself smiling at them, then turn back to the man. I frown.

Who is he? I'm the house-sitter: shouldn't I know about guests? I'm here to look after the house, I remind myself firmly, not to leave doors open when I've been out and had a couple of glasses of Rioja. I feel bad all over again. Nor should I be letting strangers onto the farm.

'Um, hello?' I say, following the stranger over the stony ground in my inadequate flip-flops, gripping the towel across my chest with my arm. 'If you're looking for Pedro, I'm not sure where he is, but I can tell him you called, if you want to leave your name.'

He stops and turns. 'Pedro?'

'Yes.'

'Pedro is gone,' he says, and starts to walk towards the barn. The same one Pedro practically shooed me out of.

'Sorry? Erm, excuse me. Pedro? Pedro the pig man?'

'*Sí, Pedro.*'

'Gone?'

'*Sí.* Gone.'

'Gone where?'

He shrugs.

My phone, which I'm holding against me, pings into life. I glance at it. It's the family WhatsApp group.

Mum, how do I find out about the bus timetable? Oh, and where's the ironing board?

I sigh.

I reply while I watch the man in the barn. *Sorry. Can't talk. I need to find Pedro!*

Mum?

Who's Pedro?

I'll explain later! I lock my phone.

'Excuse me,' I say, having made my way across the yard in my towel. He's come out of the barn, blocking the door.

'*Sí?*' He looks at me in surprise.

'Who exactly are you?'

'Miguel,' he says, as if I should know exactly who he is.

'Right. Well, Miguel, where is Pedro?' I say slowly.

'I just here for the pigs. He tell me he's leaving and to look after pigs.'

'In that case, I should phone Pedro's boss, Josep,' I say. I scroll through my contacts to find Josep's number. I dial, feeling Miguel staring at me.

It goes straight to voicemail.

'Just a moment,' I say. He leans against the door frame, rolls a cigarette and lights it.

I try the number again: voicemail.

'Look, Miguel, I'm not sure you should be here. I need to check with Josep.'

He shrugs again. 'I feed the pigs. The young ones leaving their mother's breast.' Perhaps I'm imagining it, but I think his eyes are dropping to mine. 'They need help starting to . . .' He makes a scrabbling motion with his hands.

'Scratch?' I try to help.

He shakes his head. 'Scratch a bit. For food.'

'Scratch for food?' I say.

He mimes picking bits off the ground and bushes, then putting them into his mouth.

I'm playing charades in a towel, I think in disbelief. 'Scratch, pick, eat . . . forage!' I say, pointing at him, as if it's Christmas afternoon and I've just won.

'*Sí*,' he says slowly. 'Forage,' he repeats.

'Okay, you have to feed them now, while they start to forage,' I confirm.

'*Sí*.' He turns back to the barn.

'I'll do it,' I say quickly. 'Tell me what to do.'

I gaze at the tumbling circus troupe of piglets, an unruly, energetic crowd, and try to swallow my uncertainty.

'You? You look after the pigs?' A smile tugs at the corners of his mouth in his unshaven face, confirming what I'm thinking. He looks me up and down, and inside I'm cringing – but although I'm wearing a towel it doesn't mean I can't look after pigs. I do know that I have no idea who Miguel is and that I'm here to look after things. And if that means the pigs as well, I'd better get on with it. How much harder can pigs be than dogs?

'Okay, you feed,' he says, and turns to go.

'Wait!' I call after him. 'You have to tell me what to do!'

But either he hasn't heard me or has chosen not to. He gets into his car and leaves in another cloud of dust.

I turn to the herd of little pigs, looking at me expectantly. 'Okay, we can do this,' I tell them. 'We just need to find out how.'

I try Josep's number again. No answer. I resolve to work it out for myself.

12

I step cautiously into the barn, which contains boxes and equipment I can't identify – I have no idea what any of it is – and a large tub with a scoop. That must be the piglets' feed. If I can just keep them happy until I find out what needs to be done – until I can contact Josep . . . I lift the lid of the tub and scoop out some of the contents. I walk out of the barn towards the piglets, which squeal excitedly, reminding me of the huge animal that ran at me, determined to take me out.

I have no idea what to do with the food, terrified that one piglet will bowl me over, or just attack me.

'Now, now, steady on,' I say, to calm myself. They're like a mob of children at the end of a birthday party, clamouring for party bags, high on E numbers, fizzy drinks and adrenalin. Something inside me clicks.

'Calm down,' I say, as they grunt and squeal and jostle

each other. I didn't know what I was doing when I had a roomful of excited kids, just had to wing it – it's what parents do, follow their instincts. You don't always get it right, but you have to do what *feels* right and keep going. I know the longer I stand here with a scoop of feed, the more overexcited they'll get, and it could all end in tears, possibly mine as the gate they're behind begins to shake. So, I do the only thing I can think of to keep the crowd happy. I stand as far as I can from the gate, aim at it, and launch the feed from the scoop. At that moment my towel lands at my feet, and the pigs scatter, happily snuffling the pellets, foraging. Done it, for now! I bob down, grab my towel from the dust, shake it, clutch it to me and run back to the *cortijo* as fast as my thin flip-flops will allow, sharp stones piercing the soles and making me squeal.

Showered and dressed, I check my phone again. No return call from Josep. I lock the *cortijo*, put the dogs on their leads and walk as quickly as I can into town. The sun is creeping up the sky and it's hot, really hot. My breathing is short, my mouth dry, and I'm practically gasping for water when I arrive at the bar.

'Juan!' I say, leaning against the counter, hot, sweaty and out of breath from speed-walking along the dusty track and the road into the town, then up the cobbled street to the square.

'Eliza! What's up?' He hurries around the bar. 'What on earth happened to you?'

I try to catch my breath to take a good run at what's happened. 'I was . . . swimming, heard squealing . . . in towel . . .'

'Stop!' He puts up a hand. He's wearing his usual beautiful silver thumb ring and leather bracelets. 'Take a seat!' he instructs firmly and points at the bar stool. Then he goes to the other side of the bar and pours me a glass of water. 'Drink this,' he instructs, as if I was one of my kids. I sit, and do as I'm told. I suddenly feel less out of control, the anxiety starting to ebb.

Then he pours a bowl of water for the dogs. They lap thirstily and noisily.

'Now,' he says, pouring me a drink in a beautifully shaped schooner.

'What's that?' I ask, looking at the amber colour in the sunlight.

'Sherry,' he says.

It's like the one I had from the supermarket. Lovely, but it's a bit early in the day for it. I want to refuse, but I don't think it's an offer: it's an order. 'Now,' he says, once I've accepted the glass and my fingertips are wrapped around it. I can smell its warm spicy scent. 'Start from the beginning. Tell me what's happened,' he says. He pours himself some sherry and leans against the bar.

I explain that Pedro the pig man has gone missing as Juan pours the occasional beer and tells the customers he'll be back in a moment. I'm so grateful to have him to listen to me.

The orders are backing up when Sebastián, the washer-upper, arrives, bang on time, pulling his apron around his waist. '*Hola*,' he says to Juan.

'*Hola*, Sebastián. Could you have a look at those orders and start working on them? I'll be there in just a moment,' he says, and turns back to me. 'So, this pig man has disappeared and a complete stranger turned up at the farm, Miguel. But you didn't ask him who he was, and why he was there?'

'I did. He said he was Miguel, there to look after the pigs!'

'But nothing else?'

'No!' I say, feeling more than a little stupid.

'And what about your partner – Josep, isn't it?'

'That's the thing. I can't get hold of him.'

'He's away?'

'Just for a few days,' I bluff, taking a big sip of the sherry. It hits the spot, taking my voice away and giving me the lift I need. 'I told Miguel he should probably leave until I'd spoken to Josep.' I look at Juan. 'And he did.' I take another gulp of the sherry. 'Delicious!' I'm momentarily distracted.

'It is, isn't it? Wish I could get more people trying it instead of cheap lager and cappuccino.' He sighs.

'Let's do a tasting with the Spanish Conversation Club, a sherry pairing with the tapas,' I say.

'Do you think they're ready for that?' He's doubtful.

'We can but try,' I say enthusiastically.

'And in the meantime, you've got a herd of pigs to look after and no idea what to do,' says Juan.

Suddenly, the effect of the sherry evaporates. I look at him. 'What do you know about pigs?' I ask.

He holds up his hands. 'Keeping them? Absolutely nothing.'

Sebastián is behind Juan holding an order in his hand, checking his handwriting.

'Serrano ham is made from a white pig, and Ibérico ham is from black pigs. Smaller pigs, much more flavour, nutty, sweet. Much more expensive!' says Sebastián. We turn to him.

'Hang on, more customers.' Juan spots a couple sitting down on the decking outside and rushes off with his pad and tray, muttering, 'What's the betting it'll be *café au lait* and asking if I do all-day breakfast?'

'Maybe you should do an all-day breakfast in a tapas!' I say, and laugh.

He stops. 'That's not a bad idea!' He waves his pen at me, then goes to take the order.

I sip my sherry, trying to work out the best thing to do. I have a herd of pigs to look after and I'm seriously regretting sending Miguel away. At least he seemed to know what he was doing, and I now have no way of contacting him. How stupid could I be, not taking contact details?

Juan is turning on the coffee machine, which hisses and spits. 'Burgers! They wanted burgers!'

'Tell them your tapas are like a burger, but deconstructed. I used to tell the kids things they wanted to hear all the time. Like beef with gravy instead of casserole or stew . . . And I always called dumplings Puffy Pillows. Somehow they went for that.'

'Ha! Sometimes you need to bend the truth a little to get the right result. Is that it?'

I drain the sherry glass. 'What am I going to do?' I take a deep breath and hold my head in my hands.

He disappears outside again, recommending the meatballs in tomato sauce with his own 'secret ingredient'. I pick up my bag and the dog leads as I slide off the bar stool. As I do, I see Sebastián and a thought occurs to me. 'Sebastián? White pigs, black pigs . . .'

'*Sí?*' he says, putting a spoon onto a saucer and handing the coffee to Juan as he sweeps back in, takes the cup and saucer and delivers it seamlessly.

'You know about pigs?'

He shrugs. '*Sí*,' he says, pouring Coke into a glass and popping in a paper umbrella. 'My grandfather is a pig farmer. He has a black boar, like Josep's. They are the only ones left in the area.'

'So you know about pigs?' I repeat slowly.

'*Sí.*'

'Could you show me about the pigs?'

'You have a problem, with the pigs.'

'Um, yes, er, sort of.' I'm not sure how much I should

be saying. 'I don't know how to feed them or what they need.'

'I can help,' he says simply. 'You need to move the older pigs around, keeping them out on the *dehesa*, but showing them new places to forage. The younger ones may need some extra feed for now while they learn to forage. But, really, it comes second nature to them.'

'Really?' I say, surprised. 'And you can show me how to look after them?'

'*Sí*,' he says, then smiles broadly. 'But first I have to finish my homework. English homework.' He pulls a face. 'My worst subject. I have to get it done today. After work here this lunchtime.'

'English homework? Well, I may not be a teacher, but I can do English. Bring it with you!'

'Really?'

'Of course. You teach me about the pigs, and I'll help you with your homework. That's something I do have experience in!'

He beams. 'That way, my parents can't complain I'm not at home doing my work. I'm getting help, proper help!'

And, just like that, it looks as if my problems are solved. Sebastián high-fives me, my first high-five, and I know my kids would be mortified, but I don't care. I have help with the pigs.

13

'Let me get this right. These pigs produce Ibérico ham?' I ask Sebastián.

'Sí,' he says.

'And that's the expensive stuff?'

'Sí.' He's walking through the herd of older pigs, patting them as if he's been doing it all his life, which, apparently, he has. 'This herd is very well known here, and, well, everywhere.' Instead of running away, as I thought they might, the pigs come up to us, inquisitive, milling around us.

'Which is why Josep left Pedro in charge of them, not a house-sitter from the UK,' I say, under my breath. I can't help but feel like I'm holding up a Banksy picture at auction, worried it's going to self-destruct in my shaking hands.

'The ham is very different from the Serrano ham,

from white pigs. The black pigs are smaller, so don't give as much meat. But the meat is sweeter, nuttier, and the fat melts in your mouth. It is very precious.'

This is the ham I've been eating in the kitchen.

'They are the athletes of the pig world. Fit and healthy. And it's all about their lifestyle and what they eat.'

I swallow and peer into the woods. 'Are there white pigs around here?'

He shrugs. 'Some people have started to use white boars. They are bigger pigs. More meat. You can have some white pig in the breeding and still call it Ibérico ham, but it is not like pure-bred Ibérico ham, from *pata negra*, black pigs. Black-label Ibérico ham is the very best. The pigs are fed acorns in the last four months of life. They can put on nearly a kilo a day. You need five acres per pig.' He nods to the countryside stretched out in front of us. 'It takes a long time to produce black-label *jamón*. Some people want quicker results, bigger legs, more money, so use white boars. They cannot be called black-label *jamón*. That is for the very best acorn-fed pigs. Like the ones from here.'

'That must have been what was in the woods when I first got here,' I blurt out.

'A white pig around here?' He frowns. 'Josep would never use a white pig.'

'How do you know?'

'He is like my grandfather. They believe that the

ham should stay pure, not . . .' he searches for the right word, 'diluted, so to speak. But . . .'

'But?'

'Some people, well, they cannot wait for the boar. It is said Josep's boar is no longer breeding. And they say . . .' He bites his bottom lip.

'Who's they? And what do they say?'

'The breeders. Most of the people at the Gastronómica Society, they breed pigs for ham. They sell them abroad. They say that most buyers from abroad can't tell the difference anyway, so use a white boar and sell at black-boar prices,' he says, and looks uncomfortable, perhaps wondering whether he has said too much.

I frown. So, they're tricking customers.

'It's not illegal. It's just . . .'

'Not quite right,' I finish. 'And that white boar . . .'

'Maybe it escaped from somewhere nearby,' says Sebastián.

'So someone nearby is keeping a white boar to service sows.' I think about Pedro telling me I must have been mistaken and narrow my eyes.

Sebastián nods.

'What if the white boar has made any of the *pata negra* sows pregnant?'

'Then the value is no more,' Sebastián replies. 'Unless, like others at the society, you can find a way to sell them to an unaware customer,' he says, seeming older than his years.

'Your English is very good. I don't know what you're worried about.'

His face lights up.

'And your knowledge about ham is incredible.'

'Thank you. I learn it all from my grandfather. He is in the Gastronómica Society, but I don't think he always agrees with how they do things,' he says. 'One day, the place in the society will come to me, handed down from father to son, and I hope to do things . . . differently. My grandfather is old. He doesn't want the fight. There are too many younger men who care about the money they can get and keeping the best ingredients for themselves. I want to change that. I want the world to see what my small town can produce. Like Josep. If there are any of our *pata negra* pigs left. True Ibérico ham. I am pleased to have seen this place. Josep keeps himself to himself. Thank you.'

This time I smile. 'You're very welcome. Now, talk me through what I need to do again. Where do I move the pigs to when I rotate the grazing? How will I get them to follow me? Which ones should I give feed to? And what about the boar?'

'Come, let's go and see if it's true what they say about him . . . if he really is on his last legs.' He gives a small smile at the English expression.

14

'Oh, God! He's dead!' My hands fly up to my mouth. The last thing I need is a prize boar croaking it on my watch.

Sebastián doesn't speak as we look at the boar in its stone sty, legs stretched out stiffly. Sebastián drops to his knees, picks up a twig and tickles his nose. Suddenly the pig lets out a sneeze that is a mix between a grunt and a snort, making me jump and stumble back, heart thumping. The big animal, with his huge floppy ears, rolls onto his belly and regards us, as if he's surprised to see us, then sighs deeply and puts his head down again.

'Not dead, just pretending,' says Sebastián, sitting back on his haunches.

'How did you know what to do?'

'I've seen my grandfather do it,' he says.

'Do you like being around the pigs?'

He nods. 'One day, I want a herd of my own. But my parents are not so keen. They think I shouldn't be wasting my time with pigs. They want me to do something more. But I am saving for my own herd.'

'By working at Juan's?'

He nods.

I'm impressed. 'But first you have to finish school!'

'Yes,' he agrees. 'I promised my parents.'

'Parents are like that!' I laugh.

'You have children?' he asks.

'Three. Just a little older than you. All trying to find their way in life.'

We finish with the pigs and make our way back to the barn to put away the buckets, wheelbarrow and forks. It could do with a good tidy-up. Maybe I will, but not now, I think, as I pull the door to and padlock it, then go into the house.

Sebastián sits in the shade of the terrace, stroking the dogs as he looks out over the pool. 'It's beautiful here,' he says, as I head to the kitchen to make lunch. I return carrying a tray, a jug of cold water and some snacks. Olives, glistening in oil and coated with dried herbs, squares of hot, freshly made Spanish omelette, layers of sliced potato and peppers, grilled to give a golden top, slices of salami, and toast with garlic, olive oil and chopped tomatoes. A small glass of beer for me and Coke for Sebastián. It reminds me of when I

115

did homework with the kids, but I would probably have given them cake, biscuits or cheese on toast. I've always found pleasure in feeding the family.

I pause to gaze over the pool to the mountains beyond and the woods below.

'It really is,' I say. I'll miss this place when I go home. I remind myself that I'm not here as Josep's friend: I'm just the house-sitter. This is temporary. I have a life to get back to. And I need to get my essay done and make sure that that life is as good as it can be. But right now, I need to keep these pigs safe and well until Josep gets back and wonder again why he hasn't returned my calls. For someone so nervous about leaving his pet dogs and home in a stranger's hands, why has he suddenly gone silent on me?

Sebastián helps himself to the Spanish omelette. 'This is good,' he says. 'You should show Juan how you make it. Better than his!'

I laugh. 'I think Juan is trying too hard. He needs to keep things simple.'

'Just like the ham,' Sebastián says. 'It needs nothing else.' He reaches for a second piece of omelette, checking with me.

'Of course!' I smile.

'Did you know that in America they're trying to raise Ibérico pigs on peanuts? Peanuts!' He tuts, eating and talking at the same time. 'That will never work. It is about the land, their diet. There are three different

116

types of oak tree here. The acorns are so full of goodness. And then, of course, you have the altitude, good for curing the meat.' He talks as enthusiastically as he eats.

'Now, you have an essay to write.'

'Yes,' he agrees, 'if only I knew what to say.'

'I think you should write about the things you love.' I smile. 'The pigs, the *pata negra*.'

A smile spreads across his face.

'Come on,' I say, 'tell me more about them. We'll get that essay done in no time.'

15

'*Gracias*. Thank you again,' Sebastián says, as he gets ready to leave.

'No! Thank you! *Gracias*.' My confidence is growing as I say it. 'I've loved hearing about the pigs and the *dehesa*, how the pigs eat the acorns because they would be poisonous to cows and horses. I understand now why the ham is so expensive. I mean, five or six years to produce it! And the pigs live such happy lives! I just hope I'll be able to look after them until Josep . . . until I can get hold of him.'

'You know where to find me if you need me,' he says. 'But, please, let's keep this to ourselves. My parents, you know?'

'Of course! Thank you!'

'Check they have water, if the lake is running low,

and do a head count every day. You will be fine. You have raised a family, you can look after pigs.'

We laugh as I lock up, then walk back into town together with the dogs trotting happily beside us. As the sun starts to lower in the sky, making the temperature more bearable, we make our way to the tapas bar, Sebastián to work and me to meet the members of the Spanish Conversation Club.

'My grandfather always says Mother Nature is a great teacher.'

'Your grandfather sounds like a very wise man,' I say. Because he's right: in life you can only do what you think is right at the time. You just follow your instincts and Mother Nature will help you. While we walk, I enjoy taking in the wildflowers on the roadside and the view I could never tire of: the mountains, the tree-covered slopes, and the whitewashed town nestled in the middle, like a jewel sitting on a green velvet cushion.

As we arrive at the bottom of the town and walk up through the geranium-lined cobbled street towards the supermarket, I hear a woman say, 'How was the cheese?' It's the young woman who served me, as smart as ever, beautiful shiny hair, nails and make-up.

'Delicious,' I say. '*Gracias!* And the sherry!'

'I'm glad you liked it,' she says, as I go inside. 'Can I help you with anything else?'

'What would you recommend?'

Her face lights up and she slips off her little stool from behind the till.

'Lots!' she says excitedly. 'These little green peppers are grown just up the road, fantastic cooked in olive oil, lots of it, and sprinkled with salt.' She hands me one. 'But be careful. They will surprise you when you least expect it. Most are mild, but occasionally you will get one that is hot, very hot! A little like men!' She throws her head back and laughs, her dark hair and big gold earrings swaying.

'And you can serve them with fried eggs and potatoes, or on their own. These eggs are from around the corner. Hardly any food miles! Cooking these for friends,' she points to the peppers, 'with a glass of fino makes me very happy. The secret is to keep it simple. Oh, and here,' she moves on, 'chorizo, simmered in red wine. This chorizo is really good.' She hands me one and I automatically lift it to my nose to smell. 'We use potatoes a lot, and eggs. Vegetables.' She points to shiny red and yellow peppers in rows, big round white onions, and bright red tomatoes, like Christmas baubles. Then she indicates bowls behind glass of glistening fat green olives and little silvery anchovies that melt into saltiness and lift the flavours of the other produce. 'And olive oil, lots of olive oil. This one is made by a friend of mine.' She waves to silver cans with handles. 'Much better than the one there.' She gestures to the shelf. 'With good bread,' she says, handing me a loaf. 'This one.'

I pick up a can of the oil, take a handful of the Padrón peppers, tomatoes, more eggs and the chorizo.

She smiles as I take the basket to the till and she rings them through.

'Let me know if you need any help, but keep it simple and let the ingredients speak for themselves,' she says, popping a jar of salt into my shopping. 'From me. Good salt makes all the difference. And come back next week. I'll have more cheese from my friend.'

'I will!' I say, but my time here will be coming to an end by then and my excitement dips. I thank her again and walk out with my heavy bags into the bright sunlight, collect the dogs from where they're waiting and walk slowly up the hill, breathing in the hot Spanish sunshine. As we reach the square, I hear a guitar playing from the open windows of an apartment over the Gastronómica Society.

Juan is standing on the terrace, listening to the guitar with a smile on his lips.

'Hey,' he says, seeing us and snapping out of his thoughts. '*Hola.*' He opens his arms, welcoming us.

'*Hola,*' I reply, smiling.

'All good?' he asks.

'All good.'

'Great,' he says, and kisses my cheek. 'I'm pleased.'

Sebastián heads to the kitchen, pulling his apron around his slim waist and tying it.

'Who is that?' I ask, meaning the guitar player.

'That,' he sighs, 'is a man I've never met, but I hear him play every day. Apparently his name is Thiago. And I think I may love him.'

'Have you told him?'

'No. I told you, I've never even met him.'

'Well, maybe you should. Invite him over for a drink.'

Juan flaps a hand shyly. 'Oh, no, I couldn't. I've been hurt by wearing my heart on my sleeve before.'

We listen to the music and I realize how happy I am, here and now. Eventually I let Juan guide me to a seat and my happy bubble is burst by a blast of laughter and loud conversation from a group gathering around the door to the Gastronómica Society. Something suggests that the laughter is directed at us. And my worries about my new charges rise again. 'Maybe I should go and check on the pigs.'

'The pigs will be fine, I'm sure,' Juan says reassuringly. 'Come and sit with the group. Have a sherry.'

I'm so happy to have found such a lovely friend and wonder what my time here would have been like if I hadn't.

'We are planning tapas,' he says. 'And it was your idea!'

How could I say no?

'Actually, I may be able to help there,' I say, and lift

my shopping bags to him. 'I may just have found the answer to the perfect tapas. Let's have a beer and I'll tell you all about it. Loads of local produce, totally ignored by the Gastronómica Society. This could be the answer!'

His eyes light up.

'So, let me get this right. You're now looking after a herd of pigs?' asks Marianne, sipping her wine.

I nod, but I don't tell them that Sebastián has been over to help me or that I haven't been able to get hold of Josep.

'And this Pedro was supposed to be looking after them, but he's disappeared.'

'Yes.' I nod again, enjoying the new sherry that Juan insisted I try.

'So, Josep isn't there?'

'Just gone to, um . . . see a client. He'll be back soon.'

'Well, rather you than me!' says Eileen, and once again I'm reminded of how out of my depth I am. I check my phone yet again to see if Josep has contacted me. He hasn't.

'Try these.' Juan arrives at the table holding small hot plates instead of the usual bowls of chips and puts them in front of us. The other women look at each other, uncertain, reminding me of watching a drunken aunt at a wedding as she tries to chat up the bride's father.

'Tell us what we've got here then, Juan,' I say.

'Well, having spent time in San Sebastián, I really want to show you how amazing tapas can be.' He holds his hands together. 'I've taken the traditional and blended them with some of the more experimental versions I've had!' he says. 'See if you can detect the flavours.'

I try to work out what the little plates contain but I really have no idea.

When we've all tried the dishes there's still quite a lot left and, frankly, I'm none the wiser about what he's put with what. They're just too busy.

'They're really . . . experimental,' I say, the flavours ricocheting around my mouth. The sensation reminds me of moon dust from when I was a child: it sat on your tongue, fizzled, and you waited for it to explode, pop, bounce and sting on the roof of your mouth.

'Didn't you like them?'

'Loved them,' I say quickly. 'In fact, if there's any left, I'll take them home with me.' I don't want to hurt his feelings or for him to feel defeated. He picks up the plates and disappears to parcel them up. At this stage, I'm not sure they're going to win the tapas competition. Maybe I shouldn't have stuck my nose in at all.

I follow him to the kitchen with my shopping bags and put them on the side. 'Now, what do you think of this?'

Sebastián is there and turns to see the shopping on

the side. 'Padrón peppers.' He steps forward. 'These look fantastic!'

'And this.' I open the olive oil, then hold it out to Sebastián to sniff.

'Wow!'

'With this salt. Simple!'

'Oh, yes!' he says, raising his eyebrows and nodding slowly. 'And these olives are good. My grandmother would stuff them with feta cheese, fry them in bread-crumbs and serve with a tomato sauce. And the feta is great with artichokes and lemon on skewers.'

'I can go back for artichokes,' I say excitedly. 'And these anchovies look amazing.' I show him and Juan, who is still watching us as we hand the peppers and tomatoes between each other, smelling, cutting and tasting the tomatoes and chorizo, accompanied by 'Oooh, delicious!'

'This stuff is for sale just down the road,' I tell Juan excitedly. 'The flavours are amazing. They don't need anything else doing to them. We can just let the fla-vours speak for themselves, with a glass of fino!'

'Spoken like a true Spaniard!' Sebastián laughs.

Juan's shoulders slump. 'You're suggesting I serve up these ingredients naked?'

'Yes!' Sebastián and I respond, laughing.

'With a bit of help from olive oil, salt, lemon and garlic, this cheese and these peppers will taste deli-cious and, best of all, they're wonderful and mostly produced by women in the area. Friends of the woman who runs the supermarket. She says the Gastronómica Society ignores them, but this is what she and her friends eat when they're having tapas. She says cooking them makes her so happy, and if it's not making you happy, you're not doing it right.'

Juan looks at me, and then at Sebastián. 'And this is how your grandmother cooks tapas, Sebastián?'

'Uh-huh,' he says, popping a piece of cheese into his mouth, followed by an olive.

I'm crossing everything that he goes with this idea.

'Do you think . . .' Juan pauses, and I can see this is a big step for him. Suddenly he shakes his head. 'It's no good. It wouldn't work,' he says. 'I need to do something to really stand out.'

'But these ingredients speak for themselves. They stand out! You need to do hardly anything to them.' I try to persuade him.

He shakes his head again. 'I need to do something extraordinary!'

Sebastián and I look at each other sadly. And I can see he's not going to be convinced, not today anyway.

Later in the evening, when I get back to the farm, the setting sun silhouetting the mountains around us, I go straight out to check on the pigs, letting the dogs off their leads. I carry out Sebastián's instructions and, much like when the children were small, do a head count, first of the little ones, then the other family groups in different fields. I re-count when I think I've included a couple twice. They all seem happy enough, if rooting for food or snoozing under a tree is happy. I think it is. But there's still no sign of the boar coming out of the sty to eat. He can't just stay in there and not eat. I take a scoop of the nuts I gave to the piglets earlier, push open the gate and approach the sty. I take a deep breath, remembering the huge animal that came hurtling towards me on my first day. I'm ready to run if anything happens.

'Hello?' I say nervously, approaching the sty. *'Hola?'* He probably doesn't speak English – and I laugh at myself because he wouldn't speak Spanish either. I wonder if the sherry's gone to my head. I listen for sounds, snuffling, anything. But there's nothing. Suddenly an awful thought hits me. What if this time he really is dead? I wish Sebastián was here. And I'm the one who sent away Pedro's friend Miguel. Why hasn't Josep got in touch? I told him everything would be fine, but what on earth will I do if the boar is dead?

I peer into the sty, preparing myself for the worst, but thankfully he's just lying there, his head between his front legs. He raises his eyes to me, then lowers them again, like a teenage boy who's lovesick and can't get out of bed. It reminds me of Luke's reaction to his break-up.

I look at the boar again. Well, he hasn't got up and dashed at me, baring his teeth, which is a good thing. He seems smaller than the one I saw in the woods. And Sebastián told me people were using a white boar in the area.

He looks up from under his long eyelashes and flappy ears again.

'Hello, fella,' I find myself saying. This time he lifts his whiskery chin just a little off his straw bed, sighs loudly, then puts his head down again. The other pigs sleep out in the *dehesa*, Sebastián told me. The younger ones are brought closer to the *cortijo* at night, back to the nursery, and let out again in the morning. But this fellow seems to have given up on life out on the *dehesa*, like he's given up altogether.

I stare at him with no idea what to do. I have been left with a herd of pigs to look after, and if the boar is as important as Sebastián says he is, I need to do something.

I crouch down, heart pounding, hoping he doesn't launch himself at me. But by the look of it, this fella isn't going anywhere.

'How about some food, eh?' I hold out the scoop to him, but he doesn't budge. I take a few of the pellets in my hand and hold them to him. He lifts his head, sniffs, then lays it down again.

'Hmm,' I say. 'What are we going to do with you?' I look around the sty as if I'm assessing one of the kids' rooms. We need to get this place tidied up, I think. What happened to Pedro? Why isn't he here doing this?

There's only one thing for it. I'm going to have to do it myself.

'Come on, buddy, let's get you moving,' I say, from inside the sty. I move backwards, shaking the food as I go, but he doesn't move. Right. What else? I reach out my hand towards him, from interest as much as anything else, and touch his big back. He doesn't flinch. I stroke it, like a dog. After a while he seems to make a sighing sound. I give him a bit of a scratch and he grunts in response.

He's enjoying it, and so am I as I continue to pet him. I start to hum to myself – something I used to sing to the children when they were little. After a little while, he lifts his head.

'Come on, boy,' I say, cajoling him out into the setting sunlight, but he doesn't move.

Then he lifts his head and sniffs the air, as if he's interested in something. He gives a little grunt, which makes me smile. He pushes his snout towards me, which surprises me and makes me laugh. He does it again and I realize he's pushing at my bag, which I'm wearing across my body.

Intrigued, I slip it off. And he nudges it again.

'Is this what you're interested in?' I ask, and he gives another grunt, his curiosity obviously piqued. It's the most active I've seen him. Then I realize what it is: Juan's tapas.

I think about Sebastián's grandfather's words. If you start down the right route, Mother Nature will show you the way.

I pull one of the foil-wrapped parcels from my bag. He grunts a little more, sniffing at it.

'Is this what you want?' I ask, unwrapping it. A little of what you fancy does you good, I think, my mind turning to our nightly meet-ups at the Spanish Conversation Club. We may not be speaking much Spanish, but a glass of something and connecting with others has kept those women going – me too for the time I've been here. If it wasn't for them, I would have left Pedro to it and gone, after the white pig's attack.

I put down a little piece of the extraordinary-tasting finger rolls in front of him. He sniffs and I think he's going to feel the same way we did about it, but suddenly he grabs it and gobbles it. Then he grunts and looks at me for more.

I break off another piece and put it in front of him. He hoovers that as well.

Excited, I get to my feet and drop pieces of the bread and sauce, while I step backwards. As I move back into the *dehesa* and put the last morsel just outside the stone sty he staggers to his feet and steps towards it, eating with a satisfied grunt.

He's about to lie down again, now that the finger roll has gone.

'Wait! I've got more,' I say, pulling out one of the other parcels and hoping Juan never finds out I've fed his creations to a pig.

I unwrap the miniature paella in filo and place it just outside the sty, trying to encourage the boar to take small steps. Slowly but surely he makes it out into the setting sun while I scatter the last of Juan's tapas under a tree. He happily munches them, then lies down.

He ignores the sows gathering under another tree in the distance. Sebastián pointed them out to me – the fully grown sows that are waiting for a mate. They're clearly not impressed by his lack of attention. The pigs forage all day, then take a big drink from the lake and have a siesta, getting up to forage and feed again before gathering together under a tree to sleep. I look at the boar, on his own, not with the rest of the herd as he should be. Well, at least it got him out of bed. I go to work cleaning out the sty as quickly as I can. As if sensing I've finished, and there's a clean bed to go to, the boar gets to his feet and wanders back into the cool stone sty, lies down and falls asleep. I'm happy to have made some progress: he now has a clean bed, fresh water and food to forage for if he wants it.

I'm hot and sweaty but satisfied with my efforts. I check the water butts, top them up from a hose in the yard, and look around at the young herd, as they play, run and chase each other, counting them again, just to be on the safe side, then attempting to drive them into the barn. Eventually successful, I head back to the house for a shower, pulling out my phone as I go.

Seven missed calls on WhatsApp! That can't be good.

16

Having sorted out the row over whose turn it is to borrow my car and established a rota with my children, I decide to have an early night. Tomorrow I really must focus on my essay. I have only seven days left here. At least I've made the boar and the children happy. Happiness: that's what I'm supposed to be writing about. But, so far, none of the women from the Spanish Conversation Club have given me the happy story I was looking for.

First thing next morning I let the piglets out into the closest paddock. I say 'paddock', but it's huge and dotted with big trees. The ones with the bark missing are cork trees, Sebastián told me. The bark is stripped to make corks for wine bottles. I breathe in the early-morning air, walking the farm with the dogs. There are cobwebs covered with dew and the air smells fresh, as if the earth is waking up as the sun rises over it.

The piglets tumble, fall over and chase each other outside, and I laugh as I feed them the pellets, like Sebastián showed me. I count them, then re-count, checking I haven't lost anyone in the night. All present and correct. Then I walk to the neighbouring field where the older pigs are, count them from afar and check their water. I look out over the dense woods that Sebastián told me is where the pigs feast on acorns once the first rains come. They stay out on the *dehesa* until February, enjoying free range for the last four months of their life and the best diet. These pigs have the ultimate flavour, and I can see why. As I breathe in the smells of the countryside, letting the sun warm my face and massage away any tension in my shoulders, I appreciate the perfect ecosystem: the animals, trees and other plants work in harmony with each other. Large bees buzz around me and birds make the most of the early-morning cool to gather food. I could live my best life here, I think. And shake off the idea. I don't live here. I have a home to go to.

I turn back from the *dehesa* and check on the boar, or Banderas as I've named him, after Antonio Banderas and *The Mask of Zorro* – I loved watching that film when the kids were younger and he's a very handsome boar, hence Banderas. I wonder if I'm not going a little mad, on my own on a remote farm in Spain with only the Spanish Conversation Club, the dogs and the pigs for company. Although I've loved getting to know the women at Juan's, I shan't go there this evening. I'm going to work out what to write about, then start to compose my final essay. I'm going to start running out of time if I'm not careful.

By five o'clock, my brain is hurting. I rub my sore eyes and look at the sun starting to dip in the sky. The dogs stare up at me, ready for their trip into town to the tapas bar. But we're not going. I need to work, no matter how hard I'm finding it.

Over the following five days, I do the same. Check on the pigs, feed the piglets, count them and encourage Banderas out of his sty with titbits from the kitchen. I scratch his back on the place that makes his snout turn up and his back leg lift off the ground to jiggle with pleasure.

Then I head back to the *cortijo* with the dogs at my feet, a constant questioning look on their faces, their heads tipped, as if they're wondering why we're not going to the tapas bar. But, as tempted as I am, I can't forget why I'm here. I need to finish this piece of work before I leave here.

I shower and, instead of dressing, I slip on one of the men's cotton shirts from the airing cupboard over my bra and pants. It's so much cooler than shorts and T-shirt. It's boiling hot and any help to cool down is welcome, so I roll back the sleeves and leave an extra button open at my cleavage to let in any breeze. I must remember to wash it and put it back before I go. Then I pour myself a cold glass of water and make some coffee, wishing it was a glass of red wine or sherry. I feed the dogs and head back out to the terrace to start work again.

As I sit down, my mind is full of pigs, rather than what I should be putting on the page. I count and re-count the words I've managed to squeeze out about looking for happiness and why being happy is important to our health. Nowhere near enough!

I let out a long, slow breath, throw down my pen and look out from the terrace, down the long, dusty drive. For a moment I think I'm imagining things.

I blink and rub my eyes as the outline I can see in the distance becomes clearer. I stand up. I'm not imagining it. A smile spreads across my face. What a welcome sight.

17

'We were getting worried about you!' says Josie, with a smile, despite looking very hot under the punishing Andalucían sun.

'May I have a glass of water, please, love? It's quite a walk,' says Eileen, flapping her big sun hat at her face.

'Of course, of course! Come and sit down. What are you all doing here?' I say, ushering them all to the cool of the terrace and pouring water for Eileen, who is very flushed.

'Well, like Josie says, we were getting worried,' says Eileen, catching her breath.

'We haven't seen you for days!' says Marianne.

'We wanted to make sure you were okay,' says Sally. 'Just to check you weren't poorly or anything.'

'And now we can see you're fine!' says Eileen, still fanning herself.

'So, we thought, if you won't come to the bar, we'll come to you!' Marianne says, with a broad smile, bright lipstick, and bangles jangling up her arms. The wings of her kaftan float in the gentle mountain breeze.

'And I've been trying out more tapas recipes,' says Juan, kissing me on both cheeks. He's carrying a tray covered with silver foil, as are Marianne and Josie. 'I've spent a lot of time in Catalonia so I've gone for *pinchos*, with a stick through the middle of the snack to hold it together. Same as tapas but a bit bigger.'

'Sounds fabulous!' I say, overwhelmed by their thoughtfulness, then remembering how many of Juan's tapas I fed to Banderas the boar.

'So, where have you been?' Juan asks, like a teacher asking for a note explaining absence.

'Working.' I smile. 'The work I told you I was here to do. I'm trying to finish an essay for my online foundation course. But I'm delighted to have a distraction. It wasn't exactly going to plan.'

'Wow! This place is amazing,' Marianne says.

'Rural, but what views!' says Sally.

'It is lovely, isn't it?' I say, looking out at the hazy sun over the forest where the sows are foraging contentedly.

'We tried to get Sebastián to come,' Juan says, 'but he has some schoolwork to catch up on. He says he'll try to come later if he's finished. He asked us to pass on his thanks for all your help. He got top marks in his essay!'

'He's much better at writing than I am. How come you're here?' I say suddenly. 'What about the bar?'

'Water's off. Can't open, so we came to you,' says Juan, with a shrug, making me smile.

'How long has Josep had this place?' Eileen asks. 'Is he here?'

'Oh, yes. Josep. Um . . . I'm not sure. Quite a few years.' I blush, the fibs tripping off my tongue because he doesn't want anyone to know why I'm here.

'Will he mind us being here?' asks Sally.

I hesitate, wondering if I should ask them to leave and meet them at the bar instead, but after all the effort they've put in to visit me and bring tapas – and there's no water at the bar . . . I can't remember when anyone did something like this for me, if ever.

'I bet he'll be delighted you've made friends,' says Juan.

'Now.' I clap my hands together. 'What can I get everyone to drink?'

'Pass the opener,' says Marianne, pulling out a bottle from her large, sequinned handbag. 'Sangria coming up!' And the others make a fuss of the dogs – they seem to have missed seeing them in the bar.

I walk barefoot into the *cortijo* to get glasses, and stop to savour the sensation of the cool tiles underfoot when I see the photograph of the couple on the sideboard, clearly in love, a young Josep. The one the Spanish Conversation Club believe is my 'good friend'. But the only time I've met him was when he was telling me the house rules and 'no parties'. Well, it's not like I can get hold of him. I put the photograph face down to push him out of my mind. After having only pigs for company, I deserve to let my hair down a little. I mean, it's not like we're teenagers wreaking havoc.

My phone vibrates and I check to see if it's the WhatsApp group. It's an unknown number, probably some scam. I decline it and walk back with a tray of glasses and plates to find my friends laying out platters of tapas. Suddenly there's an almighty splash as Marianne launches herself into the pool in her brightly patterned swimsuit, which is holding up her ample bosom like scaffolding. We all laugh and it feels so good. And that can't be a bad thing, can it? For the first time in ages, I'm just enjoying myself. Where's the harm in that?

18

'I have some amazing tapas for you to try!' Juan claps his hands together, his silver jewellery catching the light. Everyone is relaxed with a drink in hand and we are enjoying some large fat green olives I've brought out from the kitchen in a bowl. Looking out over the gently sloping land around the *cortijo*, I can see the sows wandering between the trees and lying in any patches of mud they can find to cool themselves. I hope Sebastián comes later and sees he was right: I'm doing okay, me and the pigs. I followed my instincts and Mother Nature has shown me the way, just like he said. Right now, I feel like a proud parent looking out on the children playing happily. When I went to check earlier, even Banderas was out of his sty, lying under the nearby tree. I really would like to show Sebastián and thank him again.

Josie has music playing from her phone. Marianne is floating like a starfish and it feels like heaven. I can smell the heat in the air, tickling the hairs up my nose. I wonder whether to change out of the man's shirt I'm wearing but, actually, it's comfortable and cool and I'm among friends so I stay as I am.

Juan is wearing a brightly coloured shirt, with three-quarter-length white trousers and flip-flops.

'I'm really going out there with some amazing flavours.'

Everyone's face shows slight concern.

Juan puts his hands on his hips and rolls his eyes. 'Yes, I took your advice and went to visit your friend at the supermarket. Sebastián has been showing me how his grandmother makes her tapas. He's a lot better at it than I am, but I'm learning and now I'm practising on you. You were right about the young woman in the shop – she knows so much about what she's selling, and loads of producers who don't get a look in around here, because they're not part of the Gastronómica Society.'

'You mean because they're not men?' I can't help but fill in the gaps.

'And she wished me luck in the competition.' He beams – he's started to make real connections in this community.

'Brilliant!' I say. 'That's great.' My eyes prickle with pride for my new friend.

'And I have a special surprise,' says Juan. 'A really special surprise,' he teases, as he disappears into the kitchen. We top up our drinks in preparation for Juan's 'amazing flavours' and his 'special surprise'!

In the cool, dark kitchen, he's unloading another basket he's carried all the way from town. He starts unpacking parcels and laying them out on the table. In no time all the kitchen surfaces are covered with bottles of sauce and packets.

'Ta-da!' he says, holding up something that's covered with a tea-towel. He whips it off to reveal a leg of cured ham, much like the one on the side in the kitchen.

'Juan!' I wonder how much it cost him. If what Sebastián says is right, they go for huge sums. I'm stunned by his generosity.

'Like I said, I wanted to do something special for the tapas competition. Thought I'd try it with a combo of different flavours. And, to be honest, it was a steal. Here.' He cuts off a slice with his penknife and puts it on a plate for me to try. It's soft and salty as it sits on my tongue.

'I thought I could pair it with some bold flavours as it needs jazzing up a bit. Bit bland, but it's local and, with a bit of Juan sparkle, it could really shine.'

I look at the leg of Ibérico ham and at the label, the same label I've seen on the ham here. But something is niggling at the back of my mind. I study it again. It's not like the ham I've had here: it isn't melting on my tongue. I pick up a piece and lift it to my nose. It doesn't smell or taste the same either. I look at the label . . . There's something about it, I'm not sure what. It's not quite the same but . . . My brain is starting to tick over and . . . It's the same sketch of a view I'm sure I recognize.

'Juan, where did you get this?' I ask brightly.

He touches the side of his nose with a smile. 'A guy I met. Got offered it for a really good price. These are really expensive usually.'

'And where did he get it from?' I say.

Juan shrugs. 'Who knows? I was just delighted to be offered it, to be honest. It was one of the members of the Gastronómica Society. I felt like I was being accepted finally! They barely speak to me, but that tall fella who stopped the other night when we were all outside, he came over and offered me one for a good price. I think it was his way of building bridges. I think I'm really starting to be part of this place.' He stops carving, looks at me and smiles, and I really don't want to burst his bubble. For now I decide to say nothing. After all, wherever this ham came from, and whatever Juan does with it, he feels accepted and he's brought it here to cheer me up. I wonder, though, if something is going on that caused Pedro to leave. From what little I know, that isn't the Ibérico ham I've tasted here with that label on it. But I'll say nothing until I can work out what's happening and why Josep chose now to go away, with a boar that has lost interest in sows. And why won't he return my calls?

I sigh, then look at Juan who is holding a glass with ice in it.

'Sherry?'

I take the glass of golden liquid poured over ice: whatever is going on, it has nothing to do with me, and I should keep my nose out of it. I won't be here for much longer and I'm going to enjoy the time I have left.

19

'Ha!' I find myself laughing so much that my sides ache as we play ping-pong. 'You lose!'

'Ooh, my turn for a swig! Who knew sherry could be so moreish?' cries Eileen, picking up a paper cup of sherry. We've finished Juan's and moved on to some I found in the cupboard, making a note to replace it before Josep gets back.

'And I barely noticed the strange sauce you poured over those little sausages. In fact, they were really tasty. But the meatballs need a bit more give in them,' says Sally, bouncing one on the table. It rolls off and one of the dogs snaffles it.

'I need to check the pigs,' I say. I should do it now, while I can still see straight.

'Ooh, I love pigs! Come on, we're feeding the pigs,' slurs Juan, waving everyone to follow.

'It's fine. I won't be long.' I laugh as the dogs get to their feet.

'No, no, we're here to help!' Juan says. 'You know, if I wasn't gay, I'd find you a very attractive woman, Eliza Bytheway.' He's swaying slightly.

'Thank you!' I smile, almost a little disappointed that he is. But that's just the drink, the sun and the fun time. I definitely don't want a man, but maybe it would be nice to be held again – I can't remember the last time.

'Right, to the pigs!' I snap out of it.

'It's dead!' Josie is pointing to Banderas under his favourite tree, near the stone sty. But at least he's outside, which is progress.

The group's faces as they stop in their tracks and stare in horror, bumping into each other, make me splutter with laughter.

I climb over the five-bar gate, rather than opening it as I usually would, and land heavily on the other side in my flip-flops. 'He's not dead,' I tell them, with a smile.

'What's she *doing*?'

'Is it safe?'

'Juan, go and help!'

'I'm not going in there! I thought they'd be cute little piggies!'

I walk over to Banderas and crouch next to him. 'Hello, fella!' I say.

'Are you sure she should be that close?'

'He's definitely dead!' shouts Josie.

I start to scratch his back and hindquarters, then start humming. He wakes from a deep sleep with a loud snort, making the group, who are leaning over the gate, jump back and stumble into each other.

'He just does it sometimes.' I'm still scratching him. 'He's friendly. Do you want to come and say hello?' As one they shake their heads.

I pull a snack from my pocket I'd sneaked off the table for him.

'Hey, is that one of my *pinchos*?' Juan points a waving finger, and I stifle a giggle as I feed it to Banderas, who grunts appreciatively. 'He's a big fan of your work,' I say. 'He's a very fussy eater and he loves this.' Banderas is chewing the meatball.

Juan breaks into a wide smile.

I stand and focus. The youngsters have seen me and are bundling towards the gate, desperate to gobble their pellets. On the outer fields, leading to the woods, the ground is dry so I check the water butts. The head count takes a lot longer than usual. '*Uno, dos, tres . . .*' The piglets run, scramble, barrel, and I lose count again. The others are falling into each other, laughing.

Even Banderas seems to be enjoying the company, his face held up to the setting sun. It's the longest he's stayed out of his bed since I've been here.

'Right, let's give them some pellets,' I say, climbing back over the gate. That'll make the job easier.

I go to the barn and trip over a hessian cloth. It seems to be covering some boxes, but nothing I know about. I kick it out of the way and come back to the group with plastic scoops full of pellets.

'Like this,' I say, showering the pellets through the air in the direction of the tumbling, squealing, excited piglets.

'Brilliant,' Marianne says. 'Can I have a go?' She takes the other scoop from me, pulls back her arm and flings the pellets, letting go of the scoop, which flies into the field and lands under a tree.

Finally, with the piglets and the sows on the dry pasture in front of the thicker woodland all counted, we leave them to it. Banderas stands, stretches and goes back to his sty, contented if not interested in the girls around him.

'Last one back to the ping-pong table has to do a forfeit!' shouts Juan, getting a head start.

'Hey!'

'Not fair!'

'Wait!' We run after him, like superfans after a boy band.

'Wait!' We turn the corner around the *cortijo* and, in the light from the setting sun, see a car moving slowly down the dusty drive.

'It must be Sebastián,' says Juan.

'Hooray!' says Marianne.

And we all wave.

And pull faces. Why not? It's not like my kids are here to see me and be embarrassed by my disgraceful behaviour.

As one, we turn and wiggle our backsides at him.

The car comes to a stop. A taxi. The driver gets out and opens the passenger door slowly. And I wonder briefly why Sebastián didn't walk, like everyone else. As the door opens, we all cheer and Marianne takes another huge leap into the swimming-pool. Feeling like one of my children, I let out a joyous laugh and a whoop.

'Geronimo!' she shouts, but as the waves begin to subside, a strange silence falls over the terrace and the group. Slowly, a figure gets out of the car and ever so slowly straightens. Seeing him, my smile drops. My heart sinks like a stone to the bottom of a lake.

You can hear us swallow, one by one.

'That's not Sebastián,' says Juan.

20

I stare at the figure in front of the car. His face is dark, glowering and he's clearly in pain.

'Josep!' I finally manage.

The group shuffles uncomfortably, sobriety washing over them.

'What's happened to you?' I blurt out. He looks a very different man from the one who left here just over a week ago. Not least because of the sling around his arm, the crutch he's leaning on and the bruising on his face. He looks furious as he takes in Marianne in the pool, the music, the food and the drink.

He says nothing. The group shuffle towards the terrace, gathering their belongings and quietly saying something about giving us space.

'We'd better go, lovey,' says Marianne, taking in Josep's

thunderous face as she and the others clutch their bags to their chests.

'Or we can stay and help clear up?' Josie asks.

I shake my head and swallow the lump in my throat. 'I can do that,' I tell them, then try to smile and say everything will be fine. Even though I can tell by his face it won't.

'We'll make ourselves scarce,' says Eileen.

I watch as shoes are slipped on, sun hats plonked at tipsy angles before they leave, like naughty teenagers caught out having a party while the parents are away. Part of me wants to giggle nervously, but Josep's expression and, indeed, his injuries make me feel thoroughly ashamed. I'll be fifty in a few years, for goodness' sake. A mother! This is a job and I'm here to look after things – what was I thinking?

Only Marianne has lingered. 'I can see you've got things to catch up on here, but it was lovely,' she says. 'Thank you.'

'Thank you.' I hug her tightly, knowing this may be the last time I see her, the rest of Spanish Conversation Club and Juan. I wish I could tell them how much I've loved meeting them, how I'll miss them, and how grateful I am to them for helping me feel a little bit more like me, even if I'm thoroughly ashamed that I let myself down professionally and, well, personally. I made a promise and didn't keep it. I made a mistake and wish I hadn't.

We hug again, and they all set off down the track towards the road and back to the town, supporting each other and passing around the half-bottle of cava that has been liberated from Marianne's bag. God, I'm going to miss this place.

Josep tries to shut the taxi door, but pain is etched on his face, possibly from bruised or broken ribs under the sling. I step forward to help him, but he puts up a hand, a barrier to stop me.

Finally, the taxi leaves. Neither Josep nor I say anything or move, just stare at each other, wondering where to begin.

21

'It's – it's not what it looks like,' I say, the age-old excuse.

His face is drawn and pale. He stares at the mess in front of him, paper cups strewn everywhere and remnants of Juan's tapas. I know how bad it must look. I'm the house-sitter, for goodness' sake. I was employed to care for his home, not turn it into Party Central. My toes curl, my cheeks burn. I'm mortified. How could I have been so stupid?

He opens his mouth – and suddenly the dogs recognize him, tearing down from the terrace, wagging their tails. I worry they'll knock him over and try to calm and settle them to sit, which they do. He bends stiffly to greet them with gentle words before he straightens and looks at the debris again. Not even the pleasure of being back with his dogs can deflect his attention from the pain, and his disappointment is clear on his face.

I am not his girlfriend or even his friend. I was employed to look after his house and, clearly, I haven't done a good job.

It goes quiet, apart from the birds chattering in the shrubs, and the ever-constant breeze shushing through the woods as the day draws to a close.

I regard the detritus around the pool. The inflatable lilos in the shape of unicorns and flamingos, a soggy T-shirt floating, forgotten, in the pool.

'I can explain,' I say, attempting to be a grown-up again.

'Good, and when you have, you can organize your flight home. I won't be needing your services any longer,' he says. Although I was expecting it, it stings as though I've been slapped in the face.

22

'Wait,' I say, as he leans heavily on his crutch and moves slowly towards the *cortijo*, the dogs pacing with him. I watch, rooted to the spot.

'I can explain,' I repeat pointlessly, as he slowly hobbles away.

He stops. Maybe he's taking a breather – moving seems to involve a huge effort. 'I'm not sure I need much more explanation,' he says. 'I asked you and paid you to look after my house, not turn it into a student party.'

I'm not sure you could describe any of us as students.

'And perhaps you'd leave my shirt behind when you go.'

I look down at it, crumpled, sangria-stained, and die inside all over again.

My phone rings, but I don't accept. It rings again. I glance at my screen and see a deluge of messages.

Mum, Luke's had friends over and the place is trashed. And one of his friends seems to have moved in. You need to come home.

Mum, Ruby's dogs have peed on the living-room rug!

Mum, I lost my job. Can I borrow £100?

I'm about to tell them how disappointed I am, but I'm really in no place to judge. I send a quick reply to say I'm busy and will reply properly later.

What? Aren't you going to say anything else? Are you just going to let him get away with this?

This is one you need to sort out for yourselves, I type, then nothing more. I slide my phone into my pocket.

'Can I help you inside?' I ask Josep, even though he's turned me down already.

'I'm fine,' he says, leaning heavily on his crutch. Every step seems to make him wince.

'What . . . what happened?' I ask again tentatively. Clearly he is not prepared to share that information with the house-sitter. 'I had . . . an accident,' is all he says. I nod, knowing I'm being dismissed. I begin to clear up around the pool, picking up the soggy T-shirt, the fallen glasses and the remnants of the tapas, which the dogs are toying with. Even they're not taken with Juan's cooking. Fat tears roll down my cheeks and I can't tell if the sherry caused it, or if it's because those people were so kind and now I'm leaving. I'll never see any of them or this place again. Not the dogs or Banderas the boar. Then there's also the fact that I've let Josep down – someone who put his trust in me. How can I tell my children what they should be doing when I've messed things up so spectacularly here?

I sniff, and the fat tears fall into the empty paper cups and plates that I stack. But I won't stop until everything is as he left it, untouched, unspoilt. I'm determined to leave it as if I was never here at all.

Finally, with my head starting to thump, I go back into the *cortijo* with a loaded tray and a pile of discarded clothes, hats, shirts and towels, which I put by the back door. I hold the tray tightly as if creating a barrier between me and Josep's wrath.

'I won't be seeing anyone,' I'd told him. 'I'm here to work!' So much for me hiding away to finish my essay. Instead, I've hardly written anything and socialized more than I ever did at home. He has every right to give it to me with both barrels, even demand his fee back from the agency. I take a deep breath and brace myself.

But instead of waiting to tear strips off me, Josep is sitting on the settee, the dogs lying on him, his eyes shut, pale, drawn and exhausted. I right the photograph on the sideboard, which is of a very different man from the one in front of me. As I take in his dark hair falling over his bruised cheekbone, the cut over his eyebrow, his resting arm in a sling and a crutch leaning against the settee, I wonder, again, what on earth happened.

I notice a footstool. I put the loaded tray on the side, lift the stool and move it towards his injured foot. Then I put my hand gently under his ankle, lift it slowly and lower his foot onto the stool. As I straighten, I step back into the leg of the coffee-table and knock over the candle holder that stands on it. His eyes fly open and he shouts out.

'Sorry.' I grimace. He sees me, looks around, and then his eyes close again. I breathe a sigh of relief.

I pick up the tray, go into the kitchen and clean it to within an inch of its life. Then I make up a plate of food from the leftover tapas, cover the rest with cling-film and put it into the fridge.

I walk back into the sitting room, put the food, a glass of wine and some water on the coffee-table, hoping the dogs don't feel entitled to help themselves to the food and show me to be a terrible house-sitter, which, clearly, I am.

He's still fast asleep, so I take the dogs out and visit the pigs one last time before nightfall. Now all I have to do is explain to Josep that Pedro has gone and he is without a pig man.

I lean on the gate and look out on the *dehesa*, the trees and the land, and wish I could see this when the autumn rain comes, the acorns fall and the pigs fatten, just as Sebastián described it to me. I hold my face to

the warm evening breeze and gaze out at the view . . .
the one I saw on the label of the ham that Juan brought
with him. By the look of it, someone is trying to pass
off a lesser ham as a much higher-quality product
from a well-known supplier. I have no idea if Josep
knows about this or wants to hear about it from me.

I walk over to Banderas's sty, his self-imposed isolation zone. He lifts his head when he sees me.

I sit down next to him and let out a long sigh. I
stroke his back and he lifts his head higher, letting me
know he likes it.

'Well, fella, take care of yourself. Your owner is back.
And take care of him. He looks as if he needs it.' I stand
and dust myself down. I feel sad saying goodbye. I
really hope he keeps improving.

The family WhatsApp group pings into life on my
phone.

Mum . . . the message starts.

I sigh and push my phone back into my pocket.
Whatever the problem is, I'll sort it out when I get
home, which is going to be sooner rather than later. I
leave the farmyard, walking back to the *cortijo* in the
warm night air, as the sun sets on my last day in Spain.

In the *cortijo*, Josep is in the kitchen, attempting to take
the lid off some painkillers. One foot is off the ground
and the bottle is tucked into the crook of his arm in
a sling.

'Here, let me,' I say.

'Really, I'm fine,' he says, although he's evidently struggling.

'But I'm here. I can help.'

'I think you've done enough, don't you?' he says, with dark circles around his deep-set eyes.

I swallow. 'Look, I'm sorry, it was just . . .'

'I specifically said no guests to the house. So, as I said, I no longer require your services. I'm back. And I'm fine.'

'There is one other thing.' I take a deep breath. 'It's Pedro.'

'Pedro, the pig man?'

'Yes.'

'What about him?' He still hasn't managed to get into the pills, and it's taking all my willpower not to grab the bottle from him.

'He's gone.'

His head snaps up and he drops the pill bottle. I pick it up, open it, put two tablets on the side and pour him a glass of water in the blink of an eye. It reminds me of multitasking with three small children. Actually, it reminds me of multitasking with three grown-up children.

'What do you mean, Pedro has gone?' he says, and swallows the tablets with the water.

'He left. Without a word to me. Sent someone called Miguel in his place.'

'Miguel?' He frowns. 'Miguel who?'

I shrug.

'The pigs!' He hops around on his crutch, and I can tell he wants to check his herd.

'The pigs are fine. All there. All happy and fed,' I say. 'Well, apart from Banderas.'

He frowns. 'Banderas?'

'The boar. It's what I called him.'

'Is he okay?' he says, dismissing the frivolous part of the conversation.

'Oh, he's still here, just not really joining in with the others. But he's definitely a little happier. He could just do with . . .' He might think I'm some kind of nutter when he finds out I've been scratching his prize boar's back and singing to him.

He sits down heavily at the table, as if exhausted by the news that Pedro has left.

'You should eat something,' I say. I fetch the plate of food from the coffee-table and place it in front of him.

He practically glares at me. And then says, 'So, who has been looking after the pigs and . . . Banderas?'

I'm not sure if he's laughing at me, intrigued or irritated. 'Me. I've been looking after them.'

'You?' He coughs, which pains him. He's getting weaker by the minute.

'You need to eat,' I say. 'Unless you eat, I shan't tell you any more of what I know.'

He picks up a wooden stick with some of Juan's stranger combinations on it.

'I should warn you, some of Juan's experimental tapas are a bit unusual . . .'

He shoves one into his mouth, chews and swallows.

'Happy now?' he asks, as sullen as a teenager.

I'm glad he ate something. He looks like he needs it.

'Now, please tell me everything that has been going on here.'

'That's as much as I know, really. I was here looking after the house and the dogs. One day, I was walking them in the woods and this huge animal came tearing at me through the trees. I thought he was going to kill me and the dogs.'

'What did it look like?'

'A huge white pig with its ears sticking up.'

He nods. 'Someone round here is using one to breed from again.' He shakes his head. 'Someone close by. Must have escaped.'

'Then I walked the dogs into town, and met a Spanish Conversation group. They were here tonight.'

'Even though I said no house guests.'

'I didn't know they were coming. They came to surprise me.'

'Did they know I was away?'

'I . . . I just said for a night or two.'

'Did anyone else know?'

'Just Pedro.'

'Pedro,' he repeats.

'After the attack, I went to tell him about the animal in the woods. He said he could stay and look after the place if I was too scared to be here on my own. I told him I was fine.'

Josep nods.

'I rang you.'

'I was indisposed,' he says, indicating the crutch. 'In hospital.'

A chill runs down my spine. Although I really want to know what happened, I definitely don't want to get involved. 'What's going on?' I ask, even though I know I'm leaving in the morning.

'I'm not sure,' says Josep. 'It was one of the things I was hoping to find out when I was away. Did you ever leave the house unattended, or unlocked?'

'No,' I say firmly, then remember the night I went to the tapas bar and forgot to lock up. 'Well, there was just one occasion, but nothing had been moved when I got in. It was the night we had a storm. The only thing was a door blowing open in the hall.'

He looks at me and I know something's wrong.

23

It's late and my head is banging but, given the look on Josep's face, this can't wait. He stares at me, processing the information. Then he eases himself up, still not accepting my help, and hops into the hallway that separates the living room from the bedrooms. He stops at the door there and tries to open it.

'Here, let me!' I reach out.

'I'm fine!' He's trying to balance on his crutch while grappling with the door handle and nearly toppling over. I catch and steady him. This time he has no option but to accept the help.

'Clearly not. Now,' I say. 'I don't know what you're looking for, but I'm going to help you, whether you like it or not. Or you'll have another accident.'

I recognize submission in his dark eyes when I see it.

One thing I've learnt from being a mum is to pick your fights carefully.

I open the door and peer down the tiled steps leading to the cellar. 'Tell me what you're looking for and I'll go down,' I say, not keen on the prospect but it's by far the most sensible approach.

He shakes his head. 'You won't know what you're looking for.'

There's that distinctive smell from the cellar again. A smell I recognize, stronger in the cellar than it is in the *cortijo*. It's a smell I've come to associate with this place.

'Surely it can wait. Is it really that important you go?'

'It is,' he says. His face softens. 'I'm sorry, but it's really important I get down there. Please, will you help me?'

'Okay.' I take a deep breath. 'If you think it's really necessary.'

'It is,' he repeats.

'Right then.' I have no idea how this is going to work but we'll give it a go. 'Use my shoulder instead of the crutch,' I say. 'I'll go in front. Take it slowly.'

He leans the crutch against the yellow, rough-plastered wall and puts his hand on my shoulder, placing his trust in me once more. This time I cannot let him down.

We go to the first step and my phone pings into life, making us both jump. I pull it out and glance at it.

'Just my family,' I say and shove it deep into my pocket. The dogs stand guard at the top of the steps. 'Ready?'

He nods.

We're on the edge of the first step. I move down and feel his hand on my shoulder squeezing a little, tensing. I give him a nod. He takes a deep breath and winces. Then, I feel him lean on my shoulder and take a little jump down on his good foot. He wobbles and straightens.

'Good,' I say, trying to sound reassuring.

There is a cool breeze coming from the cellar and the smell of the mountains, the wild herbs, the rosemary and thyme, the smell of the *dehesa* I have come to love.

'Okay, and again,' I say, as we manage the next few steps. His balance is becoming more unsteady with each one so I put my arm around him for extra support. As we descend deeper, I pull out my phone to use the torch.

'Sorry, stop,' he says, out of breath.

I turn to see sweat on his brow and down his neck, making it shine, and his shirt is clinging to his chest. 'Need a break?' I ask.

He nods.

'Are you sure I can't go the rest of the way and you tell me what I'm looking for?'

He shakes his head, still holding my shoulder and

breathing deeply, dragging in the cool fresh air that is drawing us down into the dark cellar.

We stand in silence and slowly, ever so slowly, he raises his head and meets my concerned stare. His chest is heaving, his forehead still glistening with sweat. We are strangers, yet sharing an intimate moment that in no time at all will be the past, a moment when our lives crossed, and we go off in our different directions, for better or worse.

Still a little breathless, but improving, he nods towards my phone in my pocket.

'You have family?' he asks, like he should know more about the person he's putting his trust in, who has already let him down on that front.

I nod. 'Three children. Well, adults, young adults.' I look at the picture of them on my phone as my screen-saver.

'And they have left home?' he asks, his breathing steadier now.

I shrug, my piled-up hair moving to and fro. 'Well, they had. But they seem to have moved back in.'

'And you're happy about this?'

'I love having them there, but we're very tight for space. And, to be honest, I worry they won't make lives for themselves. I love having them close. But I also want them to be independent, have their own lives. But it's hard. You don't want them to fall and not be there to help make it better.' Somehow the dim light of the cellar, the silhouette of his face, has me talking as if we're friends, not an angry employer and an employee in disgrace.

'And at home, what do you do?' he asks.

'I'm doing a college course, hoping to get a better job, and find a house to fit us all.' I smile, thinking about my abandoned coursework and feeling guilty about the impromptu party again. 'I thought this was the place to get my work done.'

'But you decided to revisit your youth instead!' he retorts.

I bite my bottom lip. 'I'm sorry. We really didn't mean any harm. They're good people. Friends,' I find myself saying. 'It's been a long time . . .' I trail off. 'It's strange the things you realize you've missed when you have the time to think.'

The smell is getting stronger now, carried up on a gust of wind. It's salty, nutty, briny, a smell I've come to associate with being here.

'And your husband?' he asks.

'My husband left me a long time ago. It's just been me and the children.'

He says nothing, then, 'You are very lucky to have a family.'

'I know. But they are their own people now, with their own lives, even though they're based at home. And I'm not sure they've missed me. I'm just the person who sorts out the arguments and gives cookery advice.'

'It sounds like you've done a good job if they are happy for you not to be there,' he says. Tears prickle my eyes and I sniff. Probably tiredness and a bit of a hangover. I rub my nose, remembering when they were small and I collapsed exhausted into bed at the end of each day and wondered when life would get easier.

I shouldn't have got pregnant with Luke. I just . . . I wanted the comfort. It was Rob's way of showing he loved me, I thought. And then I nearly lost the baby. I felt so guilty. Guilty for being pregnant, guilty for nearly losing him, guilty for not being over the moon and for not feeling good enough. When Rob left, I felt guilty for the kids not having a father any more, so I was determined to be the best parent I could be for both of us. I still feel the need to be there for them, catch them when they fall, but maybe it's the bruises you gather on the way that help you grow.

Josep drops his hand from my shoulder and straightens. He winces.

'I have an idea,' I say. 'I think you should go down on your bottom.'

'My . . .?'

'Your bottom. I think you should sit down and shuffle down. My son did it when he broke his leg playing rugby. He would go up- and downstairs in our house at the time on his bottom.'

'My bottom,' he repeats.

'It'll be quicker, and less dangerous,' I tell him.

'Okay,' he says, then rests his hand on my shoulder. This time I'm facing him. A shiver runs through me. I put it down to tiredness and the sherry. It has absolutely nothing to do with his deep-set, very beautiful brown eyes.

I lower my shoulders, my face coming closer to his, so close I can smell him. I move down backwards as he finally sits on the tiled step. We stare into each other's eyes and swallow.

'Okay.' I smile. 'You're down.'

He gives a small laugh.

'Feel safer?' I ask, already sensing his relief.

He nods. 'Thank you,' he says.

'Now, let's get down there. I'll go in front.' I hold up my phone as a torch, leading us the rest of the way. I have no idea what we'll find once we reach the bottom.

24

At the bottom of the steps, Josep points to a light switch. I reach up and push it down with a clunk. The lights fizzle, flicker, and finally throw out a dim glow.

I don't know what I was expecting, but not this.

It's a cave, the whole length of the property and maybe more, with barred windows at either end, a little open, letting in the mountain breeze. There are archways, and between each one there are rows and rows of tan-coloured, hanging hams. Like stalactites.

'This is where I have cured ham since I started the business,' he says. 'The newest at this end.' He gestures to the rows of hams, light in colour, and I see how they darken further along the cellar. He puts out his hand to my shoulder and I instinctively dip it for him to lean on and get to his feet.

'We cover them in salt,' he points to an alcove, 'to preserve them.' Then he hops forward.

'What are we looking for?' I ask, as he reaches to use my shoulder as a crutch. He waves towards the far end of the cellar and we walk through the silent cave, through the sea of hanging hams smelling strongly of that salty nuttiness, feeling the years of work that has gone into producing them.

'These hams, the *jamón*, are full Ibérico hams. Not diluted in any way,' he says, working to catch his breath.

'How long do they stay here?'

'Mostly up to three years,' he says. 'Some, a few special ones, a little longer. It's what gives them their unique flavour. That, the curing. The air up here and the pigs' pure breeding. It's all in the fat and their diet.' He takes a big breath.

'So I've been learning,' I say.

'A leg of ham can take five to six years to produce. It's a big investment of time, which is why they're so prized.'

I think briefly about Banderas's diet of late and decide to say nothing.

'Up here.' He nods towards the window at the far wall, and I keep moving, slowly and steadily, letting him lean on me and taking in the rows of hams hanging all around us, until finally we reach the furthest, dimmest, darkest corner of the cave and the strongest-smelling.

I hold up my phone torch in the poor overhead lighting and we stare. I feel him gasp.

And then my battery dies.

25

It's empty.

Completely empty.

'See?' I say. 'Nothing to worry about, nothing to see. There's nothing here. Now you should go back and rest.'

'Nothing . . . There's nothing here!'

'Exactly,' I say.

'There should be,' he says flatly. 'Four-year-old matured Ibérico ham joints. Extra special. Worth a fortune. They should be here.'

I turn back to the empty space, the hanging hooks, and suddenly grasp the enormity of what's missing.

'They're gone.' He confirms what is now blatantly evident.

'And these were the oldest.' I process how big a loss this is.

He nods.

'And the most expensive?' My chest tightens.

He nods again.

'And when you say gone,' I take a deep breath, 'that means they were here when you left?'

He nods a third time. I watch his outline in the shadows.

'So, stolen?'

He doesn't need to nod this time.

'Pedro?' I ask quietly.

'Someone who knew I wasn't here,' he says, his voice tight with frustration, fury and emotion. 'It's a big black-market business. It's why . . .' he doesn't need to finish what he was going to say '. . . why I wanted someone who wasn't from around here to house-sit. Someone no one would know or ask where I was.'

And I could weep. This is my fault. All my fault.

Slowly we make our way back up the stairs, him sit-ting on a step and pulling himself up with his good arm. Then I help him back on to his crutch. He hob-bles to the sofa and collapses onto it, his free hand covering his eyes. The dogs slide up beside him, and I realize that's my doing. But he doesn't say anything.

I go to my bedroom and pull out my case. I sit on my bed and let the tears that have been building up finally flow. I sniff, rub my itching nose and let the fat tears fall. The dogs eventually come to join me, offer-ing support by just being there. I look at them and stroke their heads gratefully. But the sooner I'm out of Josep's sight the better. I start to gather my clothes from the wardrobe and chest of drawers and look around the simple room that has been my home over the past ten days. I'm going to miss it – and so much else about being here.

Then I WhatsApp the family and let them know I'll be on my way home tomorrow. I don't think I could feel any worse than I do now.

26

The following morning, the sun is streaming through the slats in the shutters over my window and I can feel it as I open my eyes in the now familiar place. Somehow everything feels different. I push back the sheet, get out of bed and pull on some of my own clothes, not the shirt I borrowed from Josep. Although, right now, he has far more worries on his plate than his house-sitter making free with his wardrobe and his home. That same useless house-sitter is responsible for him losing his prized, expensive Ibérico hams.

I open the door quietly and walk out into the hall.

The dogs spot me from the living room where they've been sleeping next to their master.

Josep is still where I left him last night, asleep on the sofa. I creep out of the house, the dogs following me, and go round to the field where the young pigs are waiting to greet me noisily, like boisterous schoolkids at the bus stop in the morning.

I feed them, glad to see them one last time.

Then I visit Banderas, who seems happy to see me. I scratch him in his favourite place, and he shifts himself out of his bed to eat with the rest of the herd – I don't even have to bribe him. At least I've seen some improvement here.

'Keep going, buddy,' I say. 'You'll be fine.'

Then I walk back to the *cortijo* and feed the dogs, as has become my routine in the short time I've been here. I'll miss it. I pull my case into the hall and prop it there and the dogs follow me, panting, as if aware.

I look at my phone. If I leave now, I should be in plenty of time. I look at Josep, still sound asleep. He looks exhausted. I can't go without telling him, though. He looks so helpless and I worry how he's going to manage.

I try to wake him gently by whispering his name, but he doesn't move. I touch his hand lightly. Still nothing. So I call his name a little louder and tap his hand, a little firmer this time.

He wakes with a start, making me jump back and the dogs bark. He stares at me, bewildered for a moment.

'It's okay, it's just me,' I say, wondering if that helps or makes things worse. He gets his bearings with a shake of his head, then winces. It may be his collar bone that's giving him trouble, which is why he's in a sling.

'I thought you'd gone,' he says wearily, trying to sit up, pain etched on his face.

I take a deep breath. 'I'm just about to call a taxi,' I say. 'I thought you should have something to eat and drink before I go. I've put some food for you in the kitchen. And I've done the pigs. I've been giving the piglets feed, because I wasn't sure where to move them to in the *dehesa*, but you'll be able to decide from here.' I have no idea how he'll cope. 'I've done the bins. And don't forget to . . .' I stop. I'm not his mother. I'm his employee, who lost his stock while he was away. He looks up at me, but all his fight and anger seem to have gone.

'I am really sorry,' I say, less formally, letting down the barrier I wanted to put up before I left.

He tries to sit up again, in pain. This time I can't stand by and watch. I ease out cushions, plump them and put them behind him to prop him up.

'I had no idea. That night there was a storm. I thought the wind had blown the door open. I would have phoned earlier,' I say.

He tries to reach for the glass of water I left before I went to bed and I go over to help him.

'I'm fine!' he says, clutching his shoulder, screwing up his face.

He's not. Not by a long stretch from where I'm standing.

He tuts. 'If I eat my plate of food, will you be happy?'

'If you can.' I put my hands on my hips. We're challenging each other.

Slowly, he tries to get to his feet with his crutch. It's painful to watch. It takes all my self-restraint not to step forward and help him. All my instincts are telling me to help but I have to let him try to prove me wrong. After several attempts, he's out of breath, beads of sweat have appeared on his forehead again, but he's finally managed to stand upright. Although I'm not sure for how long.

He steadies himself on his crutch and then, painfully slowly, he begins to stagger to the kitchen, making a detour to the bathroom on the way. There is nothing I can do to help, and time is ticking by. I'll need to call a cab soon if I'm to get to the airport. Finally, after what seems like for ever, he makes it out of the bathroom and I can only imagine how tricky it must have been. Again I say nothing. Finally, he reaches the kitchen and sits down heavily on one of the chairs at the table.

'Happy?' he says, cocking his head crossly.

'I wouldn't say that,' I say, knowing he's just frustrated, as I would be. He's lost his stock, his pig man, and he can barely put one foot in front of the other without it causing him pain.

I put out the plate of ham, cheese, olives and bread from yesterday that I've toasted, and turn to make coffee.

When I turn back, he's looking at the ham leg on the table. The one Juan brought over.

He looks at the label. 'Where did you get this?'

'It's a local ham. Came from the Gastronómica Society,' I say, but no more.

'It most certainly isn't! This is not Ibérico ham! This is not my ham!'

Then he runs his nail along the black hoof . . . 'Nail polish! It's an old trick.'

'I knew it didn't smell or taste the same!' I blurt out.

He clutches his head.

'Right! That's it!' I say. 'I'm not going anywhere, not until you're on your feet and we've found out what's happening with the hams.'

'I've told you—'

'I know, you're fine!'

'I only paid for two weeks,' he argues back, but his fight seems to have left him.

'And I wouldn't say you'd had value for money.'

'I will manage.' He attempts to stand.

'Clearly not,' I say, and put out my hand to steady him. 'This is my fault. And, whether you like it or not, I'm going to help to put it right. Now, lean on me. Let me help you to bed. Please. I'm responsible for this.'

'You're not responsible. I shouldn't have thought I could be away from here and no one knowing. People round here talk.'

'You need to get better. Let me look after things here until you're fit. Now, let me get you to bed.'

'But you have family to go back to!' He's exhausted.

I take a deep breath. They're waiting for me to be at home to sort out the problems that have stacked up between them. 'They'll manage. It's what we do, isn't it, to grow up? We have to learn to manage. We need to learn to get along with people.'

Grudgingly, he extends a hand and I steady him.

'Besides, most of the people round here already think we're an item,' I confess, and give a nervous little laugh.

He stops raising his eyebrows, then narrows his eyes. 'You said you weren't going to mix with anyone.'

'That changed. I told you. I decided to learn Spanish.'

'And how is your Spanish?'

'Terrible!'

This time he smiles and lets me lead him to his bedroom where I help him sit on the bed.

'I promise not to look!' I tell him, with a grin. Then slowly, with few words, I help to peel the clothes off his battered slender body.

'What did happen?' I ask. Now that I'm here, helping a man I barely know with his most intimate needs, removing his clothes, I feel I have a right to know this time.

'Let's just say whoever took those hams didn't want me to find out where they were going.'

I gasp, as my eyes fall on the bruised ribs under the

arm that's in the sling. I watch as he tries to undo his trousers. He gives in and looks up to the ceiling. I undo his trouser button. 'Ready?' I say, and he nods.

I take off the trousers, over his bandaged ankle, and keep my eyes down all the time. I fold the trousers. 'I'll put them in the wash,' I say.

'Look, with the hams gone, I have no money. I can't pay you. Really, you don't have to stay.'

'I don't want money. I want to help you.'

'I don't need help!'

'Really?' I point him into bed, pull the light covers over him, then open the window. I can hear the sows in the woods, the mountain breeze shushing as it always does and the birds singing loudly. The sounds of the farm. A wave of guilt washes over me. I left that door unlocked. It's my fault those hams have gone. I was here to do a job, look after the house, and I couldn't have done a worse one. I was trusted by the company and by Josep. I have to put this right. I close the shutters firmly.

'You're in no fit state to look after yourself, and you may not want me here but I'm going to stay until you can look after yourself and your pigs . . . and we can find out where those hams have gone.'

27

The dogs are gazing at me as I finish making a simple Spanish omelette for later, without any of Juan's fancy additions, just potatoes, eggs, onions and a sprinkling of paprika. I've fed, watered and checked the pigs, cleaned out Banderas's sty. The sun is setting, and I know that the Spanish Conversation Club will be wondering what's happening here at the *cortijo*.

'They'll want to know everything's okay,' I say to the dogs, not needing to convince them, and maybe convincing myself. 'And I really should take these dishes back to Juan. Besides, I need to tell them I'm staying on for a while.' And that's it. I've managed to convince myself to walk into town and meet the others at the bar. But, first, I open the door to check on a sleeping Josep. He doesn't stir. He's still in the position I left him in, lying on his back, slightly raised with the pillows I put behind him, his arm across his chest. His breathing is regular and his face is more relaxed now he's sleeping peacefully – I heard him cry out in his sleep while I was cooking. His dark hair is in stark contrast with the white pillows he's propped up against. It looks as if the painkillers he brought from the hospital have kicked in and he's finally getting some rest, which is what he needs. He can't have had any since he left here. What on earth happened? His face gives a little twitch, then relaxes again and I pull the door to, happy to leave him to sleep.

'Oh, my God! How are you? How's Josep?' Juan says, as soon as he sees me arriving in the square. It feels like the little whitewashed town is welcoming me back with open arms. The guitarist is playing in his upstairs apartment with the window open, and Juan glances up to it before ushering me and the dogs to the decked terrace. It's hot and I've even stopped on the way up at a little shop, where light scarves hang outside on a rail, and bought a sun hat now that I'm staying for a little longer. It feels fabulous.

The gang's all there, and I'm guessing that I'm the topic of conversation as they all turn to face me, concern on their faces. I smile at them reassuringly, and wave.

'Come in.' He takes the dogs' leads from me. 'Sit, sit. Let me get you and these boys a drink,' he says, then promises to find them a treat in the kitchen.

'So? What happened?'

They look at me like eager gundogs, waiting for the signal to run.

'Phffff.' I let out a long sigh. 'Well . . .' I take a huge mouthful of the sherry Juan has brought me as he puts down small plates of his latest creations in front of us. I pick one up distractedly and its unusual flavour hits my tastebuds.

'Interesting,' I say, and don't ask any more but put it back on the plate.

'I'm going for a fusion style,' he tells me quickly. '*Pinchos* meets fine dining in tapas,' he adds, then sits with the others, eager to hear from me.

'So?' they ask.

'What happened?' asks Marianne.

I let out a long sigh. 'Well, he's not happy,' I say.

'Evidently. The man looked as if he'd done ten rounds with Mike Tyson!' says Eileen.

'But we were just having some fun,' says Josie, who is clearly worrying about our impromptu pool party.

'I know, but he . . . well, he's quite private and doesn't like people being at the *cortijo*. I brought your dishes back,' I say, handing them to Juan from my basket. He plants a kiss on my cheek and he smells so fragrant, a complex blend of spices, almost too much, making me cough. A bit like his tapas, I think.

'We've been so worried, dear. How did he react?' asks Sally.

'I'm sorry if we got you into trouble. He didn't look at all happy,' says Eileen.

'I remember that look so well,' says Sally, making my heart twist, 'the disappointment.' I know she's talking about her husband. 'The day I finally left him, he didn't think I would. But I did. I couldn't put up with that disappointed face any longer. The way he looked at the meals I cooked or how I did my hair.' She peers into her glass of wine. Her pain is reflected on the other women's faces, a tilt of the head, a frown, a hand reaching across the table. No one says a word, letting her take her time. Finally, she takes a deep breath and continues: 'And then, four weeks after I'd gone, putting up with his abusive calls . . . he died. Just like that. Barefoot, stabbing at his burnt bread in the toaster with a knife. Electrocuted himself. And I couldn't find a single tear to shed. I felt bad about that.'

I put my hand over hers. I remember it too, the disappointment, when I really couldn't cope and Rob just didn't understand, telling me to pull myself together, I had everything I wanted. It was then I knew we were never going to be on the same page.

'What happened after he died?' asks Rosie.

'Well, after I got the all-clear from the hospital after my chemo, and what with me now owning the house after my husband died, so I could do what I wanted with it, the kids suggested I move out here.' She sips her wine.

'And left you to get on with it,' Marianne says.

'But what about you?' Sally turns back to me.

'It's fine,' I tell her. 'He's just had a terrible shock. The accident.'

'What happened?' Marianne asks.

I have no idea. He hasn't told me. But why should he? I'm just the hired help, or not even that, really. 'He can't quite remember. But he's resting. I'm sure it'll come back to him.'

'Is he alone at the house now?' asks Eileen.

'Yes. What he needs is some peace and quiet, for me to leave him to it.'

'I don't suppose coming home to us kicking up our heels helped.'

'Like a bunch of teenagers!' Eileen says, and suddenly we're giggling all over again. 'My husband was furious he couldn't get hold of me. Said he was worried when he got in from the golf course and I wasn't there. And wondering who I'd been out with. He thinks I've taken a lover!' She laughs and is brighter than I've seen her before. There's a definite twinkle in her eye. Even if there is no lover, clearly the idea that there might have been has made her husband notice her, if only to realize she wasn't there.

'This morning I vowed never to drink again,' says Sally, accepting another glass of wine.

'It'll do you good,' says Marianne. 'Hair of the dog!'

'I feel so bad . . . and then you had to clear up all our mess,' Josie says.

189

'Don't worry. It took no time at all! And it was fun!'
I raise my glass. 'I can't remember the last time I had
fun like that. Thank you.'

We clink glasses.

'Looks like you're having fun helping him get over
his accident. It's brought a bit of colour to your cheeks.
I would have thought he was too badly beaten for any
of that!' They laugh, releasing the pressure I'm feeling
about the fibs I'm telling, but I blush bright red
anyway.

We fall into a moment's silence as we all sip our
drinks.

'I have news,' I say, suddenly excited to tell them.
They look at me expectantly.

'I was due to go back to the UK this weekend, but
with Josep as he is, I'm going to stay on. I couldn't
leave him like that.' That isn't a lie. 'And the pigs. I
couldn't just abandon them.' And that isn't either.

'Great news! I mean, obviously not about his accident. Actually, I have news too.' Sally takes a deep
breath.

'Your family are coming to stay?' I chance a guess,
beaming.

'No,' she says. 'I've decided to move home!'

'What?' we all say at once. 'Why?'

'Well, with the kids so busy that they never have
time to visit . . . Anyway, I suggested it to them a while
ago. We put the flat on the market, but no takers. But

now, finally, it looks as though I've got a buyer. And the kids have found me a flat to rent just around the corner from them.'

'Oh, Sally,' says Josie, and hugs her.

'I just don't think this is ever going to feel like home,' she says, watching the crowd of men leaving the Gastronómonica Society noisily. The guitar player has stopped and the square is filled with their joking and joviality.

I narrow my eyes as they walk towards us, laughing and talking loudly between themselves. Spotting me, they nudge each other, and the pattern of their footfall seems to change. A little more considered, rather than careless.

They nod as they pass, looking at the wine and tapas Juan has placed in front of us, and grin.

'Trying for the tapas competition, are you?' says the short fat man to Juan.

I want to leap up like a protective lioness. 'Yes!' I say. 'It's not just the Society that offers good food.' I pick up one of Juan's creations and pop it into my mouth, chew it and nearly choke on the hot chilli. Having finished my sherry, I grab Marianne's glass from her hand and quickly swig some wine in an effort to hide my coughing.

They stop beside the terrace, and I wish they hadn't. 'How is Josep? I hear he has been in an accident,' the short fat man says, this time with faux sincerity. I've lived with teens long enough to know when someone is truly sincere.

'He's fine!' I say brightly. 'Just fine!'

'Please give him our best and tell him we hope to see him in the club. He still hasn't taken up his membership – we've not seen a Santiago there since his grandfather died. The places are very sought after. As I've said, we could discuss business, man to man.'

I stare at the three men. 'I'll tell him,' I say stiffly.

They turn to go, and suddenly I can't stop myself.

'One more thing,' I say, stopping them in their tracks. They turn back to me. My heart starts banging and my mouth is dry, but I pull on my poker face, as I did so often as a parent. 'If you see Pedro, tell him I was asking after him.' I hold my nerve, although my hands are shaking. 'Tell him . . . tell him I'm keen to meet with him. Catch up on things.' I meet their stare and a chill runs through me, despite the warm night air. I get the very distinct feeling I should leave well alone.

The short fat man nods slowly, bidding us good night, and the three move on their way, their high spirits a little flattened, I'm pleased to see. But I still have no idea how to go about getting the hams back. I grab Marianne's glass again and drain it. When I hand it back empty, she says, 'What was all that about, the Pedro thing?'

'Sorry about the *pinchos*. Too hot?' Juan wonders.

'Less chilli,' I say to Juan, still trying to get my head

around what I've just done. To all intents and purposes I've laid down the gauntlet. I've told them I'm on to them and I'm a bag of nerves.

I let myself have a good cough and Marianne tops up my glass. I have another gulp of wine.

Juan is still fussing about his *pinchos*. 'Maybe I could replace the chilli with a strawberry, dipped in chocolate and some more lime juice?'

We look at him.

'I know, I know.' He holds up his hands. 'Keep it simple! Perhaps I'll pop to the supermarket, get a few ideas.'

'Or ask Sebastián,' says Sally, and we all nod. 'Ask how his grandmother would do it.'

Marianne returns her stare to me.

I let out a long sigh.

'So, you know Pedro the pig man left, which is why I'm now looking after a herd of pigs.' I take another big breath. 'But that's not the only thing that's left the farm. Josep's most expensive hams have gone missing. Four-year-matured hams. Each worth a fortune. It takes five or six years to get a ham to that stage. Years of investment.'

'And you think this Pedro has something to do with it.'

'It's a bit of a coincidence – Pedro goes missing and so do the hams,' I say.

They all nod in agreement.

'It's not just the hams going missing,' I say, practically talking out loud. 'There's something else going on.'

'What?'

'I'm not sure. It's not just stolen hams, but I intend to find out what it is.'

'How?'

'If I can get into the Gastronómica Society I'm pretty sure I can work out what's going on.'

Judging by their expressions, no one thinks that's a good idea.

28

I can do this, I tell myself firmly, but I'm nervous.

Josep didn't get up for dinner last night, so I sat out on the terrace with the dogs, watching the bats flicker to and fro, feeling good that he was sleeping soundly. Whatever happened to him, he's home and safe now.

I swapped WhatsApp chat with the children, who still wanted to know exactly how long I would be away and why my plans kept changing. I explained that I was needed here for a little longer. I can't say they seemed very happy about it. Nor was my boss at the estate agency when I explained I'd like to take some unpaid leave to finish my studies, but he reluctantly agreed: I hardly ever take leave and I'm never off sick.

After those conversations, I felt calm as I looked out over the pool, trying to work out why and how other hams are appearing that aren't from this farm. I know

Josep has said it's not my problem, but somehow it feels like it is. It was my fault that the hams were stolen. I was given a job to do and I didn't do it. I can't leave until I know what's going on.

I open his bedroom door. He's in his bed, not moving, but his eyes are open. He sees me and tries to struggle into a sitting position.

'Hey, hang on,' I say, and dash in to help. 'No rush.'

'The pigs – I need to get to them.'

'The pigs are fine,' I say, and smile.

'How do you know?'

'Because I've fed the little ones, topped up the water and cleaned out the barn. Even Banderas is out in the early-morning sunshine.'

'You did all that?'

I nod.

Then he narrows his eyes. 'Who is this Banderas? I told you no one must come to the farm.'

And I smile again. 'It's my name for the boar, remember?'

He relaxes again. 'Ah, yes,' he says, and then, with interest, 'He's out of his sty?'

'Sitting in the sunshine, near the first big oak tree. With a bit of persuasion.'

He smiles for the first time since I've been here, and it's really quite attractive, apart from the bruising and that it clearly hurts him.

I put out my hand to stop him getting up quickly and he leans back.

'So, you have been looking after my pigs on your own?'

'Yes,' I say.

'And have you looked after pigs before?'

I shake my head. 'But someone told me what to do, and said that if I followed my instincts Mother Nature would show me the right path.'

I move around the bed and open the shutters, letting in the glorious sunshine.

At first, he shields his eyes, then lowers his hand and lets the sun shine on his battered face.

'You . . . you said it was an accident,' I ask, not looking at him directly but folding the towel at the end of his bed.

He doesn't reply so I don't probe. I take a deep breath and say what I came in to say: 'You should probably shower.'

'Yes.'

'I can help,' I say matter-of-factly, still not looking him in the eye.

He swallows. I can see he wants to say, 'I'm fine.' But doesn't.

'Look, I'm training to work in care of some kind,' I say quickly, in case it would help. 'Well, doing a foundation course. Thinking about it,' I say, because I'm rubbish at lying.

He laughs.

'Look, I've brought up three kids. I can help,' I tell him gently.

Then he says, 'Thank you. That would be very kind.'

I smile and something inside me flickers. A light that hasn't been turned on for a very long time as we look at each other for just a split second longer than necessary. I drop my eyes, wondering where that flicker came from. This is the house-sitting company's client. Someone I was sent here to work for. Now I'm just here to help put right what went wrong. Why, then, does the way he looked at me make me feel like a woman, not just a mother, a house-sitter, a pig-scratcher?

'And I promise not to look,' I joke, as if I'm talking to one of the kids. I head to the bathroom to turn on the shower.

29

I put a plastic stool I've found in the kitchen into the shower and adjust it so the water pours over it. When I turn, he's at the bathroom door in the towelling dressing-gown I've helped him into. It's loosely tied around his waist, threatening to fall apart at any moment.

'I found these,' I say, holding up a pair of swimming trunks I found in the airing cupboard close to the shirt I borrowed. They're brand new, still with the label on. 'Not much of a swimmer, are you?' I say. He looks at them in surprise, then smiles.

'Swimming-pools are for tourists,' he says pointedly, still smiling.

'But your pool is beautiful! Don't you use it?'

'No. I had it built . . . It was when I was with my

fiancée,' he finishes. 'She wanted the pool.' The dogs join us and sit at the bathroom door. 'And the dogs,' he says.

I pull the label off the swimming trunks, bend down and offer them to him. He leans on his crutch and puts his foot into a leg hole, then leans on my shoulder and puts in the other with what I'm thinking are a few swear words.

'Sorry,' he says, clearly annoyed with himself and the situation.

'It's fine,' I say. 'We can do this!' I can do it if I don't make eye contact. He's just a man who needs another human's help right now. It's the very least I can do.

'So, your fiancée wanted the pool?' I ask, to distract us both.

'Like I said, it wasn't my choice. Part of her agreeing to try living here. She wanted a better life. I wanted to breed pigs, be part of this world. She didn't stay.'

I bring the trunks to his knees, then let him pull them up with one hand, just before the dark blue dressing-gown finally falls open, revealing his chest, his ribs purple and yellow from his accident. Something in me wants to trace the line of the bruising with my finger . . . but I won't, of course. Quickly I produce a supermarket plastic bag from my pocket and put his boot into it. It won't win any awards for style but it'll do the job. I move on to hang up the dressing-gown on the hook by the door next to the mirror where I see him easing himself onto the stool. He looks up at me, catching my eye, and I glance away.

The initial coolness of the water is clearly a shock as it hits his skin, but then he holds his face up to the spray, his eyes shut, and rivulets run down his face, neck, chest and back, clearly refreshing and revitalizing him.

'Here,' I say, opening the lid of the shower gel.

He opens his eyes slowly and holds my gaze, for a split second longer than I'm expecting, then stretches out his hand.

'Thank you, *gracias*,' he says. I pour some shower gel into his hand and he rubs it around his neck, under one arm, his chest, down his stomach and thighs. He can't reach any further.

'Here.' I rub the soap over his shoulders firmly – too firmly as he shouts with pain – and lower legs, just to make sure there's nothing sensual in it.

'Sorry, sorry,' I say – apologizing to him seems to be becoming a habit.

'It's fine.' Our other shared phrase.

I move on to the shampoo, thinking I can't do too much damage there.

I put it in the palm of my hand and stand behind him, resisting the temptation to put his hair into a pixie point once it's well lathered.

'So, the dogs weren't your idea then?' I stand behind him, and he drops his head back – perhaps the head massage is helping – and soaks me. It hadn't occurred to me to wear a swimsuit.

'No, not the dogs or the pool. I put them in hoping my fiancée could make this her home. But she couldn't. I went with her to the city, worked for a film company there. I am, was, an editor. I became a partner in the company. But I couldn't make it my home. We went our separate ways and when my father died, I came back here and knew what I really wanted to do. To help make sure that the *pata negra*, the black pig, stays a symbol of this area, of fine food, made simply and locally. I want the world to know how good our food is. How the life our animals have makes our food taste outstanding.'

'And your fiancée?'

'Not interested in pigs at all.' He attempts a smile, which makes me smile too, like a gift from one person to another, like a crackle of electricity passing between us. I feel my stomach fizz again, and wonder, just for a moment, if he felt it too. From the mix of emotions on his face, a frown from the pain, a smile of gratitude, and something that sparkles in his eyes, I think he did. I have no idea where that connection came from but try to dismiss it and focus on the job in hand.

'Well, I can see they might not be everyone's idea of fun. Until you get to know your way around them.'

I see him swallow, then focus on not looking me in the eye.

'She stayed in the city, with the estate agent we rented the apartment from. Went into real estate. She said the pool would help to sell this place as a holiday home. But I don't intend to sell. I'm happy here, with the pigs.'

I start to rinse his hair. 'And you've never had a white pig around here?'

'Up here? Never! The white pigs are bigger, more meat, less flavour. Some people want to dilute the breeding to get bigger pigs and sell to bigger markets, supermarkets. There is even talk of a US market wanting to breed their own black pigs. But it's not just about the pig, it's about the land they grow up on. The *dehesa*. The acorns that grow here and that they feed on in the autumn and winter. It's about the whole eco-system we have here, where animals and nature work happily hand in hand. You can't replicate that just anywhere, not if you want true Ibérico ham.'

'It means a lot to you, doesn't it?' I say, as I take down the shower head and begin to rinse the rest of his body, the wet trunks now clinging to his upper thighs. He still has stubble around his chin.

'You want me to try and shave that?' I point.

He explores my face with his eyes and I feel that energy surge between us again. He is clearly wondering how far to trust me. Finally he says, 'Perhaps, in a day or so if . . .' he tries to sound casual, and as if the attraction between us was a passing sensation '. . . if you're still here.'

'I've told you, I'm here until you're back on your feet and we've found out where the hams have gone.'

He scans my face, making me feel like a young woman – which I haven't felt in a very long time. 'Why?' The shower head is in my hand, the water jetting into the corner of the cubicle.

'Because this is down to me.' There's a slight waver in my voice. 'I lost the hams.'

He studies me again. 'And what about home? Maybe you have something you don't want to go back to.'

'Of course I want to go back!' I say, a little more sharply than I intended, confused by the feeling that has suddenly emerged. 'I'm going to stay here a little longer, until I feel I've put this right. The sooner it's resolved, and the hams are back, the better! Have you told the police? I think we should.'

He looks at me and I wonder what he's thinking. 'No. I don't think that will help. The police chief . . .' He stops. 'It won't help.'

'But surely—'

'Really,' he says sharply, then softens his tone. 'That's not always the way. Not here.'

I turn off the shower, my clothes sticking to my body. I grab the dressing-gown from the hook where I've hung it and wrap it around him, towelling him down quickly. There's only one thing left to do: the wet trunks.

We look at each other warily as he begins to ease them down with one hand.

Sometimes, I think, things are best tackled head on. I bend down, smelling his freshly showered skin, and give the shorts a sharp tug. They fall to the floor with a wet thud and we look at each other in surprise.

'Done,' I say, and turn away.

'Thank you, again,' he says quietly, and eases himself onto his crutch, then hobbles back to the bedroom, his ankle boot still wrapped in the supermarket plastic bag. 'You are . . . very kind.'

'You're welcome,' I say. It might have been awkward to start with, but we did it, I think, with a satisfied smile. And if he's not going to go to the police, I will.

'Eliza, I'm grateful to you, helping me, but just one thing. Promise me you won't get involved. With the hams, the police. Promise me you won't go near the Gastronómica Society.'

'Of course,' I find myself saying, while ridiculously crossing my fingers, knowing that's a promise I can't keep.

30

Once he's dressed, I leave him in his bedroom. The smell of freshly clean skin and hair is making my stomach fizz all over again, which is odd, because I'm still annoyed by his remark. Why would I not want to go home? Of course I do. I'm just doing what's right! Frustrated, I grab my college books, take my work out onto the terrace and sit at the table. The dogs flump down beside me in the cool as the swifts dive over the pool.

Looking at the perfectly still water, I wonder whether I might be able to grab a swim today. Maybe if Josep has a sleep I could have a quick one. It seems so sad that it's here and never used, like some kind of mausoleum. But I don't want him to think I'm trampling on the memory of his ex, so maybe I'll just leave it, despite how inviting it looks – I may never get another chance to swim in my own pool once I leave here. Let's be honest, it's not like the house-sitting company will want me back or give me a reference. I sigh. Although, I have to admit, I've enjoyed it. I've missed home and the kids, of course, but this could have been something I might have enjoyed doing long-term if I didn't already have plans to continue with my studies.

Startled by the thought, I give myself a shake. That's the point of being here. I need to find a course that will help me to get a job so I can . . . feel like I'm somebody. A bit like how I've felt since I've been here, says a small voice in the back of my mind, since I invented an Eliza Bytheway who wasn't the one who worked on Reception at the estate agent's, or shared her house with four young adults, or hid in the toilet for five minutes' peace and in the car to work. I try to ignore it.

Here, I'm Eliza Bytheway, living the dream, in a beautiful Spanish *cortijo*, feeling content with who I am: a forty-something woman who has brought up three children, has the scars to prove it, the streak of grey in her thick dark hair that, out here, seems to look so much better than it does in the morning mirror back home. Maybe it's the sun, the food, or just being able to accept who I am while I'm here, not constantly feeling I need a degree to validate myself. I'm just me. With the friends at the Spanish Conversation Club, I'm just me, and I like it.

I put down my pen, cross with myself. Where are

these thoughts coming from? I need them to go away because when Josep is on his feet I'll be leaving this version of myself behind.

The dogs suddenly stand, panting. I look up, and my heart pitter-patters, like the dogs' paws on the tiles as they dance in excitement, seeing their master in the doorway. He looks very handsome, clean and refreshed. His deeply etched worry lines soften in the bright sunlight as he looks across the pool to the *dehesa* beyond, then back at me.

'Am I disturbing you?' he asks.

'No, not at all. Come and sit down. The fresh air will be good for you,' I say. 'Would you like some breakfast, coffee?'

He puts up a hand to refuse.

'Just a coffee,' I insist, and he laughs, understanding that resistance is pointless.

He thanks me.

I make coffee for him and put together a small plate of food, some of the Spanish omelette from last night, a few olives and slices of the salami-type sausage, then carry it out to the terrace where he's still standing.

He's looking at the books on the table, tilting his head to read the spines. He turns to me as I return with the coffee, cold water and the plate of bite-size morsels he can eat with one hand. 'What is it that you're doing?' He points to the books.

'It's my final piece of work for a foundation course

I've been studying. I'm hoping to do a degree afterwards, something in the care sector, sports therapy, massage that type of thing.'

'Hoping to?'

'I'm going to do a degree if I can get a place on a course. Once I finish this and decide what I'm most interested in.'

'And what's the subject of your final piece?'

I take a deep breath. 'Health, wellbeing and happiness.'

'Big subject.'

'Yes.' I feel myself deflate a little.

'And what are you writing about?'

'Well, what makes me happy, I suppose. How we can find happiness and wellbeing in everyday life.'

He nods. 'And what makes you happy?'

Dare I say it? I don't know. I thought I did. I thought I had it all. Caring for a family, for others. Feeling needed and being busy. But being out here has changed all that. Helping Juan with the tapas. Enjoying the flavours of this place.

Josep interrupts my thoughts. 'I'm sorry, I was rude to you. I didn't mean it the way it came out, asking if you had nothing to go back to. I came out here to apologize.'

'It's fine,' I say, and we both laugh.

'I think maybe we should make a rule that we definitely won't say that any more.'

'Agreed.' I smile. 'Now, sit down, before I get nervous that you're going to fall.'

He does so stiffly, putting his crutch down and looking out over the terrace almost as if he's seeing it for the first time. Just like when I walked out here and saw it for the first time.

'There.' He juts out his chin. 'I can just see them.' He waves towards the *dehesa* and the pigs' bottoms poking out from under the oak trees there. 'So, tell me, is there anyone at home? Anyone you are in love with who is wondering why you're not back?'

I shake my head. 'Well, unless you count my children.'

'But something has put a sparkle in your eyes.' He smiles gently.

I shake my head again and blush.

'You seem very different from when we first met.' His head to one side.

'Snap!' I say.

'Touché!'

For a moment neither of us says anything, lost in our own thoughts, probably both wondering where life will lead us now. Now his business is practically broken, thanks to me. And my life back home seems to be stuck so that I can't move on. Or maybe I don't want to, because once the kids finally leave home, what will I have? An empty flat. Maybe that's why I've worked so hard to make it easy for them to stay. Maybe that's not fair on them.

'You seem happy here. I just assumed . . .'

'Really, I'm not staying here because I've met someone,' I say.

He shrugged. 'I just assumed.'

'I'm staying because I want to. I want to help. And because I still have work to finish before I go home. My kids are young adults now, like I told you. They're living in my flat and that's okay. It's just the flat's not big enough for all of us. I want somewhere new that will give us all some space. That's why I'm doing this. Well, trying to.' I toss down the pen I've picked up and am fiddling with the dried-out notebook, crinkled from the rain and the sun.

He nods. 'And that's what you're doing here? Getting some space?'

'Just while I finish this assignment for my college course. But I got distracted!'

'Ah, I see . . .'

'Maybe it's because of a pig called Banderas,' I joke, and he laughs.

'Actually, his name is Bruno, but I like Banderas.'

'Oh, God, I didn't mean to rename your boar, I'm so sorry.'

'Nothing to apologize for. That I can go along with. I wasn't here. You were. And still are. Thank you.'

'No more thank-yous,' I add.

And he gives a nod of acknowledgement as our list of banned phrases grows.

'Where did you find out how to look after pigs?'

I bite my bottom lip. 'I had some help, and I said I wouldn't say anything. I think this time I'd better stick to that promise.'

He nods slowly, popping some of the Spanish omelette into his mouth. 'This is good,' he says, and eats some more, which makes me happy.

'I cannot wait to get back to see them, the pigs,' he says, chewing and swallowing.

'I can take you,' I say. 'You'll see Banderas – Bruno – for yourself. Put your mind at rest.'

'It's not as if I don't trust you.'

'I can see why you might be a bit wary. You don't know me, after all.'

'I know you have three grown-up children, you are studying for a new career, and you have two dogs now who adore you!'

I laugh, looking at them. 'And I know that you love your pigs, have been in an accident, and have a swimming-pool you don't really want.'

We grin at each other.

'Come on, let me take you to the pigs and show you they're fine,' I say, getting to my feet and pulling on the straw hat I bought from the little shop in town, just up from the supermarket where I met the two local women who eat cheese and drink sherry together.

'I'd like that. Are you sure I'm not disturbing you?' Josep gestures to my books, the pages blowing in the breeze.

'Not at all. This can wait.' I close them, feeling a sense of relief and freedom.

31

Out of breath, Josep leans against the gate, his face softening as if he has all the medicine he needs.

'See?' I point. 'He's out of his sty, barn, bed, whatever you call it.' The big boar is lying in the shade of the oak tree, mindfully munching, like an old man chewing tobacco.

'He hasn't been this far since his partner died,' he says. I remember Pedro telling me this, wondering if he was teasing me.

'Really? That's true?'

'She died, and he refused to leave her body. We had to move it. Me and Pedro. And he just stayed there, refusing to move. That's why these piglets have needed a bit of help starting out. But the herd will die out if I can't get a black boar for the sows. He has no interest. But boars are not cheap. And now I don't have my hams to sell.' His face returns to sadness. 'Pedro had other ideas, wanted to do things differently. I didn't agree.' He takes a deep breath. 'It seems he wasn't prepared to wait to see if he still had a job in the coming months.'

I frown, remembering the pig in the woods. 'Could another boar mate with them?'

He shakes his head. 'It means it's not full Ibérico ham. They can still label it as such, but it's inferior. Like the white pigs, Serrano ham. Some people will breed with the white pigs and sell as Ibérico ham. It's not what I want from my farm.'

'So . . . hams could be packaged as one thing but be sold to those who don't know as something else.'

'Exactly.'

'I think someone is selling ham under your label but it's not your ham,' I say. 'The one in the kitchen has your label on it.'

He looks at me long and hard, fury bubbling up behind those dark eyes.

'Pedro?' I ask.

His lips tighten. 'It's what I needed to find out. I'm not sure Pedro would be working on his own. The fact that he has gone and all of my most expensive hams with him would say he's involved, yes, but I can't imagine he's doing it on his own. The hams will most likely be sold on the black market and the inferior ones pushed out to people who don't know any better.

Which is why my customers have become unhappy. Orders have been falling.'

'So, what are we going to do?' I ask, frustration bubbling up in me.

Josep looks out at the pigs. 'I don't know,' he says. 'I don't think there is anything I can do. This town, unless it's their way, it's no way. I don't know if I have the fight any more.'

'But we have to fight it. This isn't right! Pedro and whoever else can't be allowed to get away with this!' Familiar feelings rise up in me, like a lioness seeing her cubs under threat. I hated bullying when my children were little and it seems that hasn't changed. 'They can't bully you into using the white pigs if you don't want to!'

'There are farmers who have big orders from clients and need ham, *jamón*, supermarkets willing to take whatever they can get. They want me to be part of that. Like they did my grandfather. He refused. But . . . I would rather lose the herd than sell my soul to them.'

By 'them', I know exactly who he means.

We look back over the fields and at Banderas, lost in our own thoughts. This is so unjust, I think. And my thoughts turn to Josep's injuries. Surely, they wouldn't stoop that low . . . would they?

Josep says nothing, but his Adam's apple is bobbing up and down: he's holding back his upset, for his livelihood, his pigs, his product, the legacy he hoped to leave, and his land. There must be a way to stop this, I think, but I have no idea how to go about it.

'He's not mixing with the others yet, but at least he's out enjoying the sunshine. And he loves to be tickled,' I say, trying to distract him from his sadness.

'Tickled?' he asks, amused, as if this time I'm teasing him.

'Yes,' I say firmly. 'Tickled. Around his hips and tummy.'

His smile broadens and it's a very attractive smile. My stomach flips over.

'I love this view,' says Josep. 'This was the inspiration for the business when I set it up ten years ago. It wasn't handed on to me by my family.'

I'm surprised. 'But I thought your father . . .'

'My father was from here. Proud of where he was from. My grandfather kept pigs, but my father didn't want anything to do with them. He sold the farm. They moved to be nearer my mother's mother, my grandmother, in the city, in an apartment. But I missed this. This is what I felt was in my blood. This is what I missed when I went to work every day in the city.'

I say nothing, wondering if he'll tell me more. He does.

'I went to college, to study. My parents wanted their son to go to university. So I did. I became a partner in a film production company. They were proud of me.

But every day I kept thinking I was looking in the wrong direction. A college degree means nothing if it's not in your heart. It doesn't make you who you are.' He looks at me and I can tell he's wondered if he's said the wrong thing. 'That was just how I felt,' he says apologetically.

'Did you ever regret it?'

He shakes his head. 'And when I heard about this place for sale, I thought it was the perfect place to breed my pigs. I didn't need to think twice. I knew it was what I wanted, what I loved to do. It was my purpose.'

'Well, I suppose we all have dreams, but not all of us can afford to fulfil them,' I say, wondering if any of what I'm doing feels like 'my purpose'.

'I rented it at first, until I could afford to buy it from the old farmer who was retiring. Until I could make enough money for a mortgage. As I said, I was part of a group of three who owned a film production company. But when I came here I knew there was nowhere else I wanted to be. As you know, my fiancée didn't feel the same. I wanted to raise my family here, like I had been. But she didn't . . . not even with the pool!' He rolls his eyes.

'What did you do?' I ask, almost in awe of his certainty, willing to risk everything.

'I sold everything – my part of the business, anything I had of any value. But now,' his eyes sparkle with unshed tears, 'with my best hams gone . . .' He doesn't finish his sentence. I shift uncomfortably, wondering what to say, when suddenly he changes the subject. 'Over there, in the middle of the field,' he points to a patch of scorched earth, 'that was where the biggest, oldest oak tree on the farm stood when I first came here. Lightning struck it and it fell. It has left a hole in the landscape ever since.'

I follow his gaze. 'You could plant a new one?'

'I have,' he says, 'because as the old farmer told me, from little acorns, big trees grow.' He smiles widely and so do I, feeling a spark of excitement, something I haven't felt in years. A spark of hope, energy, anticipation for what might be to come and it feels delicious. I give myself a mental shake. I have no idea what I'm thinking but, whatever it is, it can't lead anywhere. I open the gate and walk over to Banderas. He lifts his head and grunts when he sees me and I think that means he recognizes me.

I talk to him, like I have done every morning for the past ten days I've been looking after him.

'*Buenos días.* Good morning. Did you like your breakfast?'

He grunts. I'd scattered some leftovers around the base of the tree and he's started rooting around again and is chewing on the bugs and whatever else he can find.

I begin to scratch his back and he lifts his head

higher, enjoying it. I even find myself humming the same song I would sing to the children, which I've sung to Banderas while he's been enjoying his early-morning rubs.

I turn to Josep, who is beaming, even laughing.

I've scratched and tickled Banderas's hind legs and he's rolled over, like a dog, to let me tickle his tummy. Eventually I stand up and walk back to the gate. Maybe I'll grab a handful more pig pellets, as a little treat. If I spread them around he'll perhaps join the sows, under the boughs of another big oak.

But first I check their water, go to the hose and turn it on, then direct the water jet at Banderas. He relishes it, creating a muddy puddle for him to lie in and stay cool. Josep is beaming with delight as he watches. He clearly loves his pigs.

'Tell me, how does it work?' I say to him at the gate. 'You love the pigs, and yet at some point they have to go to . . .'

'To be sacrificed,' he says, deadpan.

'Yes. How can you do it?'

He sighs.

'I love my pigs. But I am also a farmer. I want my pigs to have the best life they can. I also want to produce the best ham I can. The happier the animal, the better the product. They are eating all the things they want to eat, exercising and enjoying life. It is part of the natural process. There is also new life,' he points to the piglets, 'and I know that they will live well and happily. When the rains come, the mature pigs will eat nothing but acorns and grass and put on sixty kilos. They will walk and enjoy life in their natural habitat. Being an Ibérico ham farmer is about sustainability, and has been for generations, before we knew the word even existed. We grow crops for the herd to feed on in the summer months and let nature take its course during the winter when the grass grows and the acorns fall. I hoped to pass on the knowledge to generations to come.' He falls silent, looking out over the land, the oak trees where the pigs are rooting. 'Without the pigs . . .'

I nod, understanding.

I go to the barn for a shovelful of pellets, once again catching my foot on the tarpaulin. I tut and give it a tug to fold it away. The last thing I want is Josep coming in here and tripping over it. It doesn't move. I tug again and it releases so suddenly that I tumble back. I pull off the tarpaulin.

It concealed boxes, packaging for the hams. Labels. I look closer and see the image of the view from the gate over the *dehesa*. Josep's brand. I'm about to throw the tarpaulin back over them when something catches my eye. The same thing I saw on the label of the ham that Juan brought over. A piece of the landscape missing. The big oak that used to be in the middle of the field that was struck by lightning. At least now I have some proof that someone is selling his hams with counterfeit packaging.

Josep may not want to go to the police but I have to do something. I can't stand by and let him be bullied, even beaten, out of his livelihood, his home, his passion. I have to do something.

32

I stand outside the building, holding the labels tightly in my shaking hands. I recognized him as soon as I saw him: the man asking after Josep. That smile beneath his moustache. The man from the Gastronómica Society, the town's mayor, Señor Blanco, standing with the police chief, another man I had seen among the group regularly going into and coming out of the Gastronómica Society.

Now I know why Josep told me not to go to the police: not only did they try to take my labels for 'evidence', they pretended not to understand what I was saying.

I tap the labels in my hand as I stand on the street outside the police station in the hot, midday Andalucían sun, shielding my eyes from the heat haze, the dust tickling my nose. The red geraniums seem brighter than ever in the car park at the bottom of the town where the police station is.

Now what? I wonder crossly. If we can't go to the police, how can we get the hams back? I have to find a way of putting this right. I'm still shaking with indignation at being dismissed by the mayor, who was with the police chief. So, this is how things work around here. I glance at the small dark grocery shop, the myriad little caves behind it up the hillside. The bright white walls of the cobbled street. A pretty façade covering a much darker heart. No wonder my friends from the Spanish Conversation Club have never felt they belonged. This place wants to keep people at arm's length, especially from the Gastronómica Society.

I march back to the *cortijo* in the heat of the day, picking up the bread and milk I said I was going out for.

'Hey!' says the lovely young woman on the supermarket till. '*Buenos días!* You're still here. I was hoping to see you. How's things?'

'Frustrating,' is all I can say as I look around the shop. 'Did my friend Juan come to see you?'

'Yes.' She laughs. 'He has some strange ideas about tapas!'

'Yes.' I manage to laugh too. 'But he's learning, realizing he doesn't have to try so hard.' I look around the shop again, like an Aladdin's cave. 'What's new in?'

'Well, I have more of the peppers, and that cheese

you tried, made by my friend. Just serve on its own, beside some ham. Or on this bread.' She holds it up for me to smell.

'And then, of course, there are prawns and calamari, so simple but delicious to eat with fingers and lick off the juices!' she says, with a throaty giggle.

'I'll take some,' I say, my brain ticking over, happy to be distracted from the mayor and his crony. 'And what about ham? How do you know one from the other?' I think about the ham Juan bought.

'Let me show you . . .' She slides out from behind her position on the stool.

We reach the cured meats. I gaze at the hams hanging there and the meat already sliced and packaged.

'Which would you buy?' I ask.

'What I can afford and what I'd buy are different things. Go for the best you can afford would be my advice. Do nothing to it. Let it sit on your tongue and the ham will tell its tale. It is the story of where it has come from. You will know if it is a good one or not so good. I think you have a good sense for flavour. Trust in yourself.'

I nod thoughtfully and thank her. 'Do you ever wish you could go to the Gastronómica Society? You obviously have a great understanding of the food from this area, and lots of producers don't seem to be selling as much as they should. Don't you wish you could get in and show them some of it?'

She laughs. 'Mostly women producers. And I wouldn't go into that place if they paid me. They are not interested in the food they eat, its provenance, the quality. They are interested only in having the best of whatever they want, whenever they want. It's not about the food. I bet they couldn't tell one ham from another,' she says, with disgust. 'It's about the balance of the ecosystem, which means the land, soil and air are good, the produce the best it can be. The happier the produce, the happier the farmer and the consumer. To the Society, it's all about power. That club is everything that is wrong about this town. They keep what they want, sell what they don't want to the highest bidder. It has sold the heart of the town,' she says passionately, just as another customer comes into the shop. We look at each other with total understanding.

'Thank you for your help. I'm Eliza by the way.'

'Julieta.' She smiles, and I think I've made a new local friend.

I struggle back to the *cortijo* with my bags of shopping, the hot dust tickling my nose, making me sniff, and my eyes itch. I step into the cool of the house still smarting from my encounter with the mayor and his sidekick. Then it hits me. What on earth do I tell Josep?

33

The next morning, I walk out to visit the pigs. Banderas is back in his sty, playing dead.

'Good morning,' I say, and repeat it in Spanish. 'I'm not falling for that one! You coming out today?'

He grunts but doesn't move.

I put the leftovers I've saved for him by the door and he rolls onto his belly, then wriggles a little closer.

I think back to my conversation with Julieta in the shop yesterday, about buying good-quality produce. Happy ecosystem, happy produce, happy customer. Everyone is happy.

Happy. The word rolls around my head and I find myself thinking about my college essay. I haven't thought about it properly for days, not since Josep came home to find us partying in his pool. I need to!

I look at Banderas and put my hand out to stroke

him. He lifts his head to look at me from under his long eyelashes, his big black ears flopping while I stroke him and hum. Eventually, he shuffles out of the sty, closer to his food, and I crawl out, dust off my hands and get to work laying clean bedding. It's another step in the right direction as he finishes the bread, tomatoes and lettuce I've scattered, then moves to lie under his favourite tree, away from the sows regarding him coyly, like young ladies at court, hoping the newly single duke will ask one to dance.

I finish in the sty, still singing to myself as I crawl out into the bright, hot sunlight, shielding my eyes from its glare.

As I straighten, I discover I have company.

He's leaning against the gate, smiling, and I blush.

'Looks like someone's happy,' he says, jerking a thumb at Banderas, rootling around in the ground under the tree for bugs, shoots and roots, happily chewing his finds. 'Clearly he's a fan of Take That!'

My cheeks burn with embarrassment. He heard me. 'Someone else looks happy too,' I say. 'You made it here on your own!'

'I did!' He's propped against the top of the five-bar gate, and shifts his weight.

'I didn't hear you,' I say.

'You were deep in thought. I didn't want to interrupt.'

'Just thinking about my college work.'

'Have you finished?'

I laugh. 'No. I wish.'

'Have you decided what you want to study after?'

'No,' I say again. 'Maybe sports massage.'

'Well, it's certainly worked on Br—Banderas,' he corrects himself.

'It just one of the courses I'm thinking of going on to study. I'm not sure how to do it, but he seems to like it,' I say.

He laughs again and then so do I, both of us watching Banderas.

I see him counting the piglets. 'All present and correct,' I say.

His look says so much more than the words that come out of his mouth, but I know he means it.

'Thank you,' he says, the words catching in his throat.

Tears spring to my eyes. I know what this means to him. 'You're welcome.'

And we smile at each other and Banderas.

It's doing all three of us some good to be out here, feeling the sun on our faces, healing and growing in Mother Nature's playground.

'I'm sorry I doubted you. I can see you are trustworthy.'

'You had every reason,' I say quickly, hoping he doesn't find out about me going to the police, after he told me not to. Not when I've just regained his trust.

'Come on – lean on me, if you like,' I say, and we

walk back to the *cortijo* amicably. He goes to sit at his desk in the cool of the sitting room, in front of his computer, and I decide to take my moment, knowing he may be there for a little while, and have a swim.

34

Back at the *cortijo*, after my swim, Josep is still at his desk, staring at the computer screen, holding his phone.

'Is everything okay?' I ask, as I head for my bedroom, drying myself as I go.

He jumps, surprised to see me there. His face is pale again. He's on the mend physically, but I can see that the missing hams are playing on his mind, as they are on mine.

I go to the kitchen, pour us both a glass of water, pick up his medication and take it to him. I put the water next to him with the pills.

'Thank you. You are kind.'

'It's not kindness,' I say. 'I want to see you and the business on its feet before I leave.'

I gulp my water before remembering I'm wearing

nothing but a towel over my swimsuit. But he doesn't notice. Instead he looks blankly at the screen again.

'That may not happen,' he says.

'What do you mean?' I resist the urge to look at the screen over his shoulder.

He looks at me and does a double-take, apparently realizing for the first time that I'm just out of the pool. Drops of water gather around me on the tiles, but he does a little shake of his head, returns to his screen and focuses. He looks beaten.

'The orders are dropping off.' He points at the screen. I feel water trickling down my body. 'It was why I went away in the first place. Orders from people I have supplied for years were being cancelled. I needed to find out why and explain to them that I was going to change how the hams are delivered, that there'd been a problem with the company I have been using.'

He sighs. His leg is outstretched, out of the boot now, and his arm is out of the sling, but it seems as if it's not his foot that is broken, more his spirit.

He shakes his head again, sighs and shuts his laptop.

'Orders are way down. They don't like the quality of the meat. They say it has changed.'

'So someone is hijacking your ham?'

He nods.

'Swapping the good ham for less-good quality.' I think of the labels. 'Can't you just tell the customers?'

'I needed to be sure what was going on, who was doing it, so I followed the van, having collected hams from me and on its delivery. That's why I didn't want anyone to know I was going to be away.' He bites his bottom lip. And I couldn't feel worse than I do. 'But it looks like they found out. A van pulled out in front of me, then slammed on its brakes. I swerved,' his face is haunted, remembering the crash, 'and I came off the road. My leg was trapped.' His eyes have darkened. 'And my collar bone.' He puts his hand to it. 'By the time they got me out, the clapped-out old van had gone and so had the delivery truck with my hams on board, probably to be swapped for inferior ones at a point later in the journey.'

'Here.' I put the water glass in his shaking hands, cupping them around it. He sips.

'So, someone is labelling inferior hams to look like yours.' At least I know that much from the labels I found in the barn.

He nods. 'And selling my best hams on the black market, no doubt.'

'The ones that were stolen?'

He puts down the glass with a wobble.

'And someone didn't want you to find out the swap was happening?' I'm furious all over again as the pieces slot into place.

That must have been why Miguel was here: to get the printed labels. Get rid of any evidence. I must have interrupted him when I asked who he was, why he was there, and said I needed to phone Josep. He must have thrown the tarpaulin over the boxes to stop me seeing them when I said he should leave.

'What can we do?' I'm no longer bothered that I'm damp and in a towel.

'It's over. I can't fight them any more,' he says.

'What? Who?' I say, but I know exactly who he means.

'A lot of people in this town like the money that comes from selling hams to the big supermarkets. No quality in those hams. And it will be another year before the hams I have left are ready to sell for good money. I can't fight them now. And I'm not going to join them, no matter how much they ask. They want me out of business . . . to buy the farm and use its name and brand because it has become one of the best Ibérico ham producers in the area.'

'But you still have the sows.'

'Not without a boar. I have no boar and no hams to sell. It's over.'

'No! You can't just give up!' I say furiously.

'It's not giving up. It's being beaten. I've worked hard to keep this farm going. My parents didn't want me in this business. My father left. When the place at the Gastronómica Society eventually came to me, they thought they could get me on side. But I wouldn't. Now they have just beaten me and put me out of business.'

'This is my fault,' I say.

'It would have happened one way or another. It was just a matter of time once the boar gave up.'

I look at him, his face so attractive, if sad, and the one thing I want to do is take it in my hands and kiss it. My fingertips twitch, as I yearn to touch him, and my lips ache to be on his. I can't believe I just admitted it to myself. I want to kiss this man. I want to make it better, not just because I feel responsible but because . . . I see him scanning my face, taking in my features, committing them to memory, like an artist about to draw, finding the interest, and making me feel as if he's looking at something beautiful.

He opens his mouth to speak, just as I'm about to. My heart leaps. And I stop myself saying what I want to say, that I'm here because of him.

'I'm selling the farm,' he says. 'There's nothing more to do here.'

35

'I'll be fine,' he tells me, as I check he has food for the evening.

'I thought we said that word is banned,' I say, standing on the terrace as the sun is setting.

'Agreed.' He smiles. And although his injuries may be on the mend, I can see he's still as damaged and broken as he was when he first arrived back here. He rubs his hand round his eyes.

'I've done the pigs,' I tell him. 'No need to worry there. Banderas looked happy under his tree.'

'Eliza, I know you think I shouldn't but selling is my only option now,' he says calmly and clearly.

I let out a long sigh, throwing up my hands and letting them fall to my sides. 'Is there really no other way?'

'There really isn't,' he says.

'There has to be!' I practically shout, furious on Josep's behalf all over again. 'They can't get away with this!'

'They have,' he says firmly.

I want to shake him. Tell him to fight. Frustration bubbles inside me.

He stands slowly. 'I know you want to help but it's not your fault. They were going to win somehow. One man cannot fight a whole network of organized crime,' he says. 'I tried.'

The conversation is over. There's nothing more to say.

I put the leads on the dogs and turn to head into town, then stop and turn back. 'Come with me,' I say.

'What?' His face lights up and makes my stomach fizz.

'It'll be good for you, for your leg,' I add quickly. 'We'll just stroll to the tapas bar. It's not far. It'll help your walking. You must just remember heel to toe instead of limping to overcompensate.'

'You want me to come to the Spanish Conversation Club?' He raises his eyebrows.

I can't help but laugh, like some kind of release. 'No, I just want you to get out of here for a while. Have a walk. It'll be good for your leg. And you might actually forget about this business and enjoy yourself.'

He studies me intently, and I feel my insides melt. I put it down to the heat . . . or maybe the menopause.

And then he smiles, showing his white teeth, the little lines at the corners of his mouth, his dark eyes sparkling again. The fire in me rages in my belly and up through my chest to my burning cheeks. I take off my straw hat and fan my face distractedly.

'What is it with you, Eliza Bytheway? You . . .' He pauses and gazes at me again with that sparkle in his eye. 'You're quite an extraordinary lady. You don't give up . . . Your family are very lucky to have you.'

'Well, with you on the mend, you'll want me gone soon and they'll have me back to boss them around,' I say, and then we stare at each other, a huge elephant coming into the room and sitting between us. Leaving is the one thing I don't want to do but staying isn't an option. He's on his feet. I said I'd stay until he was. And now that he is, it's time I thought about going home.

'Come on. Once I know you're walking into town, I'll be able to leave here happy,' I say, knowing I'm lying to myself.

'You really could do anything you set your mind to,' he says, shaking his dark hair. 'I don't think I've ever met such a determined woman.'

'So, you'll come?'

'I'll come just to prove to you that I'll be fine,' he says, and I know, for sure, my time here is coming to an end.

*

We walk slowly into town, the last of the evening sun on our faces, breathing in warm air, the dogs trotting happily beside us.

By the time we reach the square, Josep is visibly tired but determined to make it.

He causes quite a stir at the tapas bar when we arrive. Everyone shuffles around making space and pulling up extra seats for us. Juan claps his hands in excitement, feeling he's got the local trade in at last. 'If Spanish people want to come here, I'll know I've made it,' he says. Sadly, Josep sticks out by being the only Spanish customer, but I don't say anything that will burst Juan's bubble.

The square is busy this evening, filled with summer visitors enjoying the guitar music.

'Who's that?' I ask Josep.

'Ah, Thiago,' he says, moving his chin towards the open windows of the apartment across the square. 'He keeps himself to himself. I see nothing has changed.'

'Why doesn't he play in the bars around here? Is he a professional?'

'He was. But with the traditional bars gone, he has nowhere to play. He used to play with flamenco dancers when this place had local bars. But his livelihood disappeared when this town became about the Gastronómica Society and no one else.'

Juan looks up at the apartment and then, determined to impress Josep with his new tapas recipes, he disappears to the kitchen, just as the bar fills with groups of people. Sebastián hasn't arrived, which worries me a little. I'm dying to congratulate him on his essay. That word, 'essay', is haunting me and I push it firmly out of my head. Not tonight, I think. I'll worry about it tomorrow. Along with booking my flight home. Tonight I want to enjoy a night with friends . . . and Josep, but I know that this is all it can be: a night with friends.

Juan is struggling to keep up with his orders. I can see he's flustered. I get up and go to the kitchen. 'Can I help?' I ask him, through the doorway.

'Oh, you angel! Can you take an order on the terrace and deliver these as you pass?' He hands me two plates.

I take a notebook, a pen and the two plates of tapas, and deliver them to the table. Josep is sitting on one side of the group and is answering questions on Spanish conversation from Eileen and Sally.

'So lovely to have someone Spanish here to teach us,' says Marianne, and I glance at Josep: I'll rescue him in a bit, but maybe this is what he needs, to take his mind off things right now.

I put down the plates on their table, Juan's new experimental tapas, and see Josep's confusion.

I hurry out to take a drinks order from the table on the terrace, then see another group of holidaymakers approaching and guide them to a table too.

'Eliza, your phone is ringing,' Marianne calls, as I pass.

'Oh, just answer it. I'll be two secs.'

I see her pick up the phone, talk and hang up.

'It was your son,' she says. 'I said you'd ring him back.'

'Thank you,' I say, stuffing the phone into the front of the apron I've found and wrapped around me.

'How are the tapas? Juan's asking.'

'Better.' They're all in agreement, and I can't help feeling proud.

'Just how it should be, simple,' says Josep. 'Those peppers are great, the olives too.'

'Ah, from Julieta at the supermarket. And you should try the cheese.'

'The simplest things can bring the greatest happiness,' Josep says, and catches my eye, making me shiver with excitement.

'Drinks, anyone?' I say, distracting myself.

The others all follow Josep's lead, ordering fino sherry. I hurry back to the kitchen.

'And?' Juan is keen to hear.

'The simpler the better, Josep said. Simple things can bring the greatest happiness.' Juan shrugs, but is smiling.

'Okay,' he replies, and reluctantly removes an ornate garnish of what might be gold-leafed pea shoots, leaving the plate as it's meant to be.

I return to the table with the tray of sherry. As I set it down, the occupants of the table on the terrace look in our direction and call me over. 'Could we have what they're having, please?'

'Of course! Can I suggest sherry to go with it? Or perhaps wine?'

'Lovely!' say the Australian couple.

I make a note, head back to the kitchen and hand Juan the order.

'Don't tell me, they want chips,' Juan says, a hand on his hips.

'They want the tapas that the Spanish Conversation Club are having.' I beam.

'Seriously?' His eyes widen.

'Seriously!' I confirm.

'They ordered my tapas!' he exclaims in disbelief, throwing his arms around me.

Finally, after several tables have followed suit by ordering simple tapas, wine, sherry and beer, I take a moment to call Luke. I pull out my phone.

'Best night ever!' Juan says, beaming. 'Tell me you'll be here to help me out for the rest of the week? Sebastián is away visiting his grandparents. I need you!'

'Of course!' I say, and wonder how to tell my family, and Josep, that I'm staying on just a little longer.

I dial.

36

'Mum, who was that? Is that a man in the background? Who is it? Are you with someone?' says my son, with more than a hint of disapproval in his voice. And by 'with someone', I presume he means a boyfriend.

'No, it's not—' I stop. 'Wait a minute. What's wrong about me being with someone?' I find myself saying. 'I can have a boyfriend if I like!'

'Well,' he gives the sort of laugh that makes me even more defensive, 'it's not like you need one. You have us!'

'Your father's got a wife and a baby on the way,' I retort.

'But that's Dad. You're, y'know . . .'

'No, I don't know! What?' I'm rattled.

'Well . . . just Mum!'

There's a pause. That's who I am at home: 'just Mum'. Maybe I'm not quite ready to go back to being 'just Mum'. He swipes the conversation aside.

'Mum? There's a problem.'

My heart jumps into my mouth. I thought it was unusual for him to pick up the phone.

'What's happened?' My blood runs cold as my brain zips through all the possibilities.

'Don't panic, but there's been a bit of an accident. I had a few people back. Nothing big, y'know . . .'

'What's happened?' My mind is still swirling with blue lights and defibrillators trying to jump-start the heart of one of my children.

'Well, I didn't realize—'

'Luke, *what's happened*?'

'There's a leak. From the bathroom. The radiator's come off the wall,' he says quickly. 'I've no idea what to do. Can you come back?'

I take a deep breath. The blue lights and hospital rooms recede into the deeper, darker corners of my mind where worry lives and won't move out.

'Mum! I don't know what to do!'

I should go, says a voice in my head.

'Mum!'

'Yes, Luke?'

'It's a leak! It's serious!'

My mind immediately turns to how quickly I can get a flight back. When I look at Josep and my friends,

I snap out of it: the kids need to learn how to cope without me.

'Put a bowl under it and then do what I would do, Luke. Phone a plumber.'

'When are you coming back?' he says crossly.

'I'm staying on, just for a little longer.'

'Is this anything to do with that man, your boyfriend?'

'Yes, that and . . .' How do I say, a grieving boar and missing hams? '. . . I have some things to sort out. I'm needed.'

'Mum? We need you here!'

I let out a long sigh. 'Do you? Or is life just easier when I'm there, Luke?'

Josep is struggling to his feet. 'I'll be back soon,' I say. 'But you can do this without me. You just think you need me, but you don't.'

Feeling weighed down with guilt and 'Mum' ringing in my ears, I hold the phone to my lips for a moment. I feel as if I've just ripped off a plaster and am waiting for the pain to pass. As the initial shock of what I've just done wears off, I go back to the kitchen and to helping Juan.

Josep's looking at me and I try not to meet his eyes, but I can feel them on me.

'Problems?' he says, as he gets stiffly to his feet. I put out a hand, which he clasps gratefully and lays his other on my shoulder to steady himself.

I shake my head, not looking at him directly. 'No,' I say wearily.

'Look, if you need to leave, I'll manage,' he says, attempting the steps down from the terrace and not managing at all.

'It's fine. It's my kids . . .'

'Your kids?'

I nod. 'A mess that maybe they need to learn how to put right.'

He's standing so close to me that I can smell his citrus shower gel. The one we used when I helped him to shower.

'It's just hard not to step in and fix it for them.'

He moves even closer and takes my hand in both of his, sending a bolt of electricity through me. 'Thank you, Eliza,' he says, almost in a whisper, his voice full of pent-up emotion, making it husky. 'I don't know what I would have done if you hadn't been here.'

I can smell a hint of sherry, feel his breath and the heat from his body.

And suddenly that fire is lit, giving off a warm glow inside me that I haven't felt in so long. I find it best not to look straight at him because that glow could turn into a raging inferno if I let it. And I definitely can't do that.

Suddenly, the door to the Gastronómica Society opens across the square. The lanterns at each corner are illuminated, throwing a golden light over the cobbles, the water fountain and the openings to the side-streets. There is laughter, singing and people chatting in the warm night air.

We turn and Josep tenses. The fire in me has been well and truly doused.

It's Señor Blanco, the mayor, with the police chief and Miguel.

They spot Josep, then walk towards him. I feel his grip tighten on my shoulder. My chin lifts.

'Josep,' Señor Blanco says, by way of greeting. He looks at me. 'Señora.' He returns to Josep. 'How are you?'

'I'm very well,' Josep says. 'And you, Señor?'

'I'm well. You could have joined us at the Society this evening.' He's evidently not impressed by the company Josep is keeping.

'Why would you think that, Señor?'

'Something tells me you will . . . soon,' the mayor says, with a smug smile. 'We're keen for you to join us.'

If you can't beat them, join them, I hear in my head. I hold my breath.

'Thank you, but no,' says Josep. 'You may have access to the finest food in these parts, but the company would leave a bad taste in my mouth.'

Señor Blanco glowers, pulls his trousers up over his belly and instructs the other two men to walk on. But then he stops. 'I hear you have had some problems at the farm, Josep?'

He frowns. 'How would you hear that, Señor Blanco?' The unsaid is as clear as what's been said. Marianne, Sally, Josie, Eileen and Juan are watching as closely as they would a Wimbledon final, not daring to breathe.

'From your girlfriend.' He looks straight at me. 'She did tell you, didn't she? She wanted to report a crime, counterfeit goods, with a handful of labels.'

Josep looks at me, and the colour drains from my cheeks.

'I'm surprised she didn't mention it. I hope nothing else happens for you.'

The three men smirk as they disappear into the night.

37

'You should have told me,' says Josep, crossly, as we walk home slowly and the evening slips away.

'I'm sorry. I thought I could help.'

'I asked you to promise not to do that.'

'I'm sorry,' I repeat, and he walks more determinedly back to the *cortijo* despite his obvious pain.

'What are you going to do now?' I speed up to keep up with him.

'I told you, sell!'

'And what will happen to Banderas?'

'It's a farm. If he has come to the end of his working life,' he's clearly finding it hard to contemplate, 'I won't be able to keep him. But without another boar, the herd will die out anyway. I have explained this.' He marches on, clearly fuelled by fury.

'What will you do, when you sell?'

'Look for work.'

'And leave this place?'

'Yes,' he says, and stops, tiring now. 'Go back to what I did before.'

'So, it was all for nothing?' I say angrily, tears not far away. 'Selling your business, leaving the city, building the herd, the name!'

'It would seem so.' He takes a huge gulp of air, as he looks out over the town and the mountains at either side of it. Then he starts to walk again, but limps and winces.

'Here, put your hand on my shoulder,' I say firmly. At first he hesitates but then he does so. Somehow, it feels as supportive to me as it seems to be to him. We start to walk again, a little more steadily this time, as the huge ball of the sun dips between the two mountains in the distance.

'And what about you? What will you do when you leave here?' he says breathlessly.

'Well, I have my family to go back to, and hopefully a new career path. At least I have a plan.'

'And you've never wanted to meet someone else, start dating again?'

His question catches me off guard.

'What? Oh, no.' I wave a hand in front of my face.

'What's the matter? What's wrong with dating?' He looks at me and then straight ahead.

'Ha! I wouldn't know where to start! I haven't been

on a date in a very long time. My dating days are well and truly over.'

'Nonsense,' he says, as he leans on my shoulder and we take our time walking back to the farmhouse in the warm night air. 'But he would have to be as strong-minded as you.'

'What's that supposed to mean?' I stop.

He shrugs. 'Just, well, you think you know what's best for everyone.'

'I told you, I was just trying to help.' His words sting. I think of the children. Have I always thought I knew best instead of leaving them to discover for themselves?

His limp becomes more pronounced as we near the farm.

'Are you in pain?' I ask.

'A little,' he says.

'Remember, heel to toe,' I instruct, very firmly.

He smiles and nods. 'I know.'

We walk on in silence, lost in our own thoughts, and I admire the beautiful countryside, the stars appearing in the clear dark sky behind the mountains, and breathe in the cooler air, while all the time I'm thinking about what he said: that I think I know best, how I should have done as he asked. I wonder what I can do about it. Nothing, Eliza! Nothing is what you should do about it! I tell myself crossly. You've done enough.

38

Back at the farmhouse, Josep's face is screwed up in pain as I help him onto the worn leather sofa. The dogs lap noisily from their water bowl, then join him, water dripping from their open mouths.

I fetch Josep a glass of water. He takes it and sips.

'Thank you,' he says hoarsely, and I can tell he hates being incapacitated. He bends and rubs his ankle. But between the collar bone on the mend and the ankle, I can tell it's too much.

'Would you like me to look at it?' I point to the ankle and raise my eyebrow. 'And you're not allowed to say, "I'm fine".'

He chuckles.

'I could massage it, see if it helps. It seems to work on Banderas. To be honest, you'd be helping me too.

See whether it's something I'm any good at – I told you I could do sports massage as a course.'

He sets the water on the little coffee-table and considers my suggestion. And I suddenly wish I hadn't offered. 'Oh, don't worry. I just thought . . .' I don't know why I even mentioned Banderas. I feel ridiculous. I suppose I was trying to take anything suggestive out of the idea, make it as matter of fact, mundane, even as unattractive as massaging a grieving boar. I turn to go.

'That would be good, thank you,' he says, surprising me. 'I'd like that. It's very kind. As you say, it seems to work for Banderas.'

'Right.' Now I'm unsure how to approach the situation.

'I suppose you'd better take your trousers off,' I say tentatively.

'I am a client,' he says, stepping into the role. 'You'll have to be more direct than that if you want to do this for a career.'

'Of course.' I smile, pull back my shoulders and lift my head, taking on the persona of Eliza Bytheway the professional. It helps. 'If you'd like to remove your trousers and show me where the pain is,' I say confidently, still smiling.

At which he stands, unsteadily at first, then straightens and lowers his trousers. Although I've seen them before, I try not to look at his long, slim legs.

'It was a long walk for you. You did well. A swim may help too,' I say, kneeling down and adding some of his painkiller gel to my hands.

'I told you, I've never used that pool,' he says firmly.

'I know. But it would help your recovery,' I say, as he flinches at the cold gel I put onto his ankle. I begin to work it in.

'And there was no one after her, after your fiancée?' I feel entitled to ask as he asked me about dating.

'This is rural Andalucía, mountains, farmland, the *dehesa*. No one to meet for miles,' he says. 'I'd made my choice. I couldn't have it all ways.'

'So how come you keep the pool? You could just empty it,' I say.

'Habit, I suppose. It takes effort to move on, to break a cycle.'

I chance a glance at him and he seems to be relaxing: his face softens as I massage his ankle, his heel, run my fingers along the high instep and over the top of his foot to each toe, as slender and attractive as his legs, I think, and wish I didn't.

'That feels good,' he says, his voice quiet. We slip into silence. And then he says, 'Is there anything you can't turn your hand to, Eliza Bytheway?'

It's a compliment. I blush.

'Well, clearly relationships aren't my forte!' I say, and once again wish I hadn't, but focusing on his foot has me talking in a far more relaxed way.

254

'Why not?' he asks.

'I've told you, my dating days are long gone,' I reply. Then I remember: 'I did get asked out a while ago. By Mick, our local parcel-delivery driver. I see him a lot. The kids order stuff but are rarely awake or in to get the package. We got talking. He asked me to his local pub for quiz night. But it's tricky with a houseful of young adults, thinking you're over the hill for that sort of thing. I'm not sure they'll ever leave home. And I really don't like quizzes. They remind me of all the things I don't know.'

I really should phone Luke and see if he got the radiator sorted.

'And your husband? Is he still involved with your family?'

'Not really. Not unless you call turning up with a card that has some money in it sometime during the month of our children's birthdays. He's remarried. Actually, he's having a baby. With a woman the same age as my children.' He gets a second chance at getting it right. And, all of a sudden, I'm not smiling. In fact I feel choked. Why now? Why has this hit me as if I'm saying it for the first time? My children have a stepmother the same age as them. Their own children will have an uncle or aunt of a similar age.

'Sorry, not very professional. Must make sure I don't cry when carrying out massages on clients!' I try to joke, as I wave a hand in front of my face, knowing how silly and blotchy I must look.

He stops me in my tracks, leaning forward and taking my shoulders as I put the back of my hand to my nose and sniff. 'You should be kinder to yourself. You're amazing, Eliza. I can't imagine anyone else who would put themselves before others like you do. Look at you here, helping me. It's time you started to think about yourself. Your children are grown-up. Find something or even someone who makes you happy.'

'I couldn't. I feel too . . .' I'm sure my face is getting blotchier by the second.

He puts his finger under my chin. 'Look at me, Eliza,' he says, and slowly I lift my face to his, despite the blotchiness.

He cocks his head and my heart starts to beat faster.

'You have been hibernating and the Spanish sun is bringing out the best of you.'

My cheeks burn – I must look like a big red radish now.

A tear lands on his foot. I rub it away, trying to focus on what I was doing, but my eyes blur. I can't even pull off a leg and foot massage now without having a breakdown.

'You need to be kinder to yourself,' he says again, as if reading my mind. 'When you get home, go out. Have dinner. You don't have to work all the time. You deserve some time off. You could go on Tinder.'

'I'm not sure my children would approve of that!' I

laugh. 'Luke was very disapproving when he thought I was with a man when he phoned last. Right now, they're still miffed that I'm staying out here longer.' I sit back on my haunches and sigh.

'Ah. In that case, I have a reputation to live up to. I'm a bad influence!' He laughs and, as he holds my gaze, I think about staying here for just a little longer. My stomach flips again.

39

'He's gone! Banderas has gone! He's not in the sty! He's been stolen!!' I shout, as I run back to the *cortijo*, tripping over the dusty, uneven ground. Something stops me in my tracks.

Josep is standing, dripping, in just a pair of swimming trunks, the ones he wore for the shower, at the top of the steps leading down into the pool. I catch my breath and wish I could look away.

'What?' He turns and nearly stumbles. I rush forward, but he steadies himself.

'It's Banderas – he's missing!'

He climbs back up the steps of the pool.

I want to ask him what made him want to swim as I watch him get out.

'I took your advice. Thought it might help my leg,' he says, answering the question quickly, without me asking it. 'No point in having it if I'm not going to use it.'

Without my help, he grabs a towel and dabs himself all over, then throws on a loose T-shirt that billows in the breeze, and attempts to pull on trousers and trainers. I want to step forward and make the process quicker, but I know I can't. He's got to do this for himself.

Finally, with his trousers on, the belt hanging open, his trainers pulled on and tied loosely, we hurry, as quickly as his limp will allow, into the yard and look into the stone sty. It is indeed abandoned and empty.

Josep chews his bottom lip, his jaw twitching. Then he sighs deeply and tips his head back as if grasping the painful truth.

If Banderas has gone then that's it, it's over. There is no chance of the herd carrying on and he will have to sell, no matter how much I've badgered him to keep going. Señor Blanco and his cronies will have won, and this farm will become like any of the others, using a white boar, producing mediocre ham for the widest possible market. Its unique special quality will have gone. I look out on the beautiful fields.

He drops his head forward and rubs his temples with one hand.

I don't know what to do or say. Do I put my hand on his shoulder? What I want to do is step into his arms and share his pain, but I can't. That isn't how this works. I have to remind myself that I'm here to help him, not because I'm finding him more and more attractive by the day. And, what's more, if his herd is gone, Josep won't be here for much longer either.

I reach out. I can't stop myself. I want to put my hand on his shoulder, offer some kind of comfort . . . when suddenly we hear it and I stop.

His head snaps up, as does mine. My hand is still stretched out. We listen and finally look at each other.

It's the pigs, the sows. There a rumpus in the woods.

40

We stare at each other, eyes widening.

Clearly, I'm going to be the faster of the two of us. I look at the woods with a split second of trepidation, then think about everything that is at stake here. The herd will be gone if the white boar gets in among them. There's no way I'm going to let anything else happen on my watch.

Without a second thought, just like I reacted when the kids cried as babies or toddlers, I run. Faster than I have in years.

My chest wobbles and I trip, stumble, right myself and carry on running, like I'd never stop.

My heart is pounding. I near the sound of the noise and, slowing, bend to pick up a long stick, which I hold out in front of me. I take a deep breath, then race towards the clearing where the noise is coming from and open my mouth to yell, as if one of my kids was being picked on in the school playground. Just make a noise! Surprise the pig-snatchers! I tell myself, as I build up the biggest shout and throw myself into the clearing. Then I stand and stare, not daring to make a sound.

Faster than I was expecting, Josep joins me. I turn when I hear him coming and put my finger to my lips. He's breathing heavily as he comes to stand behind me.

I turn to him. He smiles.

'Banderas,' I say.

'Looks like he took himself off to the woods,' he says, still beaming.

The sows are snorting, like a group of fans gathering at the stage door. And Banderas seems to be enjoying the attention.

'He hasn't been taken,' I say, with relief, my cheeks hot with exertion.

Josep shakes his head. 'Looks like he's finally found his love for life again – thanks to you.'

I wipe my eyes, feeling my nose redden. 'Sorry . . . sorry.'

'There's nothing to be sorry for. You have helped him back onto his feet. A bit like me!' he says, waving his arms, showing me he's not walking with a stick. A limp maybe, but not a stick. He puts his hand on my shoulder, and I look at him, suddenly wishing I could just be wrapped in a hug.

'Come on, let's go for a swim together.'

And he leans on my shoulder and walks beside me, out of the woods, back to the *cortijo*. Maybe I'll come to the woods again, just to see how Banderas is getting on. There's nothing to be frightened of, not any more. Good old Mother Nature led him down the right path.

41

I climb down the first few tiled steps so the water is over my knees and dive in before I can change my mind – literally taking the plunge. The refreshingly cool water wraps around me and is so welcome. I kick forward, my vision blurred, enjoying the feeling of weightlessness the water brings me. I rise to the surface and reach for the end of the pool, then turn. Josep is standing on the steps and slowly making his way down them.

'Come on,' I call.

He makes the last step, dives in and starts to swim. I can see the relief it brings him on his face as he surfaces and swims towards me. Reaching the end of the pool he stands, the rivulets of water rolling off his glistening shoulders.

He looks at me and for a moment I feel delicious:

my face and shoulders are warm from the sun, and I'm tingling all over.

'Come on, I'll race you.' He smiles happily, making me feel like a woman, not a mum or a carer but a woman, standing in a pool with an attractive man. It's like I've slipped into a parallel universe where there are no leaking radiators, ex-husbands, calls in the bathroom from irate house-buyers and sellers. It's just here and now and I feel very much alive.

I bob my shoulders back into the water. Smile to let him know I'm up for the challenge, then push off from the wall.

We swim quickly to the other end, but this time, we don't stop: we push away, swimming side by side, our eyes exploring each other's face. I can feel the ripples of water from his body next to mine as we swim, practically touching, but not.

We swim another length, side by side, our legs pushing the water out behind us, in time with each other, and when we touch the side we're practically chest to chest, heaving with a mix of exertion from the exercise and an excitement that seems to have us both caught in its spell under the hot Andalucían sun.

His face is in front of mine and I feel like I'm drinking it in, as he is mine. His face moves closer to mine. I look at his lips, then back at his eyelashes where water sits like tiny diamonds.

Suddenly I hear my phone ping into life from the

table on the terrace, reminding me of the Eliza Bytheway in the other universe. The real one. The one I'm going back to. I look at him, hesitating, and he looks at me, realizing what I'm about to do. The phone pings again, catapulting me back to real life. With a sinking feeling, I climb out of the pool. This may be here and now, but I have a whole life to go back to in the tomorrow and beyond. I walk towards the terrace and my phone.

There are two messages. The first is from the estate agent's, wondering when I'll be back. They've been very tolerant, as I've extended my leave, but this message tells me I've run out of goodwill: either I start back with immediate effect or I should hand in my notice. There's another message from the house-sitting company, asking if I'm available for another job. I'm pretty sure if ever I wanted to work for this company again, kissing the home-owner, as well as practically bankrupting his business, is not going to get me a good reference. Far from it. I'm just an employee, here to repay a debt . . . If only I wasn't, I think, as I watch him step out of the pool, dripping, with a look of regret on his face. I wonder if it's the same as I think I'm feeling.

42

'I need to talk to you,' I say, as Josep hands me a glass of water on the terrace, his hair still wet from the swim. His bruising has faded and the cut above his eye is settling to a scar.

'I need to go back,' I say, finding the words difficult to get out. 'In the next couple of days, really. My employers need me. More and more people are selling up and moving further away from the towns. More people want home offices. I have to get back. They need me to help with the workload.' I sip the water to steady my nerves and it catches in my throat, shooting water up my nose.

Taking another big gulp of water and letting it go down properly this time, I can feel him staring at me.

'Of course you must. You have been so helpful,' he

says, and I hear him rush to tell me it's the right thing to do. 'You've done more than enough.'

'I just tried to repay what went wrong when I was looking after things,' I correct him, and slowly look up at him.

He smiles kindly. Something inside me flips over, like it has before but bigger this time. And my heart squeezes as I take in what he's saying. There's no more here and now. It's over.

'Your family need you. Your employers need you. I understand,' he says, and I'm wishing he would add, 'I need you.' But he doesn't.

He's right. It's time to start getting ready to go home. The sun is dipping in the sky behind him. It's been quite a day, one way or another.

'Will you be okay?' I ask.

He smiles. The smile I have come to find so attractive. 'It seems to me,' he says, putting his hand on mine, 'you spend your life helping others, putting them first. It's time you put yourself first.'

'I'm fine. I'm happy!' I say, but it catches in my throat and I blush.

'You are a kind and caring mother.' He crouches in front of me, and I wonder if it's hurting his ankle. Then he lays his hands on my knees, making me shiver, and looks up into my eyes. I wish I could stay like that for ever. 'You put your children's needs before yours. Look at how you have helped me. I'm back on my feet. And you helped your friends in town. Now, it's time for you to go home and start living your own life. Get that qualification you wanted.'

I look back into his chocolate-brown eyes and suddenly feel like I've been soaked in a cold shower. I freeze. 'My deadline!'

'For your essay?'

'I was so busy thinking about Banderas, then sorting out the piglets and us moving them to the new pasture, checking the lake for water levels before we swam that I forgot! I've got so much to do! In fact, it's rubbish! All rubbish!' I pick up my notes that have been sitting there, ignored, since Josep came home. I shuffle through them roughly. 'I'll never get anything in!' I say and toss them back onto the table.

I put my head in my hands, covering my hot angry tears. He's right! I've done nothing but try to sort out other people and now I'm going to miss my deadline. Everything I came out here to do, leaving my family to fend for themselves. And life will go back to being just as it was. Nothing will have changed. It will all have been for nothing.

'Let me help you.' He takes my hands, and I'm not sure if it's for balance or because he needs me to hear him.

I shake my head, tears now streaming down my cheeks. I've blown it. Everything I'd planned when I came out here. Everything I've been planning for the last year and the years before that to make something of myself. It wasn't about showing anyone else I wasn't a failure for not going to university the first time round when I should have studied for A levels and could have. It was about proving to myself that I could do it! I didn't have to be like my mum, bringing up her child on the minimum wage. I wanted to show her I could break that cycle.

'Looks like my mum was right all along. College isn't for the likes of us.' I toss the notes to one side.

Josep picks them up and pages through them. 'Your essay is about health, wellbeing and happiness, yes?'

I let out a long, slow sigh. 'Yes.' The dogs come and sit by me, one lying down, the other nudging my hand.

'But what's it actually about?' He frowns, trying to make sense of my scribbles.

'It's about . . . about . . .' More tears roll down my cheeks. 'It's about what makes us happy.'

He sits down next to me and puts his arm round my shoulders, comforting me. 'And are you happy?' he asks.

I gaze into his dark eyes. 'Yes,' I say, and sniff. 'I am, very.' And sniff again.

'Then write about what makes you happy. Is it doing college work?'

I shake my head.

'Is it about trying to make others happy?'

'Yes.' I shrug. 'I think so.'

'Is it . . . about being here?'

I take a deep breath. 'I love it here. I love how this place has made me feel. I love getting up, visiting the pigs. I love the rhythm of life, watching the animals happy in the *dehesa*. I love how these animals are living the best life, working with nature, happy in their environment. How each part of the ecosystem here relies on the others and balances.' I look out. 'Every first breath I take in the mornings, my last at night before going to bed, the friends I've made, the sense of belonging, I love it. Yes, this place makes me happy. I've never felt better, happier with who I am.'

'Then write about it. Write about this place. The pigs. Your sense of wellbeing . . .'

I look at him.

'Write about why you came here, how you fell in love,' I hold his gaze, 'with the place. Write about what you've learnt from Mother Nature.'

And everything falls into place. The words are pouring into my head before I can even get them on the page. I quickly open my iPad with trembling fingers and begin to write, and write, and write, and don't stop, only to ask questions about the pigs, then tell of how I've learnt the importance of their wellbeing, the freedom they have, the happy lives they live, over the pursuit of commercialism. I find myself writing about why it's important for these pure-bred pigs to survive and not be diluted for a fast buck. Why happiness is about the importance of their wellbeing, their growth. I write about the highs and lows. The stolen hams, Banderas returning to the herd. I write it all. Stopping only to be fed tapas that Josep makes for me as afternoon turns to dusk and throughout the night. This time it's his turn to insist that I eat.

'Here, try this.' He puts a plate beside me. I have no idea what time of night it is. I stop writing. It's the Ibérico ham, neatly and thinly carved.

'It's why we're here. Why I breed the pigs. Why they have good, happy lives, fed on acorns. This is why. It's why the hams are cured and kept for three years, for optimum flavour. Without the end product, there would be no pigs.'

I pick up a sliver of cured ham.

'Let it sit on your tongue,' he says. And I do. It practically dissolves. The nutty flavour is exquisite. 'And the carving of the meat is so important. Always by hand. Like a religion. It must be appreciated.'

The words tumble out of me and onto the page.

'Remember how you helped Banderas!' he says, as excited as I am.

'Who would have thought a pig would respond to tickling and singing?' I laugh. 'I just did what I knew how to do, like I would with the kids when they were small.'

'It's all about the circle of life,' says Josep. 'After the

sacrifice, there are piglets. The anticipation of the cycle continuing. Like spring after a long winter.'

That's how I'm feeling, I think, as if spring has arrived after a long winter. I give him a tearful smile of happiness, sadness too. I focus again on the page and write about the joy of healthy animals and the breeding line continuing.

'And Sebastián. I must talk about him.'

'It is so good to hear about a young man wanting to carry on the traditions of his family. It gives me such hope to hear this. That this way of life won't die out!' I can hear the passion in Josep's voice.

I write about Sebastián, and his identity tied up in tradition.

'It's about the future,' I say. 'He's passionate about where he comes from and the farming traditions of the area. It's who he is. It's what he does. He doesn't need to go to university to follow what's in his heart.'

'I hope he finds a way, but standing up to those who just want to make money on the back of a good name is hard.' I can see what a battle it has been for Josep, and feel how important it is. I write about the forces that keep the quality food for themselves, stealing, swapping and selling on the black market. How they have tried to suck the joy from this world.

'This place has taught me so much,' says Josep. 'About the land, but also about the cycle of life, why we're here and what we need to do, how to keep the planet safe for the future, how to get the balance right.'

'It's taught me so much too,' I say. 'About who I am.'

'Like?'

'Like I'm not just a mother of three and a receptionist. I can look after pigs, on my own. I can do whatever I want if I just start down the path. I've worked out what makes me happy, what I love doing, where I feel I belong.'

We hold each other's stare for just a little longer. Then I tear away my eyes and return to the page.

'Good food,' I type, 'is like love. It's for sharing with everyone, not to be kept for a greedy few. Food produced with love should be celebrated, just like falling in love.' I finish with a full stop and then, exhausted but ecstatic and still in shock that we've done it, look up at Josep, who has stayed with me all night, and beam at him.

Outside the sun is just starting to rise.

The dogs are asleep and snoring.

'Finished!' I say, and I couldn't be happier now if I tried. Happy, teary and tired, yet wired.

'Send it,' says Josep, and I attach the document to a covering email and press send, feeling a wave of euphoria as the message goes.

'Thank you.' I turn to him, sitting next to me, his tired face close to mine. And right now, call it euphoria, call it happiness, call it love, I don't know, but

I'm happy, really happy, and this time I can't stop myself. I lean towards him, as he does to me, and kiss his lips, softly at first, then more urgently.

As we pull apart, he says, 'Now, I am no longer a house-sitting customer, or a client that you are caring for, and neither of us is in a relationship . . . so can I, please, take you to bed?'

'I haven't . . . not for a long time' I say, my voice shaky, but I'm full of excitement and anticipation. Trust Mother Nature. She'll show you the way. I hear the words in my head.

'If you don't feel . . .' He's scanning my face.

I look into his eyes, and nothing could feel more right than it does now and I take his hand, lead him to my bedroom, and close the door firmly on the sleeping dogs.

43

It's quieter than normal as I walk up into the cobbled square and stand to look up at the apartment above the Gastronómica Society. For once, no one is playing the guitar there.

I think of my essay, of how I love this place, of how I may also love Josep, and wrap my arms around myself. I've left him sleeping, the dogs keeping watch over him, a smile on his lips. I needed the walk into town, leaving a note that I had gone to the tapas bar to clear my head. How can I tell them I'm leaving when all of me wants to do anything but that? I hug my arms around me. How do I say that Josep and I have agreed to go our separate ways when every bit of me wants to go back to bed and never leave?

Just at that moment, something catches my eye, a

door opening onto the square. Presumably someone is coming down from the apartment above the Gastronómica Society.

It's him! It must be! The guitar player. Thiago.

It's now or never.

'Um, excuse me . . . *Buenos días!*' I wave and throw myself towards the unsuspecting gentleman. He has lovely greying hair, smartly cut, and a neat beard to match.

He glances around to check I'm speaking to him. 'Can I help you?'

'Well, yes, I hope so,' I say, still not having any idea of what I'll say or how I'll make this happen, but I'm not going to leave without trying.

'Well, something's certainly put a twinkle in your eye,' says Juan, that evening at the Spanish Conversation Club.

'Actually, I may have something to put a twinkle in *your* eye.' I walk into the bar, Thiago following me, carrying his guitar in its case.

Juan's mouth drops open. 'How?' is all he manages to say.

'Let's just say I told a little white lie,' I say, cringing but also pleased he's agreed.

'What?' Juan practically shrieks.

'I said you had some traditional flamenco dancers

coming for the night of the tapas competition and you were starting to have flamenco nights, purely traditional flamenco, for locals.'

'What?' If it's possible, his voice gets even higher.

'I said you were well connected in the flamenco world. Your family going back were—'

'Stop, stop!' He holds up a hand. 'Don't tell me any more.' He looks at Thiago, who is finding himself a chair and a corner. Then he turns back to me. 'Thank you!' he says, and hugs me.

'I just thought you could get talking . . . and say the dancers have let you down or something.' My deceit may not have been the best idea, but I couldn't leave without knowing if Juan had ever plucked up the courage to talk to him or was still standing in the square in the evenings listening to him playing.

Just then Thiago starts to play, filling the room and the terrace with beautiful guitar music. Everyone stops what they're doing to listen. Thiago seems lost in his music. Juan seems lost in Thiago, and I move round to take over at the bar as customers start to filter in.

'Isn't he fabulous?' says Juan.

'He is. I hope you'll be able to get to know each other better now,' I say. 'Juan, I . . . I'm going home,' I say, as he pours a fino for Thiago and one for me. I take my glass as he stares at me, and my emotions tumble over each other, like wrestling Labrador puppies.

'Oh, no!' He hugs me hard, then ushers me to our

usual table and tells Eileen, who's just arrived, my news, in a hushed but clear voice.

'Oh, love, no!' Eileen says.

'Why?' say the others, as they arrive and, one after another, put down their bags, shuffle into their usual seats on the outside sofas and pass on the latest information.

'I have to get back to work, and the kids want me home, too.'

'Eliza's leaving us!'

'Oh, no!'

'What happened?'

'We should have a party!'

'Not another! That's what got me into trouble in the first place!' I fight the urge to giggle.

'But why?' says Marianne. 'You clearly love it here.'

'But it's not my life. My life is in the UK, with the family.'

'Oh, what a shame,' says Sally. 'We must keep in touch. Especially if we're both going to be back in the UK.'

My heart sinks, like a stone in water, at the thought of being back in the UK.

'At least you'll be with your family,' I hear one of the women say.

'We'll miss you.'

My heart twists. I've missed my three children so much. But I'm going to miss this place too, and Josep.

I'm going to miss Josep very much, remembering last night and the woman I feel I've become.

'But at least you can do your university course now,' says Marianne.

I'm fighting back the tears and pushing down hard on the lump in my throat.

Juan is talking shyly to Thiago and I get up and help out as if on autopilot, taking over from him in the kitchen once more and removing the extra touches from his tapas dishes, then sending them out, just as they are. Simple, honest and full of flavour.

As I take the bins out to the back, I see a shadow in the alleyway. When a figure moves into the moonlight I instantly recognize him. Pedro.

He doesn't see me but is walking in the shadows of the tiny narrow backstreets. Right now there's only one thing I can do: follow him.

I'm back at the bar, panting and out of breath.

'Eliza?' They all stare at me. 'What on earth is going on?'

'I think I know where Josep's hams have gone!' I pant, and they all stare.

'Where?'

'Follow me!' I say, and we set off.

I stop just beyond the caves and point. My heart is racing and I'm surprised we're not heard. But we're not. We stand in the shadows, listening to Spanish voices, talking at speed. And when the door on the cave is shut, we press ourselves against the rock face. I don't think any of us breathes until we hear the sound of a moped and a car leaving.

'So, now what are you going to do?' Josie finally asks.

'Only one thing I can do. Work out how to get them back.'

44

'I've got a plan,' I say. We're back on the terrace at the bar.

As one, the others raise their eyebrows.

'A plan?'

Thiago stops playing. He looks to be part of the group already. He has a glass of fino beside him and has been teaching Josie the basics in clapping, as she sits beside him, fascinated. I just wonder how Juan is going to tell him there are no flamenco dancers.

'A plan for what?' Eileen asks.

'To get the hams back, and stop the Gastronómica Society making fools of the people in this town again!' Even Thiago's ears prick up. 'We all live here. We may not come from here, but we have made it our home. This town should be able to be proud of the food they produce here, not just them.' And not for the first time I realize this isn't about me. I'm going home.

'What's the plan?' asks Sally.

'We're going to do a ham swap!'

They stare at me blankly.

'A what?'

'Here's what's going to happen.' Everyone leans in, listening with interest. 'If what we know is correct, Josep's hams, the stolen ones from the farm, are being hidden in one of the caves at the bottom of the hill, behind the dark grocery shop.'

They all nod in agreement. It's why I always recognized the smell down there, as if it was reminding me of home.

'And if we overheard things correctly . . .' I worry that my Spanish wasn't up to it.

'They'll be leaving at the weekend to go on to the next town,' says Josie.

'Where there will be a rendezvous,' Eileen joins in.

'And the hams sold,' Sally joins in, clearly delighted at her understanding.

'Another truck will meet them with lesser-quality hams to be driven on to customers,' says Josie, who has understood the most, 'or maybe it was the other way round.'

'That's why Josep was driven off the road . . . so he wouldn't see a swap take place when he went to meet his customers,' I say.

'But we're not sure when or where this is happening,' says Marianne, her silver bangles jangling, as always.

'Well, we know where Josep's stolen hams are being hidden and that they're going to be sold on the black market. And we know that cheaper ones somewhere have been relabelled and sold on as Josep's. The townspeople and their customers are being duped, Josep too.'

My palms start to itch, and the old finger of anxiety runs up and down my legs, making them twitch.

'This all sounds a bit confusing,' says Eileen.

'How does that mean we can help?' asks Josie.

'Yes! What can we do about it?' Marianne says firmly.

'When my kids were little,' I start, feeling unsure but going with it anyway, 'they loved playing with cars and the farmyard we had. They were always mixing things up. That's what made me think about it.'

'What exactly?'

'Here's my plan. We follow the van leaving with Josep's hams in it. Take two cars. One pulls out in front.' I use a cardboard coaster to demonstrate. 'Then, as we get into the lanes, you,' I point to Josie, 'slow down and get out of the car. Yours has broken down.'

'So, I'm the decoy?'

'Exactly,' I say.

'I'll pull up behind. When they're helping you sort out your car, the others and I will steal back the hams. You start up your car. Drive off.' I use more cardboard coasters. 'They will also drive off, none the wiser to what we've done. Juan, you need to find out exactly when they're leaving.'

'Why me?'

'Because you're the only one who can get into the Gastronómica Society. You're the only man here.'

Everyone turns to him, and he agrees.

'In that time, we'll have unloaded the hams, swapped them with the cheaper ones. Then we get them away as quickly as possible. We'll be back here before anyone notices anything has gone awry.'

They sit and stare at me.

'Or something like that . . .'

'You're serious, aren't you?'

All eyes are on me.

'Deadly!'

'It's not much of a plan, to be honest,' says Eileen, doubtfully.

'We'd have to iron out the finer details,' Sally offers up.

'But it could work,' says Josie, optimistically.

'It's bonkers,' says Marianne, with a throaty laugh.

And I hold my breath.

'Everything depends on me getting those hams back!' I eyeball my friends. 'And . . .' I think of Sebastián and his grandfather's words '. . . I just think if we start down the right path, Mother Nature will show us the way. We'll work it out.'

'Well, I'm in!' says Marianne. 'Makes a difference from our usual daily routine. Perhaps we could think of it as a Club outing!' She laughs. 'Count me in!'

'And me!' say the others.

We raise our sherry glasses.

'Just one thing . . .' I say.

'What? We have to find out when they're being delivered to their contact?'

'And we need to find the cheaper hams to swap them with.'

'And the route they're taking.'

My earlier enthusiasm starts to wane.

'All that. But also no one can know, not even Josep. Actually, especially not Josep.'

'But we can't do anything about it unless we know when the hams are being shipped out to their buyer and where the cheaper ones are that they're sending out as Josep's,' says Sally.

We all fall silent.

No one says a word.

She's right. Of course she is. What was I thinking? None of this is possible.

'You're right,' I finally say. 'Of course we can't. I just wanted to try to get the hams back. But we can't do any of it without knowing what's happening.'

'You said I could try to get into the Gastronómica Society,' Juan says, trying to sound positive.

'Juan, you've been trying to get an invite to the

Gastronómica Society since you first moved here,' says Marianne, kindly but to the point.

'Well, I may have tried to ingratiate myself,' he says, his lips pursing.

'And has it ever worked?' Marianne persists.

Juan seems slightly uncomfortable now. 'Um, no,' he confirms, with a twitch of his head.

'So, it's not likely to now.' Marianne hammers home her point.

So, that's it. My plan is over before we even got it off the ground. If we don't know precisely when the hams are leaving, or have any way of getting the information, I don't know what else we can do. It's over.

Thiago finishes playing and lets out a small cough. We all turn to look at him, sitting beside Josie. He puts his guitar to one side. 'I can tell you what you need to know.'

My mouth drops open. Juan's eyes sparkle.

'How?' says Marianne.

'I live above the Gastronómica Society. I share a door to their kitchen from my apartment. I may not like them, but I hear everything. I know when the hams are being moved out. I hear everything from my flat!' he says, and smiles. As do we. My spirits soar again, and the plan could be back on.

45

'So, when?' asks Juan, at the tapas bar.

'Saturday night. That's when they plan to move them.'

'The night of the tapas competition?' Juan says.

I nod slowly.

'They've chosen to do it then because it's busy and no one will notice. So that's when the hams are leaving.'

'And the other hams you need are in a store cupboard at the back of the Gastronómica Society's kitchen. I have seen them. With Josep Santiago's label on them.'

The stolen hams are in the cave ready to be shipped out on the black market for big money. And the ones with Josep's fake label are in the club, just over the road.

'I have to get the real ones back,' I say, 'but, look, if you don't want to do it, I'll go on my own.'

'I'm in,' they say as one, and I know I have found lifelong friends here. I can't bear even to think about leaving them. But I know I must, very soon.

'So, are we all agreed?' I say quietly, leaning in to the group over the table.

'Agreed,' they say and nod.

My head and my heart are thumping. 'And no one must know about this,' I say firmly.

We look at each other and nod.

'This will come down to you being a good decoy and timing. Getting the hams out and swapping them as quickly as we can with the fake ones, then getting out of there. That should put an end to their black-market dealings, and get Josep's hams back! And, Juan, let's swap the good one that the Gastronómica Society intends to serve themselves. Give them a taste of their own medicine.'

'I can make a label for it, like Josep's!' says Mari-anne. 'I'm good at copying!'

We're all in high spirits.

Then I let out a long, low sigh. Suddenly I feel very nervous. Very nervous indeed. And, in the meantime, I have a flight to book.

For the next couple of days we meet and talk about nothing other than the hams and details of the plan to swap them, drawn on the back of napkins and beer mats. More importantly, we search for any holes in it.

I've promised the estate agency I'll be back, and I'm waiting for news on my essay. I've told Josep I'm staying on to help Juan with the tapas competition as a thank-you for being such a good friend to me. That very evening the hams are due to be driven away, when the town is distracted and busy. The biggest night in the town's calendar: it marks the end of the summer, the holidays and the move towards autumn.

After that, I'll have to leave. I'll have done everything I set out to do. I have no idea how I'll be able to say goodbye to Josep after the wonderful nights we've spent together, the mornings waking in each other's arms. But we both know it has to end and that day is coming, soon. But, hopefully, by the time I leave I will have put right what went wrong.

Sebastián is back from his grandparents' and he's sworn to secrecy. We don't want word getting back to the Gastronómica Society. They've clearly been ruling the roost around here for too long, keeping the best of the best for themselves and treating the rest of us as fools. I'm so angry when I think of how they took advantage of me, and what they've done to Josep.

I think about the man who arrived back at the *cortijo* battered, bruised and thoroughly defeated. The man I have come to love. I get a surge of anger all over again at the injustice. I can't leave here, letting those men get away with it, without trying to put things right. The loss of Josep's hams was down to me. He may have told me not to get involved but, no matter what I've told him, I *am* involved, very much so . . . and leaving will hurt so much.

46

It's Friday night. The night before the tapas competition and the night before Josep's hams leave town for good, if we don't manage to swap them. I sleep barely a wink. In fact, I don't sleep a wink.

I'm up and wandering around the bedroom, the one I have shared with Josep these last two weeks, since the night I delivered my college essay. But Josep isn't beside me. He's outside, in the hot night air, sitting by the pool, his hands on his head, clearly not sleeping either. I want to reach out and touch him. He obviously has things on his mind, as do I, but even though we've been spending our nights together, sharing a bed, neither of us seems able to share our thoughts.

In the morning, I shower and go down to sort out the pigs, but Josep is already there.

'What's up?' I ask, seeing the concern on his face

and hoping we haven't had any more trouble in the woods with escaped white pigs.

He nods to one of the sows, and my stomach flips. 'I think this one is pregnant,' he says.

'Pregnant? But that's brilliant, isn't it?' I say, delighted.

'It is . . . if it's by Banderas, and not the other boar you said was loose in the woods.'

My spirits dip again. 'And if it is the white boar?'

'There is no way I can sell them as full Ibérico pigs. Señor Blanco will have his way. I'll be selling my farm to him to breed more of the same, to sell to those who don't know the difference. No one will believe that the hams are real after the ones that have landed in the market with my label on them.'

'When will you know?'

'Three months, three weeks and three days. That's how long a pregnancy is for a pig. It's all about the threes,' he says, making me smile. We study the sow, and I breathe in the moment: the hot air, the orange-tinted dusty earth, the trees, getting thicker the further you stare into the *dehesa*. The birds are singing loudly, like they're all competing to be heard. My nerves settle and I know that today I have to get those hams back. I stop running over the plan in my head. I know what has to be done and I feel a steely determination harden inside me.

'So, all you can do is wait?' I lift my head to the breeze, feeling my longer hair brush over my shoulders.

He nods.

'And if they're Banderas's?'

'Then maybe there is a chance the line will carry on, even if only for the pleasure of Señor Blanco and his Gastronómica Society friends.'

Tears glisten at the rims of his eyes, and I know he's thinking about selling to Señor Blanco. I reach up, put my hands around his face and kiss him like I never want to stop and he kisses me back, neither of us mentioning that I'm leaving on Monday. But I do stop. I have to go. I have to try to put all this right.

'I have to go!' I say, resisting the urge and his body, which is suggesting we take things back to bed.

'Where?'

'The tapas competition – I promised Juan! Remember?'

Despite him kissing me thoroughly again, I resist temptation and pull away.

'Later.' I smile. 'I'll see you later! With any luck we'll have something to celebrate!'

He looks at me, his head cocked to one side, and my body tingles. A small frown appears on his forehead, his eyes narrow, and I blush, as if I'm standing naked in front of him for the very first time.

'What?' I'm full of nerves again, and it looks like I'm not the only one following my instincts.

'You're not, are you?' he says steadily.

'Not what?' My voice wavers treacherously.

294

He rolls his head around some more and stares at me solemnly. 'Eliza . . . tell me the truth! What are you up to?'

'I . . .' I'm tongue-tied. I take a deep breath. 'There's just somewhere I have to be!' I say quickly, then add, 'But trust me. I'm doing this for the right reasons!'

'Oh, Eliza!' He throws up his hands. 'You are impossible. I told you not to get involved. I don't want you hurt!'

'But they hurt you, and they have your hams. I know where they are!' I argue.

'You do? Why didn't you say?'

'Because you told me not to get involved!'

'You know where the hams are?'

'Yes. It's all arranged. We're going to get them back,' I say firmly, not letting him persuade me otherwise. I have to try.

I think he's going to tell me what an idiot I am. He chews his bottom lip and then, with his hands on his hips, says, 'You are one of a kind, Eliza Bytheway! I think I actually love you!' He beams and kisses me all over again, this time his hands around my face.

Finally I pull away, laughing, relieved he isn't going to try to stop me and giddy from being told he loves me. I'm so fired up I feel I could do anything. 'I have to go!' I say.

'Not on your own!' he says. 'We're in this together. I'm coming with you!'

And I have no idea whether to be thrilled or terrified.

47

My heart is thudding and I don't know if that's because of what I'm about to do or because the man beside me has helped me find myself again. He is practically marching as we head towards town and, right now, I feel anything is possible.

As agreed, none of us meets at the bar. I go in at the back and pick up the keys for Juan's van.

'All okay?' I say, putting my head into the kitchen.

Juan looks like he's been lit up. 'Yes! Fine!'

'The piggies going to market are in the back of the van,' he whispers, and giggles, with mild hysteria.

'*Phfff.*' I let out a big sigh. The first step of the plan is done. Juan and Thiago liberated the inferior hams, through Thiago's front door, early this morning, from the store cupboard at the Gastronómica Society and loaded them into Juan's van. They've also swapped the one on the bar, for the tapas competition, for one of the inferior ones, with Marianne's replica label on it. They won't know the difference until they try it – if they can tell the difference.

'Good job!' I say. I don't intend to sound like a gangster but somehow I do.

And from the sparkle in Juan's eye, I'd say his early-morning rendezvous with Thiago was everything he could have hoped for.

'And you left one piggie where it should be?' Why am I referring to the hams as piggies?

He nods. 'We did. In the bar. Thiago knows where they keep the keys for members to let themselves in. It's an honesty thing apparently . . .' The irony isn't lost on me. 'We replaced the one they had there for today's event and stuck Marianne's label on it.'

Marianne has done a great job of replicating Josep's label exactly, with the big oak tree right in the middle, before it was hit by lightning. There now sits a much cheaper ham, one of the Gastronómica Society's hams going out to less discerning customers, on their bar.

'And you've kept the other one, Josep's?' I nod at the ham on the kitchen side.

He nods firmly again. 'Josep won't mind?' he asks.

'Josep thinks it's an excellent idea,' says Josep, sticking his head into the kitchen, surprising Juan.

Josep and I can only smile at each other, the way that lovers do.

'Just . . .' says Josep.

'. . . keep it simple!' we tell him, and chuckle.

'I will. And thank you!' says Juan, waving a large flat knife.

'And slice thinly!' Josep adds. 'With care!'

'I will. And you be careful!' Juan replies, and this time he doesn't smile. He hugs me tightly. His tension is written all over his face and my nerves are back at the prospect of the task we're about to take on.

'I will!' I say.

'Both of you!' Juan says, to Josep, who is standing out in the bright sunshine. I pull away from Juan's hug, gazing at Josep: anything is possible with him there too.

I climb into Juan's dusty van, attempt to adjust the seat and look at the mirrors, both slightly cracked and scuffed. I've come to realize it's a mark of a local's vehicle around here, with all the narrow streets.

The key shakes in my hand as I try to insert it, and drop it in the footwell. I swear under my breath. I rummage for the key, suddenly very hot, my head starting to throb.

'Do you want me to drive?' Josep asks.

'No, it's fine.' He raises an eyebrow at me. But both of us know that 'fine' will do for now. His leg must be hurting from the walk into town. 'Fine' hides exactly how we're really feeling.

I remember why I'm doing this, put the key into the ignition and start the van first time.

'So,' he says, as I pull the vehicle out from its space behind the bar and we set off through the busy streets, people thronging to the square for the tapas competition.

Thiago is on the terrace and looks at me, worried, but he's performing the distraction at the tapas bar, and is finally back playing for the public, despite the lack of flamenco dancers.

I can see the doors to the Gastronómica Society: they're wide open for the first time since I've been here. As we drive slowly past, I spot Sebastián with a man I presume is his grandfather. He gives me a wave and inside, through the open door, I see the ham, taking pride of place on the bar. I hear a shout from inside the club and I get the feeling the ham swap may have been discovered. I put my head down, smile and weave along the street as quickly as the crowds will allow. There is bunting out in the streets, red geraniums bursting from window boxes, and the sound of friends meeting to enjoy the best tapas the town can create. If I wasn't going where I am, I would have loved to spend the afternoon and early evening here. But I have to concentrate on the job in hand, and wind down the window for air.

The streets are so narrow, the van barely fits through and it takes all my concentration not to scrape it along the walls of the houses, adding to the dents already on its sides. I head for the main road and my heart leaps again: Josie and Marianne are waiting in the layby to pull out when they see the van coming on its way to the ham swap.

I pull in behind them, leaving a distance, and turn off the engine. For a moment Josep says nothing. It's hot and my heart is thumping so hard he must be able to hear it.

'So,' he eventually says, 'everyone is here. It was planned.'

He's worried for us all.

I nod and swallow. 'We know what we're doing,' I say, staring straight ahead.

'These guys are dangerous, Eliza. It's not make-believe. There is big money involved in selling these hams on the black market. They won't thank you if they think you're trying to stop them. These things work smoothly and swiftly.'

'That's why we have to act,' I say, biting my lip. 'Okay, a message from Sebastián. They're not happy. And one from Eileen.' She's having a rare coffee with her husband, who is complaining he never sees her. 'The truck with your hams is leaving from the cave. Miguel is driving. We'll hang back and follow it when it comes.'

'And then what?'

'Josie will pull out in front of it, then stage a break-down. She'll get out, throw open the bonnet and stop them. Marianne will get out and help me at the back of the truck, swap your hams with these.'

300

He lets out a long, slow breath, staring straight ahead, his leg jiggling. I know that memories of the crash are playing on his mind.

'You don't have to be here, Josep. I'll be fine. I promise.'

'You don't have to do this,' he says.

He's right. We could just leave it. We could go home now and fall into bed. More than anything I want to be back there. His eyes are on mine, when suddenly something catches my eye in the rear-view mirror. Josie's little red SEAT is rolling forwards and pulls out into the road, in front of the truck with the hams on board. I gasp, as does Josep. There's a blast of a horn.

'Too late now,' I say. 'We're on! Do you want to get out?'

'Just go! Follow her!' says Josep.

I start the van, push it into gear with a crunch, and pull out behind the big Transit truck, as another car comes up behind me. Josep gasps again.

'I'm sorry, I'm sorry,' I repeat, staying close to the truck in front.

'Just keep driving,' he instructs. 'But not so close. If and when he brakes, you'll end up in there with the hams.'

I do as he tells me and back off, feeling beads of sweat roll down the middle of my back.

Josep grips the dashboard. 'Be careful. Stay back. They'll stop at nothing if they realize this is a set-up!'

'I know! I know!' The air is full of nervous energy. The van sways, trying to get around the little car.

'Keep steady, Josie . . .' I say.

'Keep back,' says Josep, and I do.

'Okay, this is where she'll stop,' I say, pointing ahead to where the road narrows. I take my foot off the accelerator, slow down and drop back. And then it happens. The truck in front comes to a stop and I know that Josie's faked her car breaking down. 'Josie was a hairdresser. She's used to pretending to be interested in people's stories about their holidays and families, she said. She can pull off a fake breakdown with a straight face, no problem,' I tell Josep. Now all we do is sit and wait for Miguel and his mate to get out and help, every second feeling like a minute.

'Any moment, Sally should come round and open the boot. She knows her way around trucks. She'll be able to sort the lock if it's sticky.'

We wait. I can hear his breathing. I see his fist tighten around the door handle, desperate to go and see if all's okay. I put my hand out.

'Wait!' I say. Suddenly the truck in front lurches forward and swerves sharply to the right. And there is Josie across the road with the bonnet of the car up. But they haven't stopped. They've gone up the verge and are disappearing down the road.

'That wasn't supposed to happen!'

Josep jumps out of the car. 'Are you okay?'

The truck wobbles in the road, then straightens and is away.

I watch in utter disbelief.

'No!' I look at Josep checking on Josie as she points to the truck in the distance. 'There was hardly any room for them to get round!'

So much for the best-laid plans. There's only one thing I can do. I can't wait for Josep to come back. I have to follow before they get away.

I drive up onto the verge, then put my foot down to catch up with the truck. I can see Josep in the cracked and bent mirror, waving at me to stop, but I can't let them get away. We've come too far to stop now.

I have no idea where I am. I can't see their truck. I've lost them. I'll have to turn back. My heart has stopped pounding. I slow down and look for somewhere to turn around. There's a petrol station ahead. And then I see it. The truck's there.

I swerve in and pull up. I have no idea what to do, other than that I can't let the vehicle carrying those stolen hams out of my sight . . . if they're still inside it. I have to find out if they're still on board.

I slip out of the van and run across the forecourt. My mouth is dry, and I feel like a schoolgirl playing a prank on her teacher. But this is no prank. Josep's right. These people aren't to be messed with.

I can see someone, wearing dark glasses, inside the petrol station paying. It's Miguel. I go to the back door and realize, in the wing mirror, someone in the passenger seat is checking their phone. It's Pedro! And I'm more furious than ever. The cheek!

I pull open the door. The hams are still there. At least, I hope it's them. I hear Miguel calling to Pedro and jump into the truck pulling the door to, so as not to be seen. I crouch down and will jump out as soon as I hear Miguel get into the driver's seat, then keep following. I turn to open the door. But suddenly the truck rocks and I'm knocked off balance, into the hams. I can smell them. I know that smell. That nutty, rich smell. They're the right hams. My heart lifts. I'd know that smell anywhere.

I stagger to my feet. I'm knocked off them again as the engine starts and the truck lurches forward at speed. I'm thrown backwards. The door swings shut. I have no idea what to do.

I crawl towards the door and grapple for the handle. But there's no way I can open it while we're moving. I can't jump out while we're travelling so fast.

Now what? I pat my pockets. No phone. It's in the van. I have no idea if the others will find me, or if they'll know where to look for me even if they find this truck. I have no idea what will happen. And I'm scared. Really scared. Scared of what will happen when this truck stops.

48

I lean against the wall of the truck and wait. It's hot in here. Really hot. I try to control my breathing as anxiety runs around me, tapping me on the shoulder, disappearing and popping up somewhere else, with a twitch, just to remind me it's there. I don't think it ever really goes away. I've been so stupid. This was totally reckless. How could I do this to the kids? They only had me to rely on. Why would I put myself in this situation? And I think of Josep – I promised him I'd be careful. Why didn't I listen to him and leave this alone? I stop the self-pitying and focus. I need to get out of here. I have a whole life ahead of me. I stand up, leaning against the wall as I feel the truck slowing down. My heart is racing and I concentrate on breathing steadily, concentrate on the smell of the hams I've come to love.

Suddenly the truck comes to a halt, knocking me off balance. I have no idea if it's traffic lights or what, but I've got to take my moment. I grab the handle on the back door and open it. I have no idea where I am. It's as hot outside as it is in the truck but I drag in lungfuls of air. I hear voices, Miguel and Pedro, and the only thing I can do is jump and hope I don't break anything.

There's a thud as I land and roll. It hurts, but I do a quick mental check: nothing is broken, although I'm scratched and covered with dust. I'm lying in the ditch by the side of the road and roll onto my stomach. I was very good at playing hide and seek with the kids in the garden of the old house: who knew that skill would ever come in useful? The voices keep talking quickly in Spanish. I crawl along the ditch, on my elbows, through the dried grasses there, hoping I don't meet any creepy-crawly inhabitants. I shuffle forward, shaded by the truck and see another in front of the one I've been in. There's a restaurant on the other side of the road. We're in the neighbouring town. I remember passing through it on my way here in the taxi from the airport. I can just see Miguel and Pedro from under the truck. They are with two other men, all shaking hands.

Now what? I have absolutely no idea.

Suddenly there's rustling behind me in the ditch and I practically jump out of my skin.

'Fancy seeing you here . . .'

I've been found!

A huge smile pulls at my lips and unexpected tears spring to my eyes.

'You came!' I can't help but hug him – hard. He found me in a ditch. Josep's here.

'Of course! There was no way—'

Sssh.

'What are they saying?'

Josep listens.

'They're going to have a coffee and they'll check the hams before settling up.'

'Do you know them?'

Josep shakes his head. 'They're just the agents . . . The hams will go to a broker to be sold on.'

They're walking towards the bar.

'Now what? This is our chance.'

'Good job Josie has her car then. Sally's driving and I have the van.'

'I could kiss you!' I beam.

'Later. Much kissing later,' he says, 'but first . . .'

Sally backs the van up to the truck. And we climb in, to the place I thought, just a few minutes ago, I might never leave. I hesitate. But I can't back out now.

I throw a ham to Josep, who straddles the two bumpers, and I worry about his leg, but he seems not to be in pain as he throws it to Marianne in the van. Eileen arrives and gets in.

'Said I had to be somewhere. Said I'd meet him for date night later,' she says, to my questioning face, and throws one of the cheaper hams to me. It lands in my arms like a baby elephant. *Phhfff!*

'Netball was my thing, not bloody golf!'

Josie is on look-out.

In no time we seem to have swapped nearly all of the hams, when we hear Josie: 'Bugger me! It's the woman from the cycle holidays. The one who my husband left me for!! But that's not my ex-husband she's with! Looks like this is the place for assignations! Oh, shit, they're coming!'

'Who?'

'The woman from the cycle holidays or the ham snatchers?'

'The pigs! Ham . . . Quick!'

Marianne, nimble as you like, jumps into the front seat of the van and Sally starts it.

'Leave them! Leave the rest!' instructs Josep.

I've only got one more to go and, as if I'm juggling youngsters and breastfeeding a baby at the same time, I tuck it under my arm and reach towards Josep as he holds out his hands to me.

'Jump!' He stretches further, and now I can see the pain on his face. 'Do it!' he says, and I don't need telling twice this time. Sally has one eye on me over her shoulder, and as I jump, Sally starts to pull away, with precision timing. With the ham under my arm and the door swinging shut as I give it a kick on the way, I fall into Juan's van on top of Josep. We lie there for a second or two, wondering if we've actually made it, sprawled in the van, surrounded by his expensive hams.

And as it speeds away, there is nowhere I would rather be right now.

The van stops and we come up for air.

Sally and Marianne are looking in the rear-view mirror and we look out the back.

The men are opening the back doors of the truck, and the hams are being transferred to the other waiting vehicle, the agents for the black-market dealer. Notes are being handed over . . . They're paying. It's a done deal. We did it! And, right now, no one is the wiser.

Whoopee! We all cheer, clenching our fists, Marianne slapping the dashboard, Sally the steering wheel. Josep and I are in each other's arms. And this time I can't stop the tears rolling down my cheeks. We're hot, filthy but elated, as Sally drives us back to the farm. A short time after we arrive the hams have been rehung where they belong . . .

49

We've agreed to meet at the tapas bar after we've showered and changed. Josie and Eileen are first there. Juan is hugging them. 'We did it!' He punches the air when he sees me.

'I know,' I say, bruised but euphoric. 'We did it! We got them all back!'

'No! I mean, we did it!' he says, waving at a trophy. 'We won the tapas competition!'

'What? Wa-hey!' We high-five and hug.

'The judges loved the Ibérico ham and want to know more about where it came from and the pigs. And the cheese that Julieta put me on to, and the peppers, all local female growers. They loved the simplicity, the flavours and sense of place. We've been packed!' He indicates the bustling, busy bar.

Then he clasps Thiago, the guitarist, to him and I think they may have overcome their shyness.

'Oh, and you've got guests,' Juan says, releasing Thiago.

'Guests?' The euphoria seeps away, replaced by a cold shiver. 'What do you mean "guests"?'

I turn to see if we've been tracked down and then I burst into tears all over again.

'Mum!'

50

'We knew we couldn't leave you alone for too long without you getting into trouble, so we thought we'd better come and check!' says Ruby.

'And bring you this!' Edie says, smiling.

They're handing me a gift bag. I look inside.

'It's not my birthday, is it?'

'Not yet, but soon!' Luke towers over me.

'What's this?' I take the box, open it slowly and frown.

'The keys to your flat. We've all moved out.' Ruby beams.

'What?'

'We've all moved out,' Edie repeats.

'And left it spotless!' Luke adds. 'So now there's nothing to stop you coming home.'

'What?' I repeat. I stare at the keys and take in their words.

'Where are the dogs?' is all I can think of saying.

'They're at home with Dan. We've worked things out and I'm back living with him. Actually . . .' Ruby holds out a finger and wiggles her engagement ring at me.

'Engaged? Oh, how lovely!' I'm delighted.

'He asked me to move back in, on one condition, that I agree to marry him! I was going to call and tell you, but I wanted to see your face when I told you and for it to be a surprise.'

'It's certainly that! It's lovely news!' I brush a tear from my eye. My little girl, getting married!

'And I've moved into a university house. I'm going back,' Luke announces.

'Oh.' My eyes prickle and I sniff.

'Only not to study law, like before, but geology. I think it's my thing. And the college trips look fantastic.'

'That's brilliant!' I can feel my nose go bright red. Maybe it's exhaustion from today. Everything seems a bit surreal right now.

'And Reggie and I are going travelling, starting here, and then we're going to work in ski resorts as chalet hosts. Reggie's got a gig in one of the bars and I get to bake cakes and have my own kitchen, not mess yours up all the time.'

I hug them all. 'I love you! I'm going to miss you!'

'No, you won't! You've got your flat back. And your spare room, your office, work space, whatever you want to do with it. You can start planning the rest of your life now!' Ruby says.

I stare at them. My three gorgeous young adults, or four if you include Reggie.

Maybe, I think, it wasn't them who needed to grow up and cut the apron strings. Maybe it was me all along. Maybe I didn't want to be without them. Maybe I needed to learn to move on in my life and let them find their own way to move on in theirs.

'It doesn't mean we won't be home to visit,' Edie says.

'Good!' I say, looking at the keys in the box with a huge lump in my throat and feeling like I want another really good cry. Only that would just make me a right old misery who doesn't stop blubbing. It's over. They've moved on and I smile. But have I? I look at Josep, and I'm trying to work out how I'm feeling. On the one hand I'm delighted for them and for me. I get my flat back. I can go to university. I have brought up three children to be independent adults. On the other, though, I'm devastated. They don't need me any longer. But I might have needed them more. Maybe that's why I always made excuses as to why I couldn't start dating again. Maybe it wasn't the kids being home that made it hard. Maybe I just used them as an excuse because I was scared. Scared to find out if the woman

I used to be was still in there. The woman I hoped might be there . . . And I may have just had a glimpse of her. Eliza Bytheway, the woman.

'And what about this boyfriend of yours?' Luke says, jolting me from my thoughts as Josep walks towards me, smiling, making my insides melt, and hands me a glass of fino. I take it gratefully and clutch it with both hands, to stop them shaking.

'Josep, these are my chil— This is my family,' I correct myself. They're not children. But they are my family.

Luke narrows his eyes and points between us. 'Is this who I heard on the phone?' He tries to find the right words. 'Is this who you've been staying with?'

Josep looks at me. My heart bangs in my chest and my stomach flips over. Then he says, 'It is.' His Adam's apple bobs up and down. 'And Eliza is very special but I know her home is with you, her family. I know how much she's missed you all,' he assures Luke, and a smile strains at the corners of his mouth. He's done it. He's handed me my plane ticket home. He's made it possible for me to go home, just like we agreed, without any complications. He's done that for me.

'Yes.' I swallow. 'I've finished everything here. I'll be home now.' That part of my life, too, it seems, is over.

My heart hits the ground, like a stone, and I take a huge gulp of sherry to help me swallow the large lump in my throat.

51

It's time to go home. In the busy bar, I feel as if I'm not a part of it any more. It was just a moment in time. I'm going home. To my empty flat . . . everything I wanted. Wasn't it? And I look at Josep as he turns away, then catch his eye as he glances back but carries on moving into the crowd. The place is packed and Juan is still celebrating with Thiago. People are waiting by the bar and I jump in to help so he can enjoy the moment. Might as well make myself useful while I can. It'll take my mind off Josep and what we pulled off today. My debt is paid. He has his hams back, I have my life in the UK, my flat and a future. I can leave, but something inside me is aching . . .

All the gang are there, mixing with locals who have heard about the tapas and are trailing in to try it. Marianne and the others seem still to be reliving the events of the day with each other and toasting a good job done, with glasses of wine. Plates of food are being passed around, shared and enjoyed.

There's sliced Ibérico ham, of course, pink and white slivers, on its own, needing nothing more. People are taking a slice and watching each other's faces as the flavour melts in their mouths. Their eyes light up, their heads tip back with pleasure, and any hands not holding glasses of golden fino wave with excitement. This is it! This is the real deal! This is everything that this place is, I hear them say. There are also triangles of Spanish tortilla, just the sliced potato in fluffy omelette, crispy top, and soft when you bite it, with a hint of paprika. And prawns, in pungent garlic and the peppery olive oil from Julieta's in little terracotta dishes. Cubes of the glorious cheese that Julieta first served me, and the Padrón peppers. There's deep-fried calamari with lemon wedges and earthenware bowls of *patatas bravas* – fried potatoes, drizzled with tomato sauce and the bite of Tabasco: hence the name *bravas*, fierce. I grab a couple of bowls and head out to the terrace.

'Some fierce potatoes for my fierce brave friends,' I say, putting the bowls of hot, crispy-edged potatoes in front of them. They ooh and aah, then raise their glasses to me.

'Thank you, all of you, for everything,' I say, and accept a glass of wine from the bottle on the table that Marianne hands me.

'So, are you going to accept the offer on your apartment, Sally?' Josie asks.

'Oh, yes,' I say. 'Are you going to take it? Move back to the UK?'

'Not on your nelly. Haven't had such an exciting time in years!' Sally says, and we laugh, raising our glasses again.

'To the Spanish Conversation Club!'

'Excuse me. Do you mind if we sit here?'

'Julieta! Hi!' I say. It's Julieta from the supermarket, and her friend from the scarf shop where I bought my straw hat.

'Hi!' She smiles. 'This place is busy! I hear the tapas is really good here!'

'All down to your recommendations,' I say.

'We're so pleased to have found somewhere to go for tapas now,' says Julieta's friend, with the short reddish hair and big gold-disc earrings.

'Somewhere that isn't chips and burgers,' agrees Julieta. 'With local food from some of our finest producers. Now we don't have to have our tapas at each other's houses. We can come out and mix with friends!'

'Because the only place that did decent Spanish food is *that*.' Her friend juts her chin at the Gastronómica Society with disgust, where we can hear raised voices, but there is a distinct lack of customers around its open door. In fact, it looks like most of them may be here.

'Well, you know where this place is now. Bring your friends! I have a very good adviser on local produce.' I smile, then suddenly, like a kick in the guts, remember again that I'm leaving this place. I look around the lovely terrace Juan has created with red and orange cushions on sofas and chairs made from wooden pallets and painted. From little acorns . . . I think about the farm, the trees, the pigs. I'm going to miss it all.

Julieta's friend is talking into her phone, at speed. She closes it. 'They're joining us now, our friends.'

'Who needs the Gastronómica Society when we have this place?' says Julieta.

'I'll get more cushions,' I say.

'Eliza, there you are! Isn't it amazing?' Juan says, passing me with a tray of drinks and more small plates. 'If this keeps up, I may regret wanting to win that competition.'

'It's wonderful,' I say, and kiss his cheek. 'Looks like you and Thiago have become close.'

He blushes and looks at Thiago, who smiles and blushes, like they're at their own private party in this crowded bar. Reggie is watching Thiago, fascinated, as he takes up his guitar to play. And I can't help it but my eyes flick to Josep, finding him in the crowd as his eyes flick to mine. He starts to make his way through the busy crowd, people stopping him on the way, saying it's good to see him, those who have migrated here from the Gastronómica Society.

'Eliza!' he calls.

'Josep . . .' I move towards him in the middle of the bar.

'I was thinking . . .' we say at the same time. And just as we do, a kerfuffle breaks out at the door of the Gastronómica Society. All heads turn to look across the square, as the talking and laughter die down. We look at each other and frown. My heart leaps into my mouth. What if . . .? My family join me.

'Who's that, Mum?'

'That's the mayor,' I say, my mouth going dry, 'and . . . the police chief for the town.'

'They don't look happy,' says Luke, sipping from a bottle of beer.

'They are also in charge of the Gastronómica Society.' Josep is standing right behind me, and I can feel the warmth of his body and wonder if he can feel my heart pounding.

We stand stock still, in the middle of the bar, as the short, fat mayor pulls his belt over his belly and marches up the steps to the terrace. Behind him, our local law enforcement officer, I think crossly, but I'm terrified that I'll be arrested, in front of my family, for the theft of Ibérico hams. But we only took back what had been stolen in the first place. I lift my chin and look at the mayor as the crowd parts to let him through. He walks up to us, stares at me, Josep, and around the now silent room.

Josep steps in front of me. 'Señor Blanco.' He nods sharply.

'Josep,' he replies, and is still looking around, as is the police officer. 'It looks as if you have had a good night.'

'We have,' says Josep. 'Everybody has been able to enjoy the tapas and the food from our area.'

Josep's little finger reaches for and curls around mine, and I feel bonded to this man, like I've never felt before. 'The food that makes this town what it is is something to be proud of.'

The mayor coughs. 'It seems that we haven't had quite the same success tonight.' He stares at Juan and Thiago, side by side.

'No, I can see,' says Josep, pointedly, pulling the mayor's attention back to himself, making sure it's on no one else.

'I, erm . . .' the mayor coughs again '. . . I hear you had problems at your farm, that some of your hams have gone missing.' He peers at the small plates, and I can just imagine the faces of the Gastronómica Society members when they realized their ham wasn't the one they were expecting. Part of me wants to smile, if I wasn't so worried about being arrested.

Behind the mayor and the police chief, the last few members of the Gastronómica Society are trailing over from the club, the door shutting as if for ever as the last person arrives in the bar and stands behind the mayor and the police chief, handing over the keys. It's Miguel.

'I've turned everything off.' Miguel shrugs. 'Closed up.'

'We cannot have a club if we cannot trust the members,' says the policeman. Once again, the irony isn't lost on me. This corrupt group of men have run the food scene around here for too long, and now they seem to be turning on each other.

Josep looks at the mayor. 'You were saying, about my hams?' he prompts, and I have the feeling he may be enjoying this conversation.

'I heard your hams went missing. We're trying to find out where they have gone. It seems, apparently, that they have been lost.'

A tiny playful smile appears on Josep's lips.

'You know why I never joined your Gastronómica Society, Señor Blanco? It was for the same reasons my grandfather left. You have kept everything that is good about the town to yourselves. Good food, like love, is meant to be shared and enjoyed, not kept for a selfish few.'

There are murmurs and shouts of agreement.

The mayor and the police chief shift uncomfortably on their feet. The mayor pulls up his trousers by the belt again.

My friends join me, as do the young women with our group.

The mayor coughs again.

'As I say, you might need some help getting back your hams. We can work together, come to an arrangement maybe. Your friend said . . .' He points at me.

'This has nothing to do with her!' Josep says fiercely.

I see Luke move forward but Josep doesn't need help. His face darkens and he steps forward, towering over the short mayor.

'As for my hams. I have no idea what you're talking about, Señor Blanco. All my hams are where they should be. Stored safely in my cave. Here, try for yourself.' He takes a plate from Juan and offers it to the mayor. 'Try it. You know how my ham tastes, from pigs that have grown up in the *dehesa*, feeding on acorns. Cured and matured.' Josep holds the plate closer to the mayor, who slowly takes a piece. He opens his mouth and puts in the ham. As he closes his mouth, his eyes shut too, as he savours it, melting on his tongue.

'It's the taste of this town,' Josep says, and the mayor agrees, his eyes open, watery with emotion. 'It's why this bar won the tapas competition. They had the best of ingredients and shared them. It is why this town is known for its tapas. Simple, quality produce. But it should be about the town and everyone who lives in it, not just a few fat men, hoping to keep the best for themselves and make money from black-market sales . . . big profits for no effort.'

'Good, good . . .'

'This is about taking pride in who we are. Not selling

cheap meat to anyone who will pay. This is about being honest about who we are and what we produce. Now my hams are where they should be, and they'll stay there. My customers will be contacted and told there has been some crime in the area. Hams going missing and exchanged for lesser-quality ones.' There is a rumbling of discontent in the crowd and the mayor looks nervous. 'And if anything happens to my hams, I have all these witnesses who have tasted my ham, and will know if anyone tries to exchange it.' He glares at the mayor and the policeman steps back, uncomfortable. The group behind the mayor starts to disperse, finding themselves plates of ham. 'Perhaps you could pass on a message when you find the middle man. No more hams will be swapped for cheaper meat from my farm or this town. Those who want honest produce, made with care and love, will have to come and get it here.'

The mayor gives Josep a short nod, then turns to the police chief and the two leave, followed reluctantly by Miguel, and Pedro, who is waiting by the door. As Miguel passes, he tips Pedro's hat off his head. Pedro picks it up and shoves Miguel, and they swing at each other down the street, squabbling like children.

It's over, I think, as I watch them go. I can breathe again. I'm not going to prison.

Thiago begins to play his guitar, and the two young Spanish women who have been joined by two of their friends, step forward and begin to clap. My heart is thumping again, but this time to a joyous beat.

'*Olé!*' And Julieta, my supermarket friend, steps forward, lifts her chin and begins to dance as the others clap. Thiago smiles. Some of the men are clapping too. The young women take it in turns to step forward, dance and clap as the guitar plays and there are more shouts of '*Olé!*'

'This is everything I could have wished for,' Juan says. 'Except more staff!'

'We can help – we can all help!' I wave to my family to come over, then introduce them to Juan quickly and get them clearing tables, serving drinks and helping Sebastián in the kitchen.

'We can all help,' says Josep, joining Luke behind the bar. 'Enjoy your night!' he tells Juan. 'And thank you!'

'Thank you!' says Juan. 'For giving me my dream!'

'And you for helping give me mine,' says Josep, and they hug each other.

The music plays louder, with the clapping, the shouts, the stamping. The smiles grow wider. My heart soars. What a night! A night I will never, ever forget.

52

Finally, as the last of the customers leave, we finish taking the last dirty glasses to the kitchen. My feet are killing me. Everything aches.

'Night, Mum!' says Edie, kissing my cheek.

'Wait, where are you staying?' I realize I haven't organized rooms for them.

'We're in an Airbnb . . . with Josie!'

'You sorted it yourselves?' I say, with renewed pride and surprise.

'Mum . . .'

'I know, I know! You don't need me any more!'

'We'll always need you.'

'Your support and encouragement will never go away.'

'But we did need to step up and do some things for ourselves.'

'Goodnight, all!' I kiss them in turn.

'Goodnight!'

We arrange to meet tomorrow, my last day in Spain.

'They are a wonderful family,' says Josep, handing me a glass of wine I'm almost too tired to hold. 'A credit to you!'

He's right. I'm so proud of them.

Juan and Thiago are arm in arm.

'Go! I'll lock up,' I say, as they laugh, grab a bottle of wine and head to Thiago's apartment. Juan tosses me the keys.

'I'll post them through the letterbox!' I call after him.

'Keep them!' he shouts back over his shoulder, one hand holding Thiago's. 'I need help here, a business partner, if this place is going to be as busy as it was tonight.'

'What?'

'Be my business partner. If you keep the keys I'll know your answer. If not, post them through the door of the flat. I'll find them in the morning.' He waves as he and Thiago hurry across the cobbles, under the orange glow of the lantern there, to the door that leads to his apartment.

Josep is looking at me. I busy myself tidying up. Juan can't have been serious. Must have been the excitement of the tapas competition, or being in love, or something.

We finish and leave the bar. I close the door behind me, then look up and around one last time. I lock up. Josep says nothing. I go to the flat door at the back of the building to post the keys. As I reach out, Josep puts his hand over mine. I turn to him.

'I've never been to England. I could come?' he asks softly.

'And leave your pigs?'

'Sebastián is going to help out on the farm.'

'Ah, you met Sebastián tonight.'

He nods. 'He asked how Banderas was. I told him to come and see the piglets when they're born.'

'He's a good lad. He admires you very much.' I look at his face, memorizing his features.

'Or maybe you'd rather have your flat to yourself for a while. Enjoy the peace,' he says again, softly.

I think about the flat. Right now, I can think of nothing worse than going home to a tidy, empty flat. I'll miss the mess. I'll miss the chaos. I'll miss . . . I look at Josep. The keys are still in my hand, the letterbox open, the keys poised. 'Or . . . I could stay?'

'But your college course, your career? I can't ask you to give that up to stay here.'

'I'm not giving anything up. I may have found exactly the job I want. Juan's right. I love this. Running the bar, local produce at its heart. I get to look after people, make them feel better, doing what I do best, with the food that goes on the table, and the drinks we serve. Make them feel at home. I don't need a degree to feel like I'm somebody any more. I am somebody.'

'You are, Eliza Bytheway, quite somebody!'

The letterbox shuts and the keys stay in my hand. I wrap my fist around them, as Josep kisses me firmly on the lips, under the warm, Spanish night sky and I know I have found me.

EPILOGUE

My hands tremble as I open the envelope. I pause before pulling out the letter. I can't bear to look. I take a deep breath and pull it out. The words jumble until at last I take in the contents.

'I got a distinction!' I say out loud, as I look around the empty, tidy flat, then hold the letter to my chest, this piece of paper telling me I passed my foundation course with flying colours.

It's so quiet. I walk into the kitchen and pull a magnet off the fridge: 'Mums are like buttons. They hold things together.'

As I walk around all I can see is the memories, from when Ruby came to stay with the dogs, and the little scratch marks on the windowsill. When Luke came back from university, and Edie and Reggie moved in with guitars and baking tins. The place is full of memories, but other than that, it's just an empty shell. I'm taking these memories with me.

I pull out my phone, just as there's a knock at the front door.

'Yes, I'm ready!' I say.

'Um,' says a voice I wasn't expecting.

'Rob!'

'I, er . . .' He peers around me into the flat. 'The place looks good,' he says, which I think may be his attempt at small talk.

'What can I do for you, Rob?'

I look past him and see his car, the baby strapped into its seat. No sign of his wife. 'I'm taking the baby for a drive, giving Natalie a rest.'

'Good for you, Rob. Good for you. Hope it works out this time.' I surprise myself by saying and meaning it. If it hadn't been for him, I wouldn't have had three amazing offspring . . . make that four, or five, if you count the new baby on its way to Ruby. I couldn't be luckier. I wouldn't have all the memories. The birthday cakes I attempted, the egg-and-chips nights when next door's cat stole the sausages, the safety we all felt in having somewhere to come home to. And that won't change, even though they all have their own lives. Their home will always be wherever I am, and mine with them. I know that.

'That your college certificate?' he says, pointing to the piece of paper in my hand.

'Yes.'

'Great. Well done. And now?'

'And now I know I don't need a qualification to help me work out where I need to be. But it did lead me to being there.'

He frowns.

The baby cries.

'I, er, I know it's Ruby's birthday, sometime now, so I thought I'd drop in a card.'

Clearly he hasn't been kept in the loop on recent developments. 'We've moved on, Rob. We all have.' I hold out my hand. 'I'll pass it on. She's visiting me next month for her birthday.'

'Ah. Tell them to get in touch. I miss them.'

'You missed a lot, Rob. But I'll pass the card on.'

'Right, okay,' he says, hesitating as he turns to leave. 'I did, didn't I?' he says slowly.

'Make sure you don't this time.' I nod towards the baby. 'You've got a second chance. Enjoy it.' He takes the hint and hurries back to the car. He looks exhausted. Maybe that little baby will teach Rob everything he needs to know . . . Let Mother Nature lead you in the right direction.

'Ready?' says the voice I was expecting, and there is Josep, so fit and well. He kisses me as he comes out of the bedroom with the last of my cases.

'Just one more thing,' I say, and dial a number . . .

'Mrs Fox? Mrs Betty Fox?' I say, when the caller picks up.

'Yes.'

'It's Eliza Bytheway, from the estate agent's.'

'Oh, yes, dear?'

'Well, I'm not actually from the estate agent's any more. I've left.'

'Did you find the peace and quiet you were looking for?' She laughs.

'Um, not exactly. But I have moved on. I was wondering, have you found a property yet?'

'Not yet, dear. Still looking.'

'Well, I know of a lovely two-bedroom garden flat coming up for sale . . . Plenty going on. Friendly postman . . .'

I finish the call and follow Josep out of the flat, pulling the door shut behind me and putting the key in the key safe, ready for the estate agents to show interested buyers around.

'Ready?' asks Josep.

'Ready. Let's not hang around – Juan will be trying to add all sorts to the tapas if he's left to his own devices. And you have a whole new litter of black-hoof piglets to get back to.'

He kisses me again. 'Let's go home.'

That night, back in the *cortijo*, the sunny September sunshine has finally turned to the first of the October rain: we wake to the sound of it on the windows. Josep gets up and opens the shutters. 'It's time,' he says.

'Time?'

'The first rain of autumn. The pigs will go out onto the wider *dehesa* now. They will eat acorns and everything they can find out there. Everything their hearts desire.'

We get dressed and together walk round to the farmyard, to the gate looking out on the *dehesa*, the rain hitting the hard, dry earth, replenishing it after the long, hot summer.

Josep opens the gate and we go to greet the field full of the mature pigs. I follow as he walks to the far side of the field, the rain falling on my face. The pigs seem to be enjoying it. He stops at the next gate and turns to me. I join him as he unlatches it, glances at me, and then, together, we push it wide. The pigs follow Josep, grunting and jogging through, their ears flapping as they begin to roam, explore and delight in the open countryside, a new adventure. I can smell the rain on the earth, energizing and revitalizing the vegetation all around. I can smell the wild herbs, the delicious life that lies ahead for these animals as they roam free, eat the acorns, the wild herbs and plants. It's time for them to enjoy life, in their mature years, to make the most of their surroundings, to be happy and content, just like Eliza Bytheway, happy and content in her mature years, enjoying life and all the surprises she can unearth along the way.

That evening at the tapas bar, everyone is there.

Juan hugs me warmly when he sees me. As does Thiago.

'So, that's it?' Marianne says. 'Here to stay?'

'Here to stay,' I tell her, raising my glass of sherry and clinking it with hers. 'What about you? What's this news you've got?'

She smiles. 'I'm going to be opening an art gallery. I got premises.'

'Where?'

'That's brilliant!' we all say.

'Here.'

'Here?'

She points across the square and pulls out a key from her big sequinned bag.

'The Gastronómica Society!' I beam.

'Yes, indeed. I'll be bringing in artists from all over the area, having some launch parties, so I'll need a place that can provide good tapas.'

'The best!' I say.

'How did you get those premises?'

'Let's just say the mayor wants to be on people's good side with the local elections coming up.'

'Derek, my husband, is joining me,' says Eileen.

'He's not on the golf course, then?'

She shakes her head. 'Let's just say that golf seems to have lost its shine. Says we should do something together. He's coming for the flamenco class later. And my son is coming to visit! I'm hoping he and Derek can bond over flamenco.'

'I can't wait,' says Josie, who has taken the new dance classes very seriously and is wearing her hair up, with a rose in it, and a delicate shawl around her shoulders. She looks very much at home, as do the rest of us. 'Julieta and Martina are such wonderful teachers, and we learn Spanish at the same time,' she says, referring to Julieta from the supermarket and Martina from the scarf shop as they arrive to join us.

'What about you, Sally? What have you been up to while I was in the UK? Any news of your family coming to visit?'

'I've got a job!' She grins.

'Where?'

'With Josie! She's snowed under and it gets me out. And one thing I know how to do is clean a place from top to bottom. And drive people to and from the airport. I'd forgotten how much I missed driving. Only thing is, my family are a bit miffed I'm not around for them to visit until the season eases off a bit. At least I'm not sitting waiting for them to decide to visit. They'll have to come when it suits me now.'

Juan comes over with a tray of drinks. 'A thank-you to you all!' he says.

'Look at this place,' I say, of the busy little bar. 'And you! Spanish through and through. You'll be running for town mayor next.'

He hands around the drinks and I'm laughing to myself.

Josep has joined us. 'What are you all looking at?'

'It's not me everyone wants to run for mayor,' says Juan, smiling and shaking his head slowly.

'Who then?' I wonder.

No one speaks. Everyone's eyes are on me. The penny drops. 'Me?'

'Yes, you!' they all reply.

'Oh, no. No, no, no, no, no!' I say, and suddenly the group erupts into excited chatter. Campaign ideas are being thrown into the mix, ideas written on the back of cardboard coasters. The conversation is loud, energetic and very Spanish. Josep squeezes my hand, and I have a feeling I'm not going to be able to say no to this, as hard as I try, because Eliza Bytheway is working from home. Her new home, her new life that she loves very much indeed.

ACKNOWLEDGEMENTS

This book was inspired by a week I spent in Spain with Katie Fforde and AJ Pearce. I was writing *Sunset Over the Cherry Orchard* at the time. But I knew there was another book to be written about the area. I remember sitting in the morning sunlight on the terrace, eating Serrano ham and melon, and it was that feeling of contentment and peace that sparked this idea.

I want to thank Miguel Ullibarri at A Taste of Spain, local culinary travel experts who organize foodie holidays. He spent so much time answering my questions and pointed me towards Dan Barber's book *The Third Plate*. If you fancy a farm-to-fork holiday, seeing how Ibérico pigs are raised, do get in touch with him (www. atasteofspain.com).

Also, a huge thank you to Martha Roberts who runs The Decent Company in Abergavenny, talking to me about pig rearing and pig habits. Do follow her and her smallholding on Twitter @martharoberts or visit her website to order the most amazing home-reared, free-range, rare-breed pork.

To my Twitter friends who I follow and love to learn from. And again, if you're thinking of going to Spain, why not look at doing a foodie tour to taste the best the area has to offer.

Thank you to Sally Williamson, who has guided this book through from inception to the shelves, and the team at Transworld. To my agent, David Headley. And to my writing friends, without whom lockdown would have been so much harder and for their continued daily support and friendship, Katie Fforde, Jill Mansell, Milly Johnson, Bernadine Kennedy, Janie Millman, Catherine Jones, Judy Astley, AJ Pearce, and of course Jane Wenham-Jones, always with us.

*Read on for
some of Jo's favourite
Spanish recipes
to try at home . . .*

Spanish tortilla

Spanish omelette . . . this, served with a cold glass of sherry . . .

Serves 4–6 people

8 large eggs
1 large onion, sliced
3 large potatoes (Maris Pipers work best), sliced
225ml olive oil
Salt and freshly ground black pepper

1. In a large bowl, mix the eggs with a fork and season with salt and pepper.
2. Heat the olive oil in a large frying pan and add the sliced onion. Cook until they soften, then add the sliced potatoes and some salt. Cook on a low heat for about 25 minutes.
3. Once cooked, add the onion and potatoes to the eggs and stir. In a frying pan, heat some more oil and tip in the egg, onion and potato mix. Cook gently until the sides start to crisp and come away from the pan.
4. Pop a plate over the pan and turn over to tip out the omelette on to it, then slide it back into the pan to cook the bottom.
5. You can add whatever you fancy to this – peppers, mushrooms, etc. – when you're cooking the potatoes and onions, or chives with the egg mix. I like to add a sprinkle of paprika for a bit of warmth!
6. Serve in slices, with a glass of something cold.

Patatas bravas

Serves 4 people

For the potatoes

800g potatoes
Olive oil
Salt and pepper

For the sauce

4 tbsp extra virgin olive oil
1 onion, finely diced
3 garlic cloves, crushed
1 tin (400g) chopped tomatoes
1 tbsp tomato purée
2 tsp sweet paprika
1 tsp chilli flakes
1 tsp caster sugar

1. Preheat oven to 180°C. Cover a large ovenproof dish with olive oil and place it in the oven until it is hot.
2. In the meantime, scrub the potatoes and cut them into 2cm cubes.
3. Once the oil in the dish is hot, add the potatoes and turn to coat them in the oil. Place the dish in the hot oven for 45–50 minutes or until crispy and golden brown, turning them over halfway through.
4. Now it's time to make the sauce. Heat the olive oil in a medium-sized frying pan and add the onion. Cook for around 5 minutes or until it starts to soften, then add the crushed garlic and cook for a further 2 minutes.
5. Add the tin of chopped tomatoes, tomato purée, sweet paprika, chilli flakes and sugar to the onion mixture.
6. Bring to the boil and then reduce the heat to low. Allow the mixture to simmer for around 20 minutes, or until the sauce has a jam-like consistency.
7. Remove the potatoes from the oven and plate them.
8. Pour over the spicy tomato sauce and enjoy!

Tapas platter

This recipe serves 4 people, but it can be scaled up or down depending on your party size.

Marinated olives with anchovies (list of ingredients in the method below)
250g cherry tomatoes
3 red peppers
150g thinly sliced chorizo
10 slices cured ham, like Ibérico in the book, or Serrano ham which is more readily available
150g Manchego cheese
2 baguettes
Olive oil

1. First make the marinated olives with anchovies. These can be made up to three days in advance and stored in the fridge. The ingredients you will need are:
   200g green olives in brine, such as Nocellara or Manzanilla
   200g black olives in brine, such as Kalamata or Arbequina
   400ml extra-virgin olive oil
   6 garlic cloves, crushed
   4 anchovy fillets, rinsed and finely chopped
   1 tsp ground cumin
   1 tsp ground coriander
   1 tsp fennel seeds
   ½ tsp chilli flakes (optional)
   1 lemon, zest and juice
   3 tbsp fresh parsley, finely chopped
   2 tbsp balsamic vinegar

   1. In a bowl, mix all the ingredients together except the balsamic vinegar.
   2. Place in an airtight container and chill in the fridge for at least 4 hours, or ideally overnight.
   3. Before serving your platter, bring the marinated olives to room temperature and drizzle with balsamic vinegar to taste.

2. Next, roast the cherry tomatoes. Heat the oven to 200°C. Place the cherry tomatoes in a roasting dish, drizzle with olive oil and season generously with salt and pepper. Place in the oven to roast for around 20 minutes or until the skin has blistered and the tomatoes are soft.
3. For the chargrilled peppers, there are several options depending on the equipment you have available. You can either place the peppers directly on the flame of a gas stove and turn them until the skin is blackened, use a barbecue grill or a very hot oven grill. Once the skin has blackened, leave the peppers to rest for 10 minutes and then remove the blackened skin and slice into large pieces.
4. Slice the Manchego cheese and baguettes.
5. To assemble, put the marinated olives and chargrilled peppers in separate bowls and place on a large wooden board. Arrange the other ingredients on the board and serve.

If you enjoyed escaping to Spain with

JO THOMAS

be sure to try her other brilliantly feel-good novels

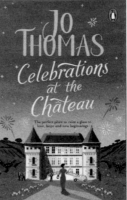